Talk of
the Town

Talk of the Town

ANNE MARIE RODGERS

Guideposts

New York

Talk of the Town

ISBN-10: 0-8249-3211-0
ISBN-13: 978-0-8249-3211-4

Published by Guideposts
16 East 34th Street
New York, New York 10016
Guideposts.org

Distributed by Ideals Publications, a Guideposts company
2630 Elm Hill Pike, Suite 100
Nashville, TN 37214

Guideposts, *Ideals* and *Tales from Grace Chapel Inn* are registered trademarks of Guideposts.

The characters and events in this book are fictional, and any resemblance to actual persons or events is coincidental.

All Scripture quotations are taken from *The Holy Bible, New International Version*. Copyright © 1973, 1978, 1984, 2011 by Biblica, Inc. Used by permission of Zondervan. All rights reserved worldwide. www.zondervan.com

Library of Congress Cataloging-in-Publication Data

Rodgers, Anne Marie.
  Talk of the town / Anne Marie Rodgers.
    p. cm.–(Tales from Grace Chapel Inn ; 41)
    ISBN 978-0-8249-3211-4
1. Sisters–Fiction. 2. Bed and breakfast accommodations–Fiction. 3. City and town life–Pennsylvania–Fiction. 4. Pennsylvania–Social life and customs–Fiction. 5. Domestic fiction. I. Title.
  PS3573.I5332T35 2013
  813 .54–dc23
                                                            2012029303

Cover design by Müllerhaus
Cover illustration by Deborah Chabrian
Interior design by Marisa Jackson
Typeset by Aptara, Inc.

Printed and bound in the United States of America
10 9 8 7 6 5 4 3 2 1

Acknowledgments

*I*n loving memory of my Teddy Bear. In my heart, you walk on four legs. I miss you, little man.

—Anne Marie Rodgers

GRACE CHAPEL INN

A place where one can be
refreshed and encouraged,
a place of hope and healing,
a place where God is at home.

Chapter One

The late March day in Acorn Hill, Pennsylvania, was bright and beautiful. Alice Howard tilted her face to the sun, enjoying the fresh air and the promise of warmer weather to come. March had come in like a lion, but the past few balmy days had been close to the "goes out like a lamb" part of the adage.

"Are you sure you don't mind raking those leaves?" asked Jane, Alice's younger sister, as she came out of the stately Victorian home that the Howard sisters had turned into a bed-and-breakfast after the death of their father. "I'll be happy to do it when I get back." Carrying a large covered basket, Jane paused on the sidewalk. Dressed in pale yellow linen trousers and a billowing white poet's shirt, she had put up her dark hair in a casual twist. Draped around her neck with an elegance Alice admired was a patterned scarf in the same shade of yellow as her pants.

"How could I mind?" Alice asked. "It's such a beautiful day. This is a wonderful excuse to be outside."

Jane smiled. "It is a lovely day, isn't it?" Her smile dimmed a bit. "I feel so bad for Mrs. Smeal. A broken ankle is no fun at any time, but it's especially bad now when she's longing to get out and do some work on her flower borders."

Penelope Smeal was a fellow member of Grace Chapel, the small white church near the center of Acorn Hill, the little town where Alice, Jane and their older sister Louise had grown up. Jane and Mrs. Smeal, an elderly widow, had bonded over their love of gardening. Ever since Mrs. Smeal had taken an ugly spill on her front steps after a late-season ice storm, Jane visited her every Sunday after church, taking a casserole or some soup that could be heated and eaten later. A chef of some repute, Jane delighted inn guests, friends and family with her delicious dishes.

"You've been such a good friend to her," Alice said. "Father would be proud of you."

"And of Louise too," Jane added as their sister's vintage white Cadillac came to a halt in the driveway. "Mrs. Smeal loves it when Louise comes along and plays a few pieces for her. She's a big fan of Mozart."

"Are you ready, Jane?" Louise called through the open car window. She waved at Alice. "I envy you. It's a beautiful day."

Alice smiled as she called back, "The sun feels marvelous. Have a nice visit and say hello to Mrs. Smeal for me."

As her sisters settled themselves and drove off along Chapel Road toward town, Alice surveyed the yard. Since Jane had returned home from San Francisco to help run the inn, the landscaping around the house was beautifully groomed and especially attractive. This year, the beds along the sidewalks already were a riot of color. Crocuses in shades of deep purple, lavender, yellow and white, sunny daffodils and bright red tulips had begun to bloom. Tiny purple grape hyacinths, commonly referred to as bluebells, sprang up in profusion.

Near the porch, Jane had planted two Hellebores, a large-leafed plant that, astonishingly, began to bloom in late winter, earning the name "Lenten Rose." The long-lasting blossoms were large and came in varied shades of pink, rose, white, green and mauve. Jane was fond of cutting them and floating them in crystal dishes for table decorations.

The forsythia hedge at one side of the house was glowing like sunbeams, while lilac and mountain laurel buds swelled in preparation for a beautiful display a bit later in the spring. Mountain laurel, the state flower of Pennsylvania, often were quite large and unruly, but Jane had found a miniature that bloomed in a clear candy pink. The little shrub with the pretty, starburst blossoms was very near the top of Alice's favorites.

Alice worked for the next hour in the front yard, using a narrow rake to pull leaves out from behind the foundation shrubs. Twice, she took the wheelbarrow full of sodden leaves back to the compost heap that Jane had established behind the garden.

When the leaves were disposed of, Alice picked up the rake and the other tools. She was just about to return everything to the garden shed when an expensive-looking black car turned in to the inn's driveway, its engine purring smoothly.

The driver braked when he saw Alice and rolled down his window. "Hello," he said. "Are you the proprietress of Grace Chapel Inn?"

Alice stripped off her work gloves. "One of them, although you might not know it to look at me," she said, smiling. She walked toward the car. "I'm Alice Howard. My two sisters and I run the inn together."

"Maxwell Alexander Vandermitton."

"It's a pleasure to meet you, Mr. Vandermitton." She saw that the man in the driver's seat was quite young, perhaps in his early twenties. His dark, wavy hair was cut in a neat, short style, and he wore a white shirt with a button-down collar.

"Your establishment is most attractive," he told her. "It has a very period feel."

"One of my sisters researched the original colors," she told him. "The body of the house is a shade called cocoa and the trim along the roofline is eggplant."

Maxwell Vandermitton smiled. "Prosaic names for such appealing colors."

Alice laughed. "That's true, but we are quite pleased with the results." She paused for a moment. "What can I do for you?"

"I am in need of lodging."

"I can help you with that," Alice told him. She stepped back a pace and pointed. "You can park in the lot at the back of the inn."

Maxwell nodded. "Is there a garage? This is a brand-new Beamer."

"I'm sorry, but there isn't. I believe your car will be safe here, if you are concerned about someone stealing it."

"One can't be too careful," he told her. "This car is attractive to thieves. It retails for seventy-four thousand dollars. My father gave it to me when I received my master's degree."

"Goodness," said Alice faintly. "That's…quite a gift. You must have done very well."

"I graduated summa cum laude from Penn with a graduate degree in positive psychology," he told her. "That's the University of Pennsylvania," he added.

"A member of the Ivy League. Congratulations." Alice was impressed. "Exactly what is positive psychology?"

"It is a new branch of psychology that focuses on the empirical study of such things as positive emotions, strengths-based character and healthy institutions."

"I see. It sounds quite interesting."

"Oh, it was. Now I'm at Stanford working on my doctorate—or I was. I've taken off this semester to do research."

"Heavens! You must love school."

Maxwell's expression seemed to grow a bit melancholy and he shrugged. "It's something I'm good at."

"Clearly." Alice smiled. "I'm sorry. I've been peppering you with questions." She pointed toward the back of the house. "While you park the car, I'll clean up. I'll meet you at the reception desk in a few minutes. Just go in the front door."

Mr. Vandermitton nodded. "Thank you very much."

After she replaced the tools in the garden shed, she hurried inside. As she went up to her room, she reflected on the young man's formal speech. She probably could count on one hand the number of people she knew of Maxwell Vandermitton's age who would use the words "proprietress" or "lodging."

More accurately, she knew no one like him. She was acquainted with a great many pleasant young people, but he was so courteous that she found his manner somewhat distracting.

Quickly, Alice washed her face and hands, then donned khaki slacks and a white, short-sleeved blouse before hurrying downstairs.

Mr. Vandermitton was standing at the desk.

"Thank you for your patience," she said, drawing the reservation book toward her. "How many nights would you like to stay with us?"

"I wish to book your best room for a month."

A month! How can a student afford that?

She cleared her throat. "A month?"

Maxwell Vandermitton nodded. "Yes."

As she perused the reservations for the next few weeks, Alice thought of the extravagantly expensive sports car and decided that Maxwell must be relying on family money. Glancing again through the reservations, she found that there were no rooms that had not been booked for some part of the upcoming few weeks.

There were two groups booked for the Sunset Room who had not asked for a specific room, unlike the honeymooning couple who had requested the Garden Room. Perhaps she could switch those two groups into other open rooms. If she did that, then she could offer Mr. Vandermitton the Sunset Room for the length of his stay.

"All right," she said, making notes at a furious pace. "The Sunset Room is at the front of the house and has a private bath."

Maxwell's eyebrows went up and his hazel eyes widened. "Don't they all?"

Alice shook her head, smiling. "Many bed-and-breakfasts have rooms that share a common guest bath. We have two with private baths and two that share one."

The young man shuddered. "Please, do book me into … what did you call it? The Sunset Room. How quaint."

Alice decided to take that as a compliment. "Thank you. My sisters and I redecorated and named the rooms before we opened for business." She finished checking him in, noticing that he had signed in as Maxwell Alexander Vandermitton III. As she handed him the key to his room, she said, "Here you go. I'll show you to your room."

As she led him up the stairs and turned toward the Sunset Room, Maxwell said, "Where is your bellboy? My bags are still in my car."

Alice stopped at his door. "We have no bellboy, Mr. Vandermitton. If you need help with your bags, I can assist you."

The look on her guest's face was comical to behold. "No bell-boy," he said faintly. "Goodness. Are all country inns like this?"

"For the most part," Alice said cheerfully. "It's a much more personal experience than staying in a hotel."

"Where they have bellboys."

She laughed. "Yes."

He nodded, and then he shrugged. "I suppose I can bring up my luggage myself."

"Mr. Vandermitton—"

"Please, call me Maxwell."

"Maxwell," Alice amended, making herself a mental note of his use of his full name rather than the nickname Max. "I have to confess that I'm curious about how you heard of us and why you chose an inn when you are not accustomed to this type of accommodation."

The young man shrugged. "I read about a bed-and-breakfast in a wine magazine and thought I would try one. I chose yours from a list of Pennsylvania establishments that I narrowed down according to the local population."

"The population?"

"Yes. I wanted to stay somewhere quite rural."

Alice chuckled. "We most definitely fit that description. Although I believe you will find that Acorn Hill has all the amenities you require as well as an abundance of charm." *Goodness, I sound like a tour guide!*

"I'm sure it shall be quite satisfactory," Maxwell said. "Quite satisfactory. Can you direct me to a good dining establishment?"

"In Acorn Hill, we have an excellent supper club called Zachary's, which you might enjoy," Alice told him. "There also are several very nice restaurants in Potterston. I have a list at the desk if you'd like a copy."

She showed him the room, then went into the bath to be sure there were fresh towels and toiletries in place.

As she came out, she said, "You'll have to tell me more about your research another time, Maxwell. Your specialty sounds very interesting."

Her new guest turned quickly from opening the laptop computer case he had been carrying. He appeared to be oddly flustered as he said, "Oh, I never discuss my work until I am ready to present it."

"Oh." His abrupt rejection left Alice nonplussed. *What is the proper thing to say in response to that?* "I see. Well, I suppose I'll leave you to settle in. If you'd like that list of dining establishments, come find me. I'll be in either the library or the kitchen."

"Thank you, Miss Howard. Your hospitality is appreciated greatly." His smile transformed his serious young face and made him quite handsome.

Alice headed back downstairs. She smiled to herself, shaking her head. What an unusual young man. It appeared that Maxwell Vandermitton was used to a very different lifestyle from her own. Costly sports cars, bellboys and monthlong stays at an inn. She could not wait for Jane and Louise to return so that she could tell them about their long-term guest.

That evening, the sisters gathered for Sunday supper. As she often did, Ethel Buckley, their aunt, was going to join them.

Jane had made an old-fashioned pot roast with potatoes and carrots. She was taking buttermilk biscuits from the oven, while Alice set the table in the cheerful kitchen with its paprika, black-and-white décor, when Ethel arrived. Tonight, Ethel was clad in mint-green slacks and a matching sweater. The color of her clothes made her incongruous dyed-red hair look even more vivid than usual.

"Hello, girls. Wasn't it a beautiful day? I can't wait for warmer weather to arrive for good. These little teasers are driving me crazy."

Jane chuckled as she placed the biscuits in a woven straw basket and covered them with a red-and-white checkered cloth. "I know how you feel. I suspect we'll get at least one more cold spell before it really begins to warm up for good."

"The first day of spring is on Tuesday," Alice reminded them. "Even if we do get cold weather again, it won't last."

"What won't last?" Louise came into the kitchen. She had been in the parlor practicing piano music for an upcoming wedding for which she had agreed to play.

"Cold weather," Ethel supplied. The older woman's pale blue eyes widened as she took in her niece's appearance. "Why, Louise! It's been a long time since I've seen you wearing something other than beige or blue. What a pretty shade of pink that is."

"Thank you." Louise actually looked a little embarrassed. She was wearing a gray wool skirt with a pale pink twin set and her signature pearls. "I looked into my closet the other day and realized what a rut I've gotten into. I'd been planning to purchase a new sweater set anyway, so I made myself choose a color other than blue or beige."

"Those colors both look very nice on you," Alice said loyally. "But this does too. It complements your complexion."

Jane set down the pot roast in the center of the table. It was beautifully presented on a white china platter, surrounded by roasted carrots and potatoes. "Shall we dine?"

The four women took seats around the table, and Ethel murmured a simple blessing while they bowed their heads. When they began to eat, Jane turned to Alice.

"So, tell us about our new guest. When I saw the book, I was overjoyed. Is he really staying for an entire month?"

"A month?" Louise repeated as she selected a biscuit from the basket.

Alice nodded. "Right after you left to visit Mrs. Smeal this afternoon, a young man in a wildly expensive car pulled into the driveway. His name is Maxwell Alexander Vandermitton the Third."

Louise raised an eyebrow. "Good gracious."

"And though he gave me permission to use his first name, I would not suggest shortening it to Max," Alice added, smiling. "He's not a nickname sort of person."

"What sort of person is he?" Ethel asked.

"Formal, extremely formal for someone in his twenties. He is working on a doctorate."

"Family money?" Ethel cut to the chase. "If he's been in school that long, has that sort of car and can afford to stay here for a month, he certainly isn't paying his own bills."

"I didn't ask. I admit I'm curious. I'm sure he'll tell us anything he wants us to know in his own good time."

Ethel chuckled. "You're such a good person, Alice. You're quite right. We shouldn't be gossiping." She leaned forward. "But if you learn anything else about him, I do hope you'll share it."

All four women laughed.

They were just finishing an excellent baklava, a deliciously sweet Greek dessert, when the telephone rang.

Jane rose. "I'll get that."

"Perhaps it's another guest booking a room for a month," Alice joked.

"Somehow, I suspect that is not the case." Louise smiled. "I'd be thrilled with a week."

They heard Jane answer the phone with the inn's standard greeting.

After an unusually long silence, Jane said. "I'm sorry. I don't … no, no, ma'am, is there anyone with you who speaks English? … Deutsch? No, I don't speak Deutsch. I'm so sorry—"

"Landsake!" Ethel pushed back her chair and went to Jane's side. "Jane, let me have that."

Jane, looking rather bewildered, slowly surrendered the handset.

"Hello? *Sprechen Sie Englisch?* May I help you?"

Jane turned to Louise and Alice. "It's a woman caller. She just kept repeating, '*Sprechen Sie Deutsch?*'"

"*Deutsch* is German," said Louise. "I have a smattering of it thanks to my music studies, but certainly not enough to communicate."

"Aunt Ethel apparently does." Jane indicated their aunt, shaking her head in wonder.

"I had no idea she spoke German," Louise said.

"And it seems quite well," Alice observed, amazed. Their aunt's first words were halting and slow, but she quickly picked up speed as the language came back to her.

"This is an inn—*das gasthof*. You may, oh, what's the word? *Reservieren?* Reserve a private room ... Breakfast is included, but not lunch or dinner, except by special arrangement ... What's that? No, we do not offer *transportmittel*, but if you need help getting to Acorn Hill from Philadelphia, we might be able to—let me think, what's the word for arrange? ... *Ordnen dich abzuholen* ..."

Ethel turned after a few moments and beckoned frantically for Jane. She mouthed, "This lady would like to book a room."

Jane nodded, and quickly fetched the reservation book. Ethel translated as more questions and answers about dates, rates and amenities were exchanged, and Jane took down credit card information.

After a few more moments, Ethel said, "*Auf wiedersehen.*" She placed the receiver back on its stand and returned to the table.

"What?" she asked, when she noticed that Alice, Jane and Louise were all staring at her as if she'd suddenly sprouted wings.

"You speak German," said Louise, restating the obvious as if she could not believe it.

"You speak German very well," added Jane.

"I don't know about the 'very well' part," Ethel said modestly. "I haven't spoken it in years."

"I've never heard you speak German," Alice told her aunt.

"Well, I don't imagine you have," said Ethel brusquely. "I've had no call to use it in a very long time."

"It's a good thing you were able to recall it so easily," Alice said with admiration in her voice. "We would have found it very difficult to help that caller without you."

"I'm glad I could be helpful."

"So give us the details," Jane said. "The caller is visiting from Germany? What brings her to Acorn Hill?"

"Her name is Clothilda Moeller. Right now she is in Philadelphia visiting distant relatives while she researches her family genealogy," Ethel told her nieces. "Though no one else was home just now to help her with the call. She said that some of her ancestors came through the Port of Philadelphia and that she believes they may have settled in this area. Ms. Moeller will be checking in at the inn on Saturday and plans to stay for a little more than two weeks. She is hoping to pursue her genealogical research while she is here."

"Gracious," said Louise. "This has been our day for long-term guests, hasn't it?"

As the women trooped back into the dining room, Ethel retook her seat and eyed the remains of her baklava. "My hips do not need one more bite of that," she said. "But my willpower is nonexistent where Jane's cooking is concerned."

"I know just what you mean," Louise said, chuckling.

Alice said, "So where did you learn to speak German so well, Aunt Ethel? Did you study it in school?"

"No." Ethel sighed, picked up her fork and took another bite of baklava. "When I was in grade school, the girl who lived down the road from us spoke German. Her parents were immigrants. Annelise and I spent a lot of time together." Her smile took on a faraway quality. "We were at her house a lot. It always had people coming and going, laughing and arguing, the way I thought a real family would be. The way I thought my family might have been if my brothers and sisters had been closer in age to me."

"I sometimes forget how much space there was between you and Father," Jane said, "even more than between Louise and me."

"Seventeen years," Ethel said. "And the other five were even older than Daniel so I barely knew most of them."

"Perhaps that is why Father never mentioned that you spoke German."

"He may not have known. He was grown and gone from home while I was still just a tot." She paused wistfully, and then seemed to shake off the moment of introspection. "At any rate, Annelise and I were great friends, and when her family realized I was picking up some of their language, it became their mission to make me a proper German-speaker."

"Apparently, they succeeded," Louise said dryly. "I can't believe you remember it so well after all these years."

"Well, I had more practice than simply those childhood years," Ethel told her. "When Bob and I married, he spoke the language fluently because his mother had been German." She laughed. "Although his accent was from Cologne and mine was from Munich, so we sometimes had to repeat things."

Alice laughed. "I suppose I never thought of other languages having local accents, but American English is sprinkled with accents—"

"Southern, Midwestern, New England..." Jane interrupted.

"Exactly," Alice said, nodding. "So why shouldn't there be a variety of German accents?"

"Aunt Ethel, did you teach your children to speak German?" asked Louise.

Ethel shook her head. "No, and I regret that. It was part of Bob's heritage, and we should have passed it on. But we didn't. We went to Germany on our honeymoon, and we spoke it to each other a bit during the early years of our marriage. And then I suppose life got hectic and we let it lapse. To tell you the truth, until today I had no idea I still would be able to speak it so well."

"Tell us about your honeymoon, Aunt Ethel," Alice requested. She could not remember her aunt ever speaking much about her marriage, although Alice knew she had loved her husband very much.

"And your courtship," Jane added.

Ethel giggled girlishly, and Jane grinned at Alice. "My courtship and honeymoon. Let's see . . . I was still in high school when I met your uncle. He was older than I, and he lived in a neighboring town. I married your uncle while he was home on furlough. My father wouldn't hear of my getting married right out of school, so I went to business school for a year."

"You said on furlough," Louise said. "He was a soldier?"

Ethel nodded. "He was in the Eleventh Airborne. He joined the army shortly after VJ Day."

"So he never actually had to fight?" Alice shuddered.

Ethel shook her head. "No. He was sent over during the Allied occupation of Japan. Oh, gracious, I still remember how desperately I missed that man."

Alice was shocked to see tears rising in her stalwart aunt's eyes. "Oh, Aunt Ethel, you don't have to talk about this. I'm sorry we pried."

"You're not prying, dear." Ethel patted Alice's hand. "And I don't mind talking about it. It's just that I haven't thought much about those sweet days of falling in love in a very long time." A small smile tugged at her lips. "Some day I'll have to show you photographs of Bob in his fatigues. He was a handsome devil. He sent me pictures from Fort Campbell in Kentucky while he was at boot camp. Back then, it was called Camp Campbell. I also have a couple of postcards that he sent from Manila. I can still feel the thrill I got each time one of those postcards arrived." She shook her head. "But you aren't interested in all that."

"Yes, we are," Louise said vigorously. "So you got married when he was still in the army?"

"Yes," Ethel said, "but we didn't go on a honeymoon right away, except for an overnight to a historic hotel down in Maryland. We went to Germany right after he got home from Japan."

"Why did you choose Germany?" Jane asked curiously. "Wasn't it in ruins?"

"A lot of it was," Ethel said. "Heidelberg wasn't bombed, but most cities were. We went there because Bob's mother had not heard from some of her family since the start of the war and she wanted us to try to find them. She was from near Cologne, which was very heavily bombed by the Allies in 1942."

"Had her family been killed?" Louise asked.

Ethel shook her head. "No, they had escaped into the country-side. Some time after the end of the war, they returned, and we eventually were able to find them. But Cologne was in shambles. The entire city looked like a huge rubble pile except for the cathedral. It had not been completely destroyed because the Allies used the largest structure in each city as a navigation point."

Jane shook her head, her artist's soul saddened. "What a pity—all those ancient buildings gone because of man's foolishness."

Ethel nodded. "It was the most unforgettable thing I have ever seen. Almost everywhere we went, the war had left its mark."

There was a moment of silence around the table. Then a plaintive "Meow" disrupted the hush. Jane laughed as Wendell, the family's gray tabby cat, leaped into her lap. Then he leaned forward, his nose twitching as he smelled the remains of their dinner. "Oh, no you don't," Jane said. "You've already had your treat for the day."

Alice smiled, leaning over to stroke a hand along the cat's soft back, making Wendell arch and close his eyes in delight. "Silly old thing," she murmured fondly. "You're just a silly, silly boy."

Louise pushed back her chair in a prelude to clearing the table. She walked around to her aunt's side and bent down to kiss Ethel's cheek. "Thank you, Aunt Ethel, for sharing those precious memories with us."

"And for saving the day as our one-and-only German-speaker," Jane said as she urged Wendell gently onto the floor and began stacking dishes.

Chapter Two

"Good morning." Maxwell Alexander Vandermitton III rose from his chair on Monday morning as Jane approached the dining room table. She smiled at the tall, slender young man. She just knew she was always going to think of him by that entire name.

"Good morning, Mr. Vandermitton. I'm Jane Howard." Jane set down a covered plate and took off the lid. "This morning we are serving ginger-pear pancakes with a side of crisped bacon and a kiwi-orange salad."

"Please call me Maxwell, Ms. Howard."

"And you must call me Jane."

"This smells delicious," he said, indicating the plate. "Won't you please sit and talk with me for a few minutes?"

Jane hesitated. There was no one else in the dining room at present. "Just for a minute," she said. "There are things in the kitchen I need to check."

He smiled at her, and then closed his eyes in sheer delight as he took his first bite of pancake. "Extraordinary. I confess I did not expect to find a four-star chef in Acorn Hill."

Jane laughed. "Thank you." She waved a hand at their surroundings. "This was our family home, my sisters' and mine.

After our father passed away, we decided to create a bed-and-breakfast. So far, it's been quite a success."

"With food like this, that's no surprise to me. Acorn Hill is a lucky little town."

"Thank you."

"So tell me about Acorn Hill." He made an expansive gesture with his fork.

"What would you like to know?"

"Anything. Everything. Is everyone as pleasant as you and your sister Alice?"

Jane smiled. "Very nearly. It's a lovely little town. I've only been back for a short time. Alice could tell you much more."

"Back? From where?"

"San Francisco. I lived there until we decided to open Grace Chapel Inn."

"How long did you live there?" Maxwell leaned forward, a frown creasing his brow.

"Longer than I lived here." Jane laughed. "Over thirty years."

"So you really aren't a small-town person."

"Oh, I don't know about that. I was raised here, and since returning to Pennsylvania I have discovered that any city veneer I might have acquired rubbed off rather quickly. I feel more at home here than I ever did in San Francisco, no matter how much I liked the City by the Bay."

"But Alice never moved away?"

"She lived here all her life, except for when she was in nursing school," Jane responded. "In fact, many of our town's residents have been here their whole lives. The downtown area, which you may not have seen yet, is picturesque and very charming."

"I have not seen the downtown section yet," he told her. "I came straight here from the highway yesterday."

"What are you planning on doing during your stay? If you enjoy hiking, there is a very nice trail not far away."

Maxwell shook his head. "I'm not much of a hiker. A brisk walk into town will suit me fine. Are there any places I should visit?"

Jane noticed that he had not answered her query, but she decided not to pry. "If you walk into town, you must visit the Good Apple Bakery. Clarissa Cottrell, the owner, makes mouth-watering baked goods. There's a good bookstore, our library, an antique shop and a tea shop, plus the usual assortment of other businesses. Outside of town, there's an old cemetery, which also might be interesting if you like that sort of thing. There are at least three graves of Civil War soldiers." She drew in a breath. "But we are not really a tourist town."

"I'm sure I'll enjoy the peace and quiet."

"Good morning." Alice entered the dining room, wearing a nursing smock with navy pants and sturdy white shoes. "I hope you slept well, Maxwell."

Their guest nodded. "The room is quite comfortable, thank you. Much more so than I was expecting, really."

Jane was taken aback by the comment, but Maxwell appeared oblivious to any insult he may have given.

Alice broke into the awkward silence. "I just wanted to let you know I'm leaving now, Jane. I'll be home in time for dinner."

"Is that what the early telephone call was?" Jane asked her sister.

Alice nodded. "I wasn't on the schedule for today." She smiled. "But I don't mind."

"See you at dinner," Jane said. "Have a good day."

"You too. Good-bye, Maxwell," Alice said, smiling as she turned and left the dining room through the swinging door to the kitchen on her way out to the parking lot.

Not a moment after Alice's departure, Louise breezed in from the hallway. "Good morning."

Jane and Maxwell turned as Louise came into the room, dressed in a tailored navy skirt with a pretty, lacy ivory blouse. Her pearls gleamed against the light fabric.

"Good morning, Louise." Jane rose from the table. "Have you met our guest yet?"

Jane performed the introductions.

"It's very nice to meet you," Maxwell said.

"And you, also. I understand this is your first experience staying at an inn."

The young man smiled. "Yes, I'm afraid my education has been limited to four-star hotels."

Louise raised an eyebrow. "Indeed."

"It's a very different experience," he told her.

"I agree," said Louise. "My husband enjoyed traveling in style when we vacationed or attended a conference. One feels quite pampered. However, at a bed-and-breakfast one has the opportunity to meet all kinds of interesting people and become as socially engaged as one chooses."

Jane bit her lip, trying not to laugh. When Louise used "one" that often, it was a sign she was irked. Jane could see why Louise would take offense, although she suspected that Maxwell was unaware of how his references to privilege and wealth came across to others. The young man had a superior air about him, although he could be charming and quite friendly.

"Louise is an accomplished pianist," Jane explained to Maxwell. "Her husband also was a musician. He taught at the university level, and they even had opportunities to travel to Europe with performing groups."

Maxwell looked surprised. "There isn't a university here, is there?"

Louise shook her head. "Oh no. I moved away from Acorn Hill to go to college and didn't return until after our father's passing. My husband and I made our home in Philadelphia for many years."

"I see."

Maxwell looked almost . . . disappointed, Jane thought, although she could not imagine what could have been disappointing in Louise's explanation.

"So your sister Alice is the only one of you who has spent her life here?"

Louise nodded. "That's correct."

"You know," said Jane, "I was planning to walk into town in a bit. If you'd like to come along, I'll be happy to introduce you to some other folks who are long-time residents."

Maxwell nodded eagerly. "Thank you, Jane. I would enjoy accompanying you."

"All right, then." Jane rose. "I'll get back to the kitchen. Perhaps we could meet in the foyer in half an hour?"

"I look forward to it." He inclined his dark head once in what looked suspiciously like a gesture of dismissal.

As she returned to the kitchen, Jane could not help grinning. It was going to be interesting to have Maxwell and Louise under the same roof for a month.

Her eldest sister was right behind Jane as the swinging door between the kitchen and dining room closed behind them.

"*Humph!*" Louise exclaimed, crossing her arms. "That young man is a bit full of himself, don't you think?"

"I believe he was raised in a very privileged atmosphere," Jane said diplomatically. "I don't think he meant to be offensive, although I grant you that he does come across that way occasionally."

"Occasionally?" Louise sniffed. "I hope I don't see much of him while he's here—Wendell!" Louise moved across the kitchen with surprising speed. "You get down from there *right now*."

Jane looked around just in time to see Wendell quickly remove himself from her chair, where he'd apparently been surveying the remains of her breakfast.

"One more minute and he'd have been munching on your bacon," Louise said.

"Thank you." Jane smiled sweetly at her sister. "I don't know if I've ever seen you move that fast, Louise."

"I rarely have the need to move that fast," Louise countered. She glanced down at the cat, who had moved to the floor but still was eyeing the table in an intense and hopeful way. "Scat," she ordered him. "If you can't use good manners, you can't be in the kitchen."

"He's a cat," Jane said laughing. "First of all, I don't think he understands English, and second, scavenging for food is instinctive. He didn't mean any harm."

"And he didn't cause any," Louise said, adding darkly, "this time."

The ringing of the bell that signaled someone at the front desk interrupted further conversation.

"Would you please get that?" Jane said. "I'll finish cleaning up these breakfast dishes."

"I'll be glad to," said Louise. She straightened her skirt. "Am I presentable?"

Jane inspected her briefly. "You look lovely, the very picture of a prosperous innkeeper."

Louise chuckled as she started toward the front of the house. "Someone had better call the bank. I do believe they forgot to inform me that I'm prospering."

Louise could hear Jane laughing as she walked through the hallway toward the reception desk tucked beneath the stairs.

"Welcome to Grace Chapel Inn. I'm Louise Howard," she said to the middle-aged man with a briefcase who stood waiting at the desk.

"Hello. I'm Lyle Jervis. I need a room for the next two nights. Do you have anything open?"

"We do." Louise took his information, ran his credit card and chose a key from the drawer while she explained their breakfast schedule and check-out hours. "May I ask how you found us, Mr. Jervis?" The sisters always tried to ask the guests that question so that they could determine where their advertising dollars were best spent.

"I found you online," he told her. "I would have called in advance except that my travel schedule is not always predictable, and I wasn't sure when or how long I might be here."

She led the way upstairs and showed Mr. Jervis into the Garden Room, then returned to the kitchen.

"Was that another guest?" Jane asked.

"Yes. He's on a business trip and will be here for two nights."

"Great." Jane glanced at the clock. "Goodness, I'd better grab my jacket. It's almost time to meet Maxwell."

Chapter Three

As Jane and Maxwell walked into the heart of Acorn Hill, two men approached them. Jane waved a hand as she recognized Ronald Simpson and Henry Ley. "Good morning, gentlemen."

"Hello, Jane. Are you t-taking a break from the kitchen?" Henry Ley asked.

"Just a short one. Henry, Ronald, I'd like you to meet Maxwell Vandermitton, a guest at the inn. Maxwell, Henry Ley and Ronald Simpson."

"Gentlemen. It's a pleasure." There was a flurry of handshaking.

"Our pleasure also," Henry said. "If you are in need of any spiritual guidance wh-while you are staying in Acorn Hill, I would be happy to visit w-with you."

"Henry is the Associate Pastor at Grace Chapel," Jane said.

"Thank you," Maxwell said politely, "but I am not religious."

Henry smiled. "You don't have to be re-religious to be in need of spiritual guidance."

Ronald chuckled, and his brown eyes twinkled. "So what brings you to Acorn Hill, son?"

Maxwell's eyebrows rose slightly, and Jane suspected he was a bit taken aback at being addressed as "son," but his response was cordial.

"I am doing a research project," he told the men. "Acorn Hill seems like a quiet, pleasant place to write my paper. I'll be here for about a month."

"I'm giving him the grand tour of Acorn Hill," Jane said.

"Well, you'll have to come down to the Coffee Shop and have a piece of pie with us a few times while you're here. June Carter, the owner of the Coffee Shop, makes terrific pies every day," Ronald told him. He winked. "And I manage to get in there for a piece nearly as often."

"In fact," Henry added, "when you and Jane finish your tour, join us at the Coffee Shop. That's w-where we're headed now."

"Thank you for the invitation." Maxwell sounded sincere as he said, "I would enjoy that a great deal."

"Jane," Ronald said, "have you heard that Sylvia has the flu?"

Jane was dismayed. Sylvia Songer was the owner of a small shop, Sylvia's Buttons, and one of Jane's close friends. "Oh no! She was supposed to go to Lancaster to a quilt sale today. She'll be so disappointed to miss it."

Ronald nodded. "The shop's closed until further notice."

"Oh, that's just terrible. I'll have to take her a meal," Jane said. "Thank you for letting me know."

As the two men resumed walking, Jane said to Maxwell, "If you want to get to know local folks, you really should drop by the Coffee Shop. People come and go all day long, and a lot of folks stop in almost every day." She grimaced. "Although most of them are in a significantly older age bracket than you are."

Maxwell nodded. "That won't bother me. I find older people fascinating. Even when I was small, I preferred the company of adults. I suppose that's a result of being an only child."

The pair took a short tour of Acorn Hill's main streets and shops. Jane stopped at the Good Apple Bakery and introduced him to Clarissa Cottrell, who was just beginning to clean up from her early morning baking spree.

"Clarissa makes amazing pastries," she told him.

Maxwell smiled. "Tomorrow I shall have to sample your baked goods," he said. "Today I have already promised to meet for pie at the Coffee Shop."

"That doesn't offend me, young man," Clarissa said briskly. "I'm as crazy about June's pie as everyone else in this town."

Walking south across Acorn Avenue from Hill Street, Jane directed her guest down Berry Lane. She pointed out Time for Tea, owned by Wilhelm Wood, before moving on to Nine Lives Bookstore. Viola Reed, the proprietress, popped up from behind the counter when the bell over the shop door signaled their entrance.

"Hello, Jane," she said jovially. "How are you today?"

"I'm fine, thank you," Jane replied. "Viola, I'd like to introduce you to one of our guests, Maxwell Vandermitton. Maxwell, Viola Reed, the owner of Nine Lives. If you need anything to read while you're in town, Viola is your woman."

Maxwell smiled charmingly. "It's truly a pleasure," he told her. "Ever since I was quite young, my favorite pastime has been reading. My father used to get quite angry with me for disappearing when it was time for my riding or tennis lessons. He never did figure out that I was right under his nose in the coat closet, reading with a flashlight."

Viola laughed. "Ah, a man after my own heart. There's something delicious about reading when one knows there are odious tasks to be done."

"Exactly." Maxwell beamed.

"Jane, I'm glad you're here," Viola said. "That Eastern European cookbook you ordered has finally come in."

"Wonderful! I am dying to try some of the recipes. The book got excellent reviews in *The Innkeeper's Journal*."

"I expect to be provided with samples of your culinary efforts," Viola pronounced.

Jane grinned. "I'll add you to the official guinea pig list."

Maxwell threw Jane a puzzled glance. "The guinea pig list?" His eyes widened as he looked askance at the book Jane was holding. "There are recipes using guinea pigs in that book?"

Jane began to laugh. She actually could see him backing away. "No, no. I only meant that I would let Viola sample my test batches."

"Oh. Yes. Of course." Maxwell's face reddened.

Jane turned back to Viola and changed the topic. "Ronald told me Sylvia has the flu."

"Yes, I heard," Viola responded. "Florence told Nancy Colwin, and when I went to the bakery to pick up a muffin this morning, Clarissa told me. I'm planning to take Sylvia chicken and stuffing tomorrow."

After another few minutes of conversation, Jane concluded her purchase and accompanied Maxwell to the door. They barely had turned the corner onto Chapel Road when Maxwell said, "How did Clarissa know about your friend Sylvia? I thought Viola said the first person, Florence, told somebody named Nancy...?"

"Florence Simpson," Jane told him. "Ronald's wife. Florence told Nancy Colwin. And Nancy bakes for Clarissa at the Good Apple."

"Ah! Mystery solved." They were approaching the intersection with Hill Street now. "News surely does travel fast in Acorn Hill. I must admit, I find this passing of information simply fascinating."

"I suppose it is," Jane admitted, "as long as you aren't the one being talked about."

He nodded soberly. "Very true." He glanced around. "Is there a local newspaper? I thought I might learn a bit more by reading it on a regular basis."

Jane nodded. "Yes, it's called the *Acorn Nutshell*. But it's only published once a week, on Wednesdays."

"Once a week?" Maxwell looked stricken. "But what happens if something interesting or exciting happens on Thursday? People have to wait a whole week to find out about it?"

Jane laughed out loud. "Not in this town. As you've seen, the gossip mill is very efficient in Acorn Hill. If I stubbed my toe at breakfast, everyone in town would know it by the end of the day."

"I see."

Jane said, "Do you have any other questions?"

"I didn't see any parks," Maxwell said. "Are there recreational facilities around?"

"There is a park. And there's a rec area near the elementary school. Fairy Lane is a good place for a country walk. It's about a mile north of the inn and there's a lovely path around Fairy Pond."

"Ah. A pond. That sounds restful."

"It's beautiful," Jane assured him. "I wish I had time to show it to you, but I must go home and get to work. If you'd like to explore the town a little more, it's hard to get lost in Acorn Hill. But if you do lose your way, just ask anyone you meet and they'll point you in the direction of the inn."

"Thank you for the tour, Jane." Maxwell paused at the entrance to the Coffee Shop. "I also have work to do but I believe I'll take Ronald and Henry up on their invitation first. I really must sample this pie everyone raves about."

"Her blackberry pie is one of my favorites—it's practically a work of art."

Just then the door of the Coffee Shop opened and Hope Collins, the waitress, stuck out her head. "Good morning, Jane. Did you hear Sylvia has the flu?"

Jane knew she would laugh if she looked at Maxwell. "Good morning, Hope," she said to the waitress. "I did hear that, thank you. Hope, this is Maxwell Vandermitton. Maxwell, Hope Collins."

"It's nice to meet you," Hope said as she held the door open for him to enter. "Are you staying at the inn?"

"Yes, I'll be there for the next few weeks."

"Weeks? Goodness, I guess we'll be getting to see a lot of you then." She turned to Jane. "Are you coming in? June has blackberry pie today."

Jane grinned. "You know me too well, but I'm afraid that I have to get back to the inn. Maxwell is going to join Ronald and Henry. Make sure he gets a great piece of pie."

Hope smiled. "That's an easy request to fill." She turned to Maxwell. "Today we have blackberry, blueberry, key lime and shoofly pie, and strawberry shortcake, which isn't pie, but it's still one of June's most popular desserts."

Maxwell shook his head. "I can see I'm going to have a tough choice."

"Oh, you have no idea," Jane said, grinning as the two parted ways. "I'll see you back at the inn."

Alice did not work at the hospital on Tuesday. In the middle of the afternoon, she carried several bags and a large box into the dining room. The ANGELs, a church group of middle-school girls that she led, had decided to put on a prom for seniors. With Alice's assistance, they had contacted a nearby nursing home and arranged to host a dance for the residents in the facility's recreation room.

Most of the residents used canes, walkers or wheelchairs, and the dancing they'd do would be mostly from their seats, but the ANGELs knew that the older people would enjoy a special night.

The girls were very excited about dressing up and were looking forward to seeing smiles on the faces of the residents at the nursing home. At their next meeting, they would be making paper corsages out of colored tissue and pipe cleaners, decorating invitations and baking cookies for the event. Alice's initial task was to organize their supplies, and she went about it efficiently, laying out all her purchases on the table before beginning to sort them by project.

"Good afternoon, Alice." Maxwell stopped in the doorway.

"Good afternoon," Alice responded. "Are you enjoying our little town?"

"Very much." He nodded, and Alice suspected the tepid enthusiasm that he showed was as much excitement as he ever allowed himself. "I visited the Coffee Shop for lunch today. One meets all kinds of fascinating characters there."

Alice had to chuckle. "That's certainly true. Jane told me she introduced you to a few folks yesterday. Whom did you meet today?"

"Well, there was Zach Colwin—I have not yet met his wife Nancy although I know she works at the Good Apple Bakery. And I was joined by an older lady who was quite entertaining. Can you guess who?"

Alice was bewildered. Acorn Hill was small, but not *that* small. "May I have a clue?"

Maxwell smiled slyly. "Red hair."

"Oh! You met our aunt, Ethel Buckley, didn't you?" Alice began to laugh. "That clue was a dead giveaway. Aunt Ethel has been using that hair color for years. It's called Titian Dreams. It's hard to miss, isn't it?"

Maxwell nodded. "It is, indeed. I doubt I'll have any trouble remembering who she is."

Maxwell stared at her incredulously. "It's amazing."

"Oh, not really." Alice shrugged. "By the time you've been here another week, you'll have most of the ins and outs of residents in Acorn Hill down pat." She rose from her seat. "Excuse me for a moment. I think I left my scissors in the library."

As she walked out of the dining room, Maxwell trailed after her. "So I understand you have lived in this town all your life."

Alice laughed. "I have lived in this *house* all my life, except for when I attended college. I imagine that seems strange to you."

"A bit." He stepped into the library behind her. "I began attending boarding school when I was eight years old. I haven't lived at home since then."

Alice was sincerely shocked. She stopped and turned around. "*Ever?*"

Maxwell shook his head. "I did have holidays, of course, but those were rarely more than a week long. In the summers I usually went to camp when I was younger. Then during my college years I traveled in Europe: Austria, Hungary, France, Germany, Poland, Italy, Portugal, the U.K....I even went to Russia on a kids' tour when I was younger."

"Russia! How fascinating. What impressed you the most?"

"That's an easy one—Lenin's tomb." He laughed. "I was ten years old on that trip and I thought a moldering, decades-dead body had to be the most enthralling thing ever."

Alice chuckled. "Oh yes. I know some ten-year-old boys who would be equally fascinated by that." She crossed the room and found her scissors lying on her father's desk. "Aha! Just what I was looking for."

Maxwell was looking around the library with interest. "This room has a certain charm."

"It was my father's study before he passed away. He used fountain pens all his life. My Aunt Ethel, whom you've met, gave him this lovely box for the special pens in his collection. And these vases are collectibles called Depression glass. Are you familiar with it?"

He shook his head. "No. I'm afraid my art education consisted largely of studies of the Old Masters."

Alice laughed. "These are a bit newer than that. Depression glass was made, as the name implies, before, during and just after the Great Depression. There were many patterns. Single pieces were sometimes packed in cereal boxes as premiums. People collected their favorite patterns and colors." She picked up one of the green glass vases. "This pattern also was made in yellow and pink. It is formally known as 'Cameo' and often is referred to as 'Ballerina.'"

"For obvious reasons." Maxwell peered at the tiny dancers in the glass's motif as Alice pointed them out.

"It's my favorite pattern," Alice told him. "Not only because of the pattern but because I like the shape of the dishes in this set.

There are all kinds and shapes of Depression glass, simple and elaborate."

"How interesting."

He didn't sound as if he thought it was very interesting, Alice thought. Although in fairness, she knew she probably could talk anyone to sleep once she got started discussing the collection.

"How did you get interested in Depression glass?" Maxwell asked her.

"My mother. She loved socializing and having parties, and part of her pleasure in hostessing was the opportunity to create a certain look with table settings and decorations. She had an entire luncheon set in a pink Depression glass pattern called Cherry Blossom, and every spring she held a tea party for the ladies she played canasta with. She would cut pink peonies and set a stunning table with the pink glass and all the ladies would dress in pink. Half the fun for her was the collecting, though. I can recall going to auctions and flea markets with her when I was small. She always had an eye for bargains." She smiled at the fond memories.

"I've never been to an auction. Or a flea market," Maxwell said.

"Really?" She smiled. "If you'd like, we can remedy that while you are with us."

༄

Wednesday morning, Louise walked into the kitchen to find Alice already enjoying breakfast. "Good morning," she said to her sisters. Then she eyed Alice's plate. "It looks and smells delicious."

"It is delicious." Alice said. "Jane, you've outdone yourself."

Jane had made rhubarb streusel muffins; an egg, basil and cheese breakfast lasagna; and chicken basil sausage, a new set of recipes. From the aroma arising from the breakfast, Louise suspected it quickly would become one of the inn's specialties.

Jane carried servings for Louise and for herself to the table. "You say that at least twice a week," she informed her sister.

Alice's eyes twinkled. "I only speak the truth."

"So what's on everyone's agenda for today?" Louise poured herself a glass of cranberry-apple juice and passed the pitcher to Jane.

"I'm off to Aunt Ethel's after breakfast," Alice informed her. "I promised to help her with her spring cleaning today, and she wanted to get started early. That's why I started eating without waiting for you." She chuckled. "I asked her if she wanted me to come by around seven and you should have seen her face."

Jane grinned. "A tad earlier than she intended?"

"Most definitely."

"Spring cleaning," said Louise reflectively. "I suppose we need to get started on that here, as well."

"I thought perhaps we could start washing windows next week," Jane said. "If we do two rooms per day, it won't seem like too much work."

"Yes, when you put it that way, it sounds manageable," Louise remarked.

Jane laughed. "I have to approach big jobs that way or I'm discouraged before I even begin."

"I'll help as I can," Alice said. "We'll make short work of it."

"Today I want to dust the library," Jane said. "I'm going to take all the books off the shelves and give everything a thorough cleaning."

"I can help with that this afternoon, if you want to wait for me," Louise said. "I have a National Piano Guild luncheon and meeting. This morning, I need to look over the judging packet."

"That would be great," Jane said. "I had a notion of putting all the books in alphabetical order by author as I went."

"That's an excellent idea," Alice told her. "It would make it much easier to find things."

The sisters ate heartily. Jane finished her juice and rose. "I need to get tea things on the dining room table," she said. "Both Maxwell and Mr. Jervis liked our selection yesterday."

Alice had risen to place her dirty dishes in the dishwasher. "I'm sorry I can't help today," she said.

"That's all right, Alice," Jane reassured her. "You're doing a kind thing for Aunt Ethel. Besides, you're probably going to work a whole lot harder today than either Louise or I."

Alice laughed. "Sadly, I suspect you're right. My taskmaster awaits."

"Yes, you don't want her to get mad at the help so early in the day." Jane glanced down at Wendell, who was winding around her legs looking hopeful. "Not a chance, buddy," she said. "This sausage is for humans only."

"Have a good day," Alice said. "I'll see you two later this afternoon."

Jane waved a tea towel at her sister.

"Have a good day, Alice. Say hello to Aunt Ethel for us." Louise rose and began to clear her place.

Jane glanced at the clock. "Oh, good. My timing is perfect for our guests' breakfast." She took a tea tray from the kitchen pantry and covered it with a linen cloth. She set a creamer and sugar bowl on it, a pretty basket arranged with several different teas that she had ordered in from Time for Tea and a woven basket holding some muffins. Adding two small teapots filled with hot water and cups and saucers, she backed through the swinging door.

"Good morning, Mr. Jervis," Louise heard her say pleasantly as she approached the table and began setting down the items from her tray. "Here is our selection of teas, with creamer and sweeteners, and rhubarb streusel breakfast muffins. Please let me know if there is anything else I can get for you. I'll be bringing the main dish within a few minutes."

A moment later, Jane returned to the kitchen, where she began cutting generous slices of the lasagna.

"Well," said Louise, "I promised Cynthia I'd give her a call this morning. Then I'll be back to help with the dishes." She walked into the hallway, intending to use the phone in the reception area. As she did, she saw Maxwell Vandermitton walking toward the dining room.

"Good morning, Louise." Maxwell greeted her with a smile.

"Good morning." She smiled determinedly at the young man. She still found herself put off by him. "How was your exploring trip yesterday?"

"Quite pleasant, thank you. Everyone is so friendly here."

"It's one of the things we love about Acorn Hill. Have a good day."

"Is Alice about?" The question stopped her just as she was about to pick up the phone. Louise shook her head. "No, she will be away until later this afternoon. Is there some way I can help you?"

Maxwell hastily shook his head. "No thank you. I simply wanted to get to know Alice a little better."

Louise could have pointed out that she had not spoken to him much more than Alice, but that would have been rude. "Perhaps this evening she will have time to visit with you. I'll try to remember to mention it to her."

"That would be quite helpful."

Louise shook her head as he entered the dining room. What an odd young man. He talked as if he'd been born in another, far more formal time.

She was again about to pick up the phone when it rang.

"I'll get it," she called to Jane.

A few minutes later, she retraced her steps to the kitchen, smiling in satisfaction. "I just took a reservation for August," she reported to Jane. "A group of ladies getting together for a girls' weekend. They want three rooms."

"It's a good thing they didn't wait," Jane said. "We're soon going to begin getting more bookings for the summer."

"Always a good thing," Louise said.

"Ah, Jane," said Mr. Jervis as Jane walked into the dining room to see if their guests needed anything more. "What a wonderful meal."

Jane smiled. "Would you like a second helping?"

Shaking his head, the businessman sat back, a smile wreathing his face. "I couldn't eat another bite," he confessed. "That was one of the best breakfasts I have ever had."

Jane removed his empty plate. "Thank you so much. I enjoy finding unique and tasty recipes."

"You certainly succeeded with this one," he told her. "I hate to leave."

"And we will hate to see you leave. You're welcome to extend your stay."

"I wish I could," he said. "Unfortunately, I have a schedule to keep. But I'm going to put Grace Chapel Inn on my list of wonderful places to stay during my travels through this area."

"Thank you. That's what we like to hear." She gathered a few more items from the table.

"Yes, Jane, this was a marvelous meal," Maxwell informed her. "I never would have expected muffins made with rhubarb to be so flavorful."

"It is an unusual ingredient," Jane admitted. "But when I read the recipe, it sounded as though it would be tasty, so I decided to try it."

"Your judgment was sound," the young guest declared as he rose, setting his napkin aside.

Chapter Four

*L*ouise needed a bag to carry some extra music and notebooks to the luncheon. Several canvas bags were stored in the pantry, and she went to retrieve one. As she came back out of the small storage area, she stopped in her tracks and sharply clapped her hands twice. "Wendell!"

The cat was on the table, hunched over a platter that Jane had yet to clear. He had been gnawing vigorously at a length of sausage, but at the sound of Louise's horrified tone, he cast a wild-eyed glance in her direction and leaped off the table.

He paused at the hallway door, though, which was his big mistake. Incensed, Louise snatched a section of the newspaper and rattled it menacingly, then thwacked it on the table. "Shoo!"

Wendell vanished as if he'd been shot out of a rocket, his black-tipped tail lashing the doorframe as he raced through it.

"What on earth…?" Jane pushed through the swinging door from the dining room.

"That cat!" Louise barely could get the words out. "He was…" She made agitated gestures. "He was on the table eating sausage!"

Jane looked aghast. "Gracious. He's never been so bold before. I wonder why he's suddenly so determined to sample table food."

"I don't know." Louise still was provoked. "But I let him know it was not appropriate."

Jane grinned. "I bet it will be a while before Wendell braves your wrath again."

○‿

Mr. Jervis checked out shortly after breakfast, promising a return visit. Both sisters stood on the front porch as the businessman's dark blue sedan rolled out of the driveway and turned onto Chapel Road. He waved through his open window as he drove off.

Louise went up to her room and dressed in one of her best twin sets with a soft beige skirt in lightweight wool. She added modest pearl earrings to match her pearl necklace and put on a new pair of taupe pumps with the sensible heels she preferred. She was attending a National Piano Guild luncheon today because she was to judge performances of students in several nearby towns this year. She brought her judging packet to the kitchen for one last review before she left. Jane had gone upstairs to clean the vacated guest room, and Louise had no intention of leaving the kitchen unattended with Wendell the Sausage Thief still at large.

Jane returned a bit later, carrying a basket of sheets and towels to be laundered. She stopped and blew a stray wisp of hair out of her eyes, smiling at Louise. "Lying in wait for Wendell?"

Louise narrowed her eyes. "I haven't seen so much as a whisker. I suspect he got the message that the kitchen table is off-limits."

"I haven't seen him either, but if you had fussed at me like that, I'd have run too." She laughed. "I wish I had been there when you caught him in the act." She crossed to the porch door, where the washer and dryer were located, then paused again. "Gracious, today is already Wednesday. Our German guest will arrive on Saturday. What would you think if I asked Aunt Ethel to teach us a few phrases in German? It might be a nice gesture to make Mrs. Moeller feel welcome."

"That's an excellent idea," Louise said.

Just then, the telephone rang. Since Jane had her arms full of laundry, Louise rose. "I'll get it." She picked up the telephone receiver. "Grace Chapel Inn, Louise speaking. May I help you?"

"Miss—Mrs.—Louise? This is Lyle Jervis. The guest who just left? I think something terrible has happened!" The man's words were rushed, his voice agitated.

Alarmed, Louise said, "What's happened, Mr. Jervis? Have you had an accident? Do you need assistance? I can call—"

"No, no, nothing like that. I'm in Potterston. I stopped for gas a moment ago. When I opened my door to get out, a gray-striped cat leaped out from behind my seat and ran across the parking lot. I was so surprised I just stood there, and when I finally did give chase, he had vanished into a heavy thicket just behind the gas station. I hate to tell you, but I'm almost positive it's the big cat I saw lounging at the inn yesterday, the one with the four white paws and the black tip on his tail."

Louise put a hand to her heart, feeling its rhythm speed up. Suddenly there did not seem to be enough oxygen in the room. "Oh no!" She sank into a chair at the table.

Jane came rushing in from the porch. "What's wrong?" she gasped. "Is it Alice?"

Louise shook her head. "Wendell," she said helplessly.

"Has he been hit by a car?" Jane glanced toward the front of the house as if she was ready to dash out to the road.

"No." Louise put a hand on her sister's arm to restrain her from rushing out. "It's Mr. Jervis." She indicated the receiver. "He stopped for gas in Potterston and a cat that looked like Wendell jumped out from a hiding spot behind his seat and took off."

"Was he sure it was Wendell?" Jane clearly was grasping at any straw. "I'll go check to see if he's lying on Alice's bed. He likes to lie there in the morning sometimes."

Louise shook her head, and then held up a finger as the man continued to speak.

"I had left my two front windows down last night, you see. The weather was so pretty and mild that I had been driving with them down and never gave it a thought when I came in last evening. Your cat must have jumped into my car sometime before I drove away this morning." He exhaled heavily. "I am so sorry. Tell me what to do."

"It wasn't your fault," Louise told him. "Tell me again where you are."

Jane rushed for a pen and paper, and Louise wrote down what the man told her. When she finally hung up the phone, she said, "It was Wendell. I'm sure it was. I scolded him and scared him, and he found a wonderful hiding place—only it turned out to be Mr. Jervis' car. He must be so frightened," she said, her voice trailing off.

Jane had tears in her eyes. The sisters all were very fond of the cat.

"Oh, dear heavens." Louise had another thought. Alice was particularly attached to Wendell. He was the last living link to their father, who had adored the chubby feline.

"How will I tell Alice?" She badly wanted to lay down her head and sob, but of course, she was not the type for that. Louise stood up, making a decision. "I'll go to Potterston right now. Wendell ran into some underbrush near the gas station. Perhaps he'll come out if I call him."

"Oh, I wish I could go with you," Jane cried. "But I still haven't made up Maxwell's room, and Miss Havishim, the school teacher from Boston on break, will be arriving soon."

"It's all right." Louise attempted to sound confident. "I'm sure when he hears a familiar voice, Wendell will be happy to come home. Besides," she added, "it's my fault that he's missing. He probably wouldn't have sneaked outside the house if I hadn't been so angry about the sausage."

Quickly, she called the coordinator of the Piano Guild luncheon and explained that she had a family emergency and would be unable to attend. Jane was trailing miserably behind her as she snatched up her purse and keys. She paused to give her sister a hug. "I'll find him," she said. "I have to."

"I'm going to start praying," Jane said, wiping tears from her cheeks. "Call me if you have any success."

Louise arrived in Potterston shortly before eleven o'clock in the morning. It had been the longest twenty-minute drive she'd ever taken.

Pulling into the gas station, she went inside and identified herself, and asked if anyone might have seen Wendell.

A young clerk with appalling black eye makeup was behind the counter. Through a wad of snapping gum, the girl said, "That man that lost him said to tell you he was sorry, but he had to get going. I walked out back on my smoke break and looked around but I didn't see nothin'."

Louise ignored the automatic urge to correct the girl's grammar and suggest that she would be more attractive without the gum and the gunk on her eyes. "Thank you," she said instead, and hurried back out.

It was a beautiful, warm March day, for which she was thankful. It easily could have been rainy and blustery, if not snowing and downright miserably cold. She called and called Wendell's name, moving from one side of the gas station to the other, and wading as far into the thicket of bushes behind the building as she dared in her dress shoes and good clothes. She had been in such a rush she had not even thought to change into something more practical.

After an hour of fruitless calling, she popped the top on a can of tuna she had brought along and set it on the ground, hoping that the scent of the enticing treat might flush him out. She opened the door of her car and sat down heavily, bitterly regretting her earlier treatment of the cat that, after all, had only been following his instincts.

Lord, she thought, *please don't let Wendell come to harm. Help me to find him and bring him home. He can have sausage every day if he likes.*

After resting a few moments, she got to her feet again. She started down the street next to the gas station, reasoning that someone in the residential area behind the main road might have found the cat.

She walked up and down through the quiet streets, stopping to talk to anyone she saw, describing Wendell and giving the inn's telephone number. Two young girls, perhaps nine or ten, joined her for a while, but they didn't find a single hint of him.

The girls finally got bored and wandered off, but Louise decided to make one last attempt. She turned down the block closest to the thicket of brush into which Wendell had disappeared. "Wendell," she called again and again. "Wendell."

About halfway along the block, a tiny woman with snow white hair coiled into a bun came stumping across the street, leaning heavily on a cane. "Here, now," she called to Louise, "don't you give him the satisfaction, missy."

Distracted from her search, Louise raised one eyebrow. "I beg your pardon?"

"Ain't no man on the face of this earth worth carryin' on like that for," the woman informed her tartly. "I've been listenin' to you caterwaulin' half the afternoon. Where's your pride, girl?"

"My pride…?" *Caterwauling?* Louise shook her head. "I'm sorry, I believe you have me confused with someone else, ma'am."

"I most certainly have not." Thumps with the cane accented the last two words. "You've been wanderin' up and down the street tryin' to find your Wendell, haven't you?"

"I . . . oh!" As comprehension dawned, Louise did not know whether to laugh or to cry. "Wendell isn't a man," she told the old lady. "He's my cat. He stowed away in a car this morning and jumped out the window at the gas station on the corner."

"Yer cat?" The woman's face softened from the ferocious scowl it had been wearing. "Well, that's another story. I like cats. Tell me what he looks like and I'll keep my eyes peeled for him."

It was nearly three o'clock when Louise's feet finally demanded immediate respite. Feeling terribly defeated, she spoke to the gas station clerk one last time. The girl gave her a piece of paper on which to write a description and then affixed it to a bulletin board inside the door.

"You'll find him," the girl said, patting Louise's shoulder encouragingly. "When he gits hungry, he'll be back."

The girl's attempt at comfort was touching, and Louise mentally asked forgiveness for the critical thoughts she'd had earlier. Then, climbing wearily into her car, she turned it toward Acorn Hill.

"Louise is back!" Alice jumped to her feet, nearly tipping over the bowl of hard-boiled eggs she had been peeling for egg salad. "I hope she found him."

"She must have," Jane said as they both rushed down the back porch steps and out to the parking lot, where Louise's car door was opening.

But one glance at their elder sister's face when she emerged told the story.

Alice stopped cold. "Oh, Louise," she said, her voice wobbling. "We were so sure you'd be able to find him."

"So was I," Louise said. "But no one has seen him, and if he heard me, he must be too upset to come to me."

The three sisters walked back into the kitchen and Louise sank down on one of the chairs and slipped off her shoes. She winced, and Alice noticed. When Alice glanced down at her sister's feet, she understood why Louise was in pain.

"Oh, my heavens. Your poor feet." She brought a second chair around and lifted Louise's legs so her feet were propped on the seat of the chair. "Jane, get me a bucket of warm water." To Louise, she said, "You need to soak your feet. I believe I have some Epsom salts upstairs."

Walking out of the room was a relief for Alice. As she hurried up the stairs, she could not suppress the tears that rose. "Oh, Wendell," she said softly. "I know Father would welcome your company in heaven, but I'm not ready for you to leave me."

The box of Epsom salts was beneath the sink in Alice's third-floor bathroom. Picking it up, she composed herself, brushed the tears away and went back down to the kitchen.

Louise shared her search efforts with Jane and Alice, and they laughed fleetingly at her tale of the elderly woman's misunderstanding. But the light moment could not overcome the gloom and sorrow that permeated the room.

As Jane gently dried Louise's feet with a soft towel a short time later, Alice said, "Let's pray."

"I have been," Jane said, "but it would be comforting to me if we all prayed together."

The sisters linked hands.

"Dear Father," Alice began, "please keep Wendell safe. Please…" She felt a sob rising and had to stop to regain her composure.

Jane took over the prayer. "Please bring him home to us. You know our hearts, how much we love him. Bless our search efforts and let them bear fruit."

"And Lord," Louise said, "forgive me for my impatience. Wendell is one of Your precious creatures, made with the instincts You gave him, and I forgot that. Don't let any harm befall him. Help him find something to eat and to drink, and give him a warm place to rest until we bring him home again. Amen."

"Amen," Jane and Alice echoed.

Chapter Five

*W*ednesday evening, Alice was sitting listlessly in the living room when Maxwell Vandermitton came into the foyer.

"Uh-oh, Maxwell," she heard Jane say, "you're tracking mud across the floor. Please remove your shoes before you go upstairs. Where on earth have you been to get so covered in mud?"

"Just out walking." The young man sounded a bit defensive. "I'll take off my shoes and set them outside the back door for now."

"Thank you, that's a good idea," Jane responded. "By tomorrow morning the mud probably will have dried and you'll be able to clean most of it off."

There was a momentary pause. "I don't know how to clean shoes," Maxwell admitted to Jane.

There was a long pause. Jane apparently was as puzzled as Alice felt by that statement. Finally, Jane said, "Most of it will fall off if you take them out in the grass and bang them together. Come find me after you try that, and I'll show you how to remove what's left."

Alice heard Jane climb the stairs as Maxwell's footsteps headed down the hallway. In a moment, he was back, his stockinged feet making soft thuds as he walked.

"Alice!"

Rats. He's seen me. Alice was not feeling very social at the moment, but she couldn't be rude to a guest. "Hello."

Maxwell dropped down on the sofa beside her, then turned and peered down at her. "What's wrong? Have you been crying?"

She nodded. "Our cat got lost today."

"How do you know he's lost?"

Alice relayed the story of Wendell's escape and Louise's futile search. "It hurts my heart to think of how afraid he must be, alone in a strange place with no food or water. I'm so afraid he'll get hit by a car or attacked by some other animal. He isn't used to fending for himself."

"Maybe someone will find him." Maxwell patted her shoulder. "And if not, you can always get another cat."

"Maxwell!" Alice was too upset now to worry about offending a guest. "Wendell is not replaceable. He's a living being, not a stuffed toy. My father picked him out of a litter when he was a tiny kitten, a few years before Father died, and he's very special to me—to all of us."

Maxwell was quiet for a moment. Alice hoped he might take her silence as a hint and just go away.

Then he said, "I'm sorry, Alice. I never had a pet. I don't really know what it's like to love an animal."

Alice sighed. He'd succeeded in making her feel petty and mean. "I'm sorry too. I shouldn't have snapped at you. It's just that Wendell is very special. No other cat will have his silly little quirks, his personality." There was a pause. Then, as his words penetrated her haze of sadness, she said, "You never had any kind of pet?"

"Not even a fish," he confirmed. "My father never would have tolerated having pets in the house. And as I told you before, I was at school most of the time. Of course, pets are not welcome at boarding school. I did learn to ride, but I never cared much for horses."

"I see."

"You know, I don't believe I've ever spoken so much to anyone about my past." Maxwell sounded surprised. "You're very easy to talk to, Alice."

She considered the fleeting exchanges that she'd had with their guest, and the few details she'd learned. How sad that he felt she had learned a lot about him. "Thank you," she said quietly, resolving to be a better hostess and a better Christian friend. "I'm happy to listen any time you'd like to talk."

"Actually," Maxwell said, "I would like to ask you some questions. I'm very interested in Acorn Hill. I can imagine that growing up here was very peaceful and secure."

"Peaceful might not be a term I'd use for a household of three girls," Alice said, smiling a little. "But we were happy most of the time. And secure—yes, I certainly felt comfortable and safe anywhere I went. The community still inspires that feeling in people, I believe."

"So you've known most of the people around here your whole life."

"Many of them, yes. Others are more recent transplants from other locales who enjoyed our atmosphere and decided to make their homes here."

"Everyone seems to know one another awfully well."

"It's a given in most small towns," Alice told him. "There are no secrets."

Maxwell chuckled. "That would be an interesting theory to put to the test."

There was something remotely disdainful in his tone, something that she couldn't quite put her finger on. But, she reminded herself, he had not grown up in an atmosphere conducive to trusting others. She imagined the concept of other people knowing all about your business was so alien that he couldn't quite grasp it.

Then her gaze lit on a bright red stuffed mouse half hidden beneath the Oriental rug and she forgot all about Maxwell's social issues.

Oh, Wendell. She glanced at her watch. She was working the night shift from eleven to seven, but when she left the hospital, she intended to go to search for him. Tomorrow was the day they would find their beloved pet. She just knew it.

The atmosphere at breakfast on Thursday morning was subdued. Jane presented sliced smoked salmon on toast with cream cheese, red onion and capers to their guests, along with butternut and bran muffins, cranberry jam, fresh strawberries in cream and their choice of beverages. Miss Havishim and Maxwell both raved about the salmon, but Jane could work up only the faintest pleasure in their enthusiasm. All she could think about was that

Wendell had missed two meals now. He had to be upset, hungry, afraid—she tried to stop thinking about him. She couldn't let herself dwell on Wendell or she would have a total meltdown.

Louise came into the kitchen just as Jane was finishing tidying up. She had had an early lesson with one of her adult students. When Jane offered to fix her a plate, Louise declined.

"Thank you, dear, but I'm just not hungry. I barely slept a wink last night." She looked as if she had been up all night. Deep circles beneath her blue eyes made her look years older.

"I know." Jane untied her voluminous white apron and hung it in the pantry. "I just got done telling myself that I can't dwell on Wendell all day. I'm going to make up the guest rooms and do a little cleaning. Then I thought perhaps I would make posters that we could take to Potterston and hang in several places."

"I hope that won't be necessary," Louise said. "I keep thinking the phone is going to ring, and someone will tell us they have found our boy." She glanced at the clock on the kitchen wall. "Where's Alice? I expected her to be home from work by now."

Jane shrugged. "She hasn't called, but you know Alice. She gets caught up helping with patients through the end of a shift and forgets the time. I imagine she'll be home soon." Then, when Jane glanced at the clock, she did a double take. "Oh my. It's nearly eleven. Shifts do run over, but Alice has never been this late before."

"That's what I was trying to say."

Jane went to the phone. "I think I'll call the hospital and check. I'm sure there's nothing to worry about, but just to be sure…" She punched in the number of the Potterston Hospital impatiently and waited for the receptionist, then asked for Alice. A moment later, she put down the phone and looked at Louise soberly. "Alice left the hospital at least two-and-a-half hours ago."

"Oh dear."

"I'm sure she's fine." Jane knew she sounded as if she were trying to convince herself. "Perhaps she had some errands to run."

"Do you think we should go and look for her?"

"Let's give her a little more time," Jane suggested, although part of her badly wanted to jump in her car and begin searching. "Our routine has been upset since lunch yesterday. She simply might have forgotten to call."

Louise glanced at the clock. "All right. One hour. We'll give her until noon but after that, if we don't hear from her, I'm going to look for her."

"All right." Jane squared her shoulders. "I'm going to get to work."

"As am I. I have more lessons to prepare."

Shortly before twelve, Jane heard the kitchen door open and close. She raced downstairs, nearly colliding with Louise, who had come out of the parlor.

"Was that the door?" Louise asked.

"Yes. Alice!" Jane was now a few steps ahead of her sister and she could see Alice shrugging out of her jacket. "We've been so worried. Where were you?"

Alice's shoulders slumped and she plopped down at the table, massaging her temples with her fingers. "I'm sorry. I went to look for Wendell after my shift ended and I lost track of time." Her air of sadness made it clear she had not found their pet.

"Did you speak to anyone who lives in the area?" Louise asked. "I thought perhaps he would go to someone's home when he got hungry."

Alice nodded. "I spoke to several people who were walking dogs or pushing baby strollers. Everyone promised to keep an eye out for him, but no one has seen him."

"It's only been one day," Jane said, trying to encourage herself as much as her sisters. "He's got to be out there."

"I'm going to call the Potterston radio station," Louise announced. "They have a lost-and-found segment twice every day, at eight AM and at five PM. Maybe someone will hear that and see Wendell, and we'll get a call."

"That's a good idea." Alice raised her head wearily.

"You should get some sleep," Jane said, concerned by her sister's atypical lack of energy. "You worked all night and searched half the morning."

"Yes," Louise said. "Why don't you rest, Alice? Jane is going to make a flyer on the computer, and tomorrow we can post copies all over Potterston."

"Yes," Jane confirmed. "And we can spread the word here as well, just in case people are traveling to Potterston. Everyone can be on the lookout for Wendell."

"All right." Alice's eyes welled with tears, and she blinked rapidly. "Sorry. I'll be steadier after I've gotten some rest."

"It's all right," Jane said. "We're all having bad moments." She pulled a travel-sized pack of tissues from the back pocket of the baggy ivory cotton pants she wore with a soft blue oversized boatneck sweater. "Here."

Louise and Alice both managed to smile.

"Trust you to be prepared," Louise said.

"All right," Jane said firmly, giving Alice a nudge. "You rest. I'm going to make that poster right now."

"And I'll call the Potterston radio station," Louise said.

Jane went to the computer behind the registration desk. Sliding into a chair, she quickly got into the program she wanted. Fortunately, one of their guests had taken digital pictures of Wendell while staying at Grace Chapel Inn. The woman had sent several by e-mail to Jane, who had saved them in a file on the computer. She selected the best one, a full-body picture of Wendell lying on his side, face turned straight into the camera lens.

Using the photo, she created a flyer offering a small reward for his safe return. She had not discussed the reward with her sisters, but she doubted they would mind, and if they did, she would pay the money herself.

When the printer spit out a high-quality flyer, Jane snatched it up and scanned it. *That should be good for a start*, she thought, and she ran off twenty copies.

Louise came into the hallway and picked up a flyer off the registration desk. "Very nice," she said, looking over the information with approval. "Oh, what a good idea! I'll be happy to share the cost of a reward, Jane."

"Thanks, Louise. I thought perhaps a reward might keep people more interested in looking for him."

∽

Shortly after three o'clock, Alice awoke from her nap. She felt lethargic and dull but she made herself rise and dress, and then went downstairs. As she walked through the hall, the flyers with Wendell's picture caught her eye.

Picking up one, she looked it over as she went back toward the kitchen.

"Hello, Jane," she said as she entered the room.

"Hi, Alice. How are you feeling?" Jane was rhythmically kneading a lump of bread dough.

Alice shrugged. "A little more rested, but I doubt I'll have any trouble sleeping tonight." She waved the paper in her hand at her sister. "These are very well done."

"Thank you. I figure it can't hurt to spread them around Potterston."

"Can you spare a few? I'm going to walk into town and I can put them up while I'm there."

"Sure. I saved the final version of it so if we run out, I can always make more."

Putting on her jacket, Alice made the short trip on foot from the inn to town. She put posters on public bulletin boards at the General Store, the library, the post office and in the front window of the Good Apple Bakery with Clarissa Cottrell's blessing. Her last stop was the Coffee Shop, where Hope Collins helpfully brought her some tape so she could position a flyer prominently in the front window right next to the menu June placed there every day.

"Thank you so much," she said to Hope and to June, who were behind the counter sorting currency during the afternoon lull.

"I hope you find him," June told her sympathetically. June was a cat lover too.

Just then a commotion interrupted the women's chat.

Two grade-school boys burst into the shop, wild-eyed. "There's a monster out there!" one of them blurted.

Alice recognized him as Jason Ransom, one of Louise's piano students. The other boy was Charles Matthews, also a piano student and a member of the Grace Chapel congregation.

"A monster?" she said, making her eyes wide. "Did you see it?"

"No, but we saw its tracks by the pond," Charles told her. Hope and June were both listening, and a few other people lingering in the shop also looked as if they were dying to hear more.

"Its tracks. What did they look like?" *A raccoon, maybe*, Alice thought. Although there were bears in Pennsylvania, they weren't common to the area around Acorn Hill.

"They were this big," Jason said, measuring an imaginary track well over twelve inches long by spreading his hands apart.

"That's big," Alice agreed.

"What did they look like?" Hope asked.

Charles clearly was so excited he could barely speak. "Like—like—like big, fat feet," he said.

"Well," murmured June, "that's helpful."

Alice swallowed a chuckle. "Where, exactly, at the pond did you find them?"

"We can show you," offered Jason.

It was barely four o'clock and Alice didn't have to get back to help with dinner quite yet, so she decided she could afford to spend a few minutes humoring the boys. "All right."

"I'll come too." The voice from behind Alice belonged to Ronald Simpson, Florence's husband. His freckled face wore a smile, and Alice read the amusement twinkling in his brown eyes. "I've always had a yen to see a monster. Let's take my car."

Alice and Ronald followed the boys out of the Coffee Shop. Ronald's car was parked along the curb, and after holding the passenger door for Alice, Ronald went around to the driver's side while the boys hopped into the back seat. Ronald headed north on Chapel Road, past the inn, to where Fairy Lane was located. As soon as Ronald parked along the lane, Charles and Jason tumbled out of the car and took off at a good clip. They were well ahead of Alice and Ronald by the time they reached the edge of the pond, but then both boys slowed and waited until the adults were close behind them before forging onward.

It had rained a bit two nights before and on one side of the pond there was a gentle incline to the water. "The tracks are over here," Jason told Alice and Ronald.

A path had been worn around the pond by people strolling along the edge of the peaceful water.

Near the water's edge there were weeds and cattails, withered and brown from the winter, but new shoots of green were beginning to show.

Now that they were at the pond, the two boys seemed strangely subdued and surprisingly content to stay near the adults. Ronald led the way along the bank, following clear impressions of sneakered feet that the boys must have left earlier in the rain-softened earth.

Suddenly, Ronald stopped. Alice nearly plowed into him.

"Holy moley!" His voice was awed. "Alice, take a look at this."

She moved around to his side. There, in the middle of the path ahead of them, were two well-formed impressions of massive feet. Whatever had made the prints had apparently been traveling beside the path rather than on it much of the time, because a third print showed toes only, suggesting that the maker of the tracks had strayed onto the path from the side and then stepped back off it two paces farther on.

"See?" Jason's voice was high with excitement. "Monster tracks."

"I think they're bear tracks," Charles said. His voice quavered slightly as he looked around, clearly more than a little concerned that the bear might be nearby.

"I don't believe these are bear tracks," Ronald said. "Bears rarely walk on two legs for any distance. Also, bears are rarely found in this area, as far as I know." He knelt, staying a distance away from the tracks. "And in ground this soft, wouldn't you think you'd see the claws in a bear track?" he said to Alice.

"I don't know enough about tracks to have an opinion," she said honestly. "But I can tell you these are the biggest footprints of any kind I have ever seen."

"How big would you estimate they are?" Ronald asked.

Alice eyed the prints. "Sixteen inches, perhaps?" she said hesitantly.

"I'd agree with that, give or take an inch," Ronald said. "Boy, what I wouldn't give for my camera right now."

"You could go and get it and come back," she suggested. "It's going to be light for another few hours."

Ronald nodded. "That's a good idea." He winked at Alice and then turned to the boys. "How about you two stay here and guard these footprints while Alice and I go get a camera?"

Jason shook his head vigorously, his eyes wide. "I gotta get home. Mom needs me."

"Um, me too," Charles said. He already was edging backward. "I mean my mom needs me, not his. I told her I'd go to the store for her before dinner and…"

Both boys turned and ran. Over his shoulder, Jason called, "See ya."

"See you," Ronald and Alice called.

As the sounds of the children rushing away faded, Alice began to laugh. "Those poor kids are half terrified."

"More than half, I'd say." Ronald took another long look at the tracks. "But, Alice, I have to tell you that I have no idea what could have made these tracks. No idea at all," he said slowly.

"Maybe it's someone playing a joke," she suggested.

Ronald's freckled forehead wrinkled. "Who would do something like that? The prints are too well-formed to be the work of kids."

Alice shrugged. "Good point."

The two of them stood for a moment longer, staring down at the "monster" tracks in the soft mud of the path. The longer they stood there, the odder Alice felt, as if there were eyes watching her from the heavy underbrush farther back from the pond.

A shiver chased itself up her spine. "Okay," she said, "I'm as ready to get out of here as those boys were. And I have to get home and help Jane with dinner."

"All right," Ronald said. "I'll drop you off and then I'm going home to get a camera." As they turned to retrace their steps back to Fairy Lane, he muttered under his breath, "And maybe someone to come along with me."

Alice chuckled. "I'm glad it's not just me who feels a little spooked."

"You know," he said, "we ought to have someone make plaster casts of the prints. Then we could take them to a biologist who might be able to figure out what they are."

"That's a great idea. Fred Humbert probably sells plaster at the hardware store."

"I've never tried to make plaster casts before," Ronald said. "I'd better find out if he knows anyone who could help me do it."

The two of them were almost back to the car when Alice felt a raindrop on the top of her hand. Then others struck her nose and her forehead. "Oh no. It's starting to rain," she said to Ronald.

"I can see that." As the drops began to fall faster, the two of them rushed the last few yards to Ronald's car. Ronald's blue shirt was spattered with dark blotches by the time they got there, and moments after they had scrambled in, the heavens opened and a deluge poured from the skies.

Not unexpected in March, Alice thought, but surely unwelcome at this moment. The tracks were going to be too damaged to view after a downpour like this. When she said as much to Ronald, he glumly agreed. "Not much point in heading back there with a camera now," he said. "I'll just drop you off at the inn and go home."

"Thanks," Alice said. "And perhaps on the way back to town you'll see the boys. I can't believe they didn't wait for a ride. They must be soaked."

"They're young," Ronald said philosophically. "They'll think it's a great adventure."

Chapter Six

*A*n hour after Alice arrived home, the telephone rang. Jane, who was in the living room, walked to the reception desk and picked up the handset. "Grace Chapel Inn, Jane speaking. May I help you?"

"Hello, Jane. This is Carlene. Is Alice around?"

"She's here somewhere," Jane said. "Let me find her for you." She glanced into the parlor and the dining room, but she did not find Alice until she stepped into the kitchen.

"Telephone for you. It's Carlene."

Alice looked surprised. "What does she want?"

Jane shrugged. "She didn't say."

Alice went to the kitchen phone. "Hello, Carlene. This is Alice."

Jane moved to the counter where she began forming the dough that had finished rising into croissants for tomorrow's breakfast menu. Although she did not intend to eavesdrop, it was difficult to ignore Alice's end of the conversation.

"Yes ... just Ronald and me ... the boys found the tracks first ... No, no, I don't believe they were human. They were really large, well over a foot long, but also they were very broad. Ronald said he didn't think they were bear tracks, either ... No, I didn't look closely at the toes ... We intended to, but it began to rain. You might take a walk back there to see, but I imagine that hard rain we had washed them out or, at the very least, damaged them badly."

By now, Jane had given up any pretense of not listening. After Alice concluded her conversation, Jane said, "What on earth was that about?"

Alice rolled her eyes and shook her head. "You'll never believe it."

"How about you tell us all about it over dinner. Would you please call Louise while I serve this potpie?"

Alice did as requested, and in a few minutes, the three sisters were sitting at the kitchen table. Alice opened the meal with a prayer for Wendell's safe return in addition to the usual blessing of the food. When she finished, there was a heavy moment of sorrowful silence.

Then she picked up her fork. "You two will never, in a hundred million years, guess what I saw today."

"I could make a lot of guesses in a hundred million years," Jane said, gamely trying to lighten the mood.

"In the interest of time, I move we dispense with guessing," Louise said dryly. "Let's hear it, Alice."

As Alice launched into her story, Louise and Jane listened with growing incredulity.

"So why did Carlene call?" Jane asked when Alice finished. "Is she going to write an article about it?"

Alice chuckled. "Apparently, after Ronald dropped me off, he went back to the Coffee Shop. Everyone who had heard the boys the first time wanted to hear what he had to say."

"And he said . . . ?" Jane leaned forward.

"The same thing I said. He had no idea what to make of the tracks."

"Could they have been a hoax?" Louise asked.

"I suppose anything's possible," Alice said, "but except for the boys', there were no human prints of any kind around. And unless the boys are terrific actors, they had nothing to do with making the prints. As for what the tracks are, I'm afraid to even guess. I keep thinking about those ridiculous Bigfoot stories, but they don't seem quite so ridiculous anymore."

"Bigfoot," Jane said thoughtfully. "Isn't that the North American equivalent of the Abominable Snowman?"

"It is." Louise picked up the salad bowl. "It is also called Sasquatch, and the Himalayan monsters are called Yeti." She spooned a portion of salad onto her plate, then realized both her sisters were staring at her. "What?"

"Interesting trivia for you to know," Jane said with a grin.

"Cynthia had to do a report on the topic in school one time," Louise said. "What else would you like to know?"

"Do you think they're real?" Alice took the salad from Louise.

"I just don't know." Louise shrugged. "I'm skeptical. There are no fossil records, no skeletal remains, no records of any hunter ever bagging one…on the other hand, there are many, many eyewitness reports and findings of tracks. There have even been a few claims of finding nests or scat."

"Scat?" Jane's brow wrinkled.

Louise gave her a look. "F-e-c-e-s."

"Oh." Jane made a face. "Sorry. Keep going."

"Some of the eyewitness accounts are extremely detailed and a significant number of them share commonalities that the average person would not have known."

"Geographically speaking," Jane said, "I don't think we are exactly in the center of Bigfoot sightings. Aren't most of them out in the Northwest?"

Louise nodded. "A lot of reports have come from areas where there are extremely large tracts of undeveloped land."

"So the four of you are the only ones who saw these tracks?" Jane asked Alice.

Alice nodded. "Ronald was going to get a camera, and we had talked about making plaster casts. And then it rained."

"It didn't just rain," Louise said. "It poured. And it's still raining, although certainly not as hard as it did earlier."

"It just kills me to think of Wendell being out in this." Alice had to voice the thought that wouldn't stop circling in her brain, despite the memory of her unusual experience during the afternoon. "It's supposed to get down into the low forties tonight."

"Perhaps he's not outside," said Jane. "Maybe he's found sanctuary with some lovely person who will call us tomorrow. Or maybe he's sneaked into someone's warm, dry garage."

"Oh, I hope so." Alice's voice quavered and Jane reached over and placed a comforting hand atop her sister's.

"Have faith," Jane said. "We just have to have faith."

Alice realized, apparently at almost the same moment Jane did, that Louise had been noticeably silent during their exchange. She reached out and clasped Louise's hand and Jane did the same.

"It is not your fault, Louise," Alice said firmly. "Neither of us blames you, and we won't let you blame yourself. If I'd been in the kitchen and caught him on the table, I'd have reacted very much the same."

"Do you remember the time he leaped onto the counter and walked right across that freshly iced sheet cake I had made for the Potterston Art Festival?" Jane asked. "By the time I found him, he had licked his feet clean, but the paw prints in the icing gave him away. I wasn't very happy with him that day."

Alice chuckled. "And how about the day he got into one of our guest rooms and knocked over the little girl's goldfish bowl that she'd won at the fair? Thank heavens I was walking down the hall and heard the crash. That poor fish was flopping around and Wendell was trying to pin it down until I scooped it up and dropped it into a glass of water."

Louise finally smiled a little at that memory. "I bet those guests will never come back."

"Probably not." Alice's eyes lost their momentary sparkle. "Tomorrow I'm going to put up some more posters if we don't hear anything by noon."

"I can help," Louise volunteered. "And we can go to Potterston to try to find him again. By now, he must be getting hungry and lonely. Maybe he'll come out if he's hiding in the bushes."

"Maybe." Alice tried to hold onto hope.

After dinner, Alice went to the telephone. Smiling to herself, she dialed a familiar number.

The phone rang once, then a second time. "Mark Graves."

"Hello, Mark. It's Alice."

"Alice! Hello. How is business at the inn?"

"Very good, thanks. We have two guests right now and another lady arrives tomorrow. How are you?"

"I'm great. I'm packing to fly to California tomorrow. The San Diego Zoo has asked me to do a consult. I'm going to help design a new pachyderm habitat."

"That's exciting. You really enjoy working with elephants, don't you?"

"I do." She could hear the smile in his voice. "Weird, right?"

"Not for a veterinarian," Alice said. "I think it's fascinating."

"When I return from San Diego, do you think there might be a room available at the inn for a weekend stay?" His voice deepened. "I haven't seen you in far too long."

"I know." Alice cleared her throat. "I'm sure we can work out something. I'd like to see you too. But that isn't really why I called."

"Don't burst my bubble. I'm imagining that you can't live without seeing me."

Alice laughed, and he said, "All right. Tell me what's going on."

❧

"I called Mark," Alice announced to Jane an hour later. Jane was at the computer. Looking over her sister's shoulder, Alice could see a recipe for some kind of pancakes.

"That's nice." Jane looked up, puzzled. "Is there some significance to calling Mark that escapes me?"

Alice smiled. "I asked him about Bigfoot."

"Ah. And he said...?"

"Well, I was hoping he could come out and take a look around, but he's leaving town tomorrow, so that's a no-go."

"How disappointing. I know how much his professional opinion means to you." Jane was grinning.

"Stop that," Alice said with mock severity. "We're just friends." She went on. "I was a little surprised at what he said when I told him how big a furor those prints have created around here."

"Let me guess. He laughed and said people are gullible."

"No, that's what I said—in a nicer way, of course. I think it's implausible that an animal that size could have escaped detection for so long. But Mark reminded me that only last year scientists got their first-ever video of a living giant squid. He seems to think it's possible that a shy creature with significant animal intelligence could evade humans for a long time."

"Wow." Alice had caught Jane's full attention. "You're kidding me. Mark believes in Bigfoot?"

"I wouldn't say he believes," Alice hedged. "But he was more willing than I was to entertain the possibility of its existence."

Despite their hopes, Wendell did not appear when Alice and Louise went to Potterston on Friday afternoon. They distributed all their posters but one and made a list of several other places that would allow them to hang a flyer.

Discouraged and disappointed, they stopped at the animal shelter located between Potterston and Acorn Hill on the way home and put up their last poster. The girl at the desk had no record of any gray tabbies brought in recently, but promised to keep an eye out for Wendell.

Riding home, Alice began to feel the first stirrings of resignation. What if Wendell was gone for good?

When Louise suggested they stop at the Coffee Shop, Alice agreed, eager to push away her morose thoughts.

The little restaurant was fragrant with freshly baked pies. As they looked around for seats, a waving hand caught their attention.

"There's Maxwell," Alice said. "Shall we join him?"

"Lead the way," Louise said. "I'll sit anywhere as long as Hope brings me a piece of that blackberry pie."

"Hello, ladies." The young man rose courteously as the sisters walked toward him. He wore pressed khakis and the rolled up sleeves of his blue Oxford-cloth shirt revealed a hefty gold watch that Alice suspected must be a Rolex. "Won't you please have a seat?"

"Thank you." Alice heaved a sigh. "What have you been doing today?"

"I was at the library doing a bit of research on their public computer," he told her. "How about you?"

"We were in Potterston again looking for Wendell."

"No luck?" He looked sincerely concerned. "I'm sorry. He may turn up yet."

"I hope so," Alice responded. "I've been praying about it. Mostly I've been praying for what I want, which is for Wendell to come home. And of course, I pray for him to be fed and warm and dry, but today I began to pray for acceptance, for God to soothe my sadness if Wendell is gone for good."

Louise nodded. "I'm at the same point. Except that I am having a hard time not blaming myself for his disappearance. I keep replaying the way I fussed at Wendell."

"Oh, Louise," said Alice. "You must let that go. You are not to blame."

There was a long silence. Maxwell looked around uncomfortably as if he didn't know how to respond to their comments. Alice suspected that Maxwell had never experienced God's love in a personal way, had never opened his life to Christ. After all, who would have guided him in a Christian path? By his account, his father had been largely absent from his life, and if the schools where he'd lived had given their students any sort of religious training, she had yet to see a sign of it. And since the young man had never mentioned his mother, she suspected that Mrs. Vandermitton either had passed away or left her family. Alice resolved to be a good role model during the remainder of his visit and to share her faith with him whenever the opportunity arose.

Louise cleared her throat. "Here comes Hope. What kind of pie would you like, Alice?"

"I'd like blackberry," she told the waitress.

Louise ordered blueberry pie, while Maxwell declined.

"I've already had two pieces," he said.

Hope smiled at him. "He's rapidly becoming our best customer," she told Louise and Alice.

As Hope left their table to get their order ready, Alice asked, "Have you heard about the tracks the two boys found yesterday?"

"Yes, indeed," Maxwell responded. "And I understand you and Ronald Simpson are the only two adults to actually see them."

"Unfortunately." Alice grimaced. "I wish it hadn't rained."

"The tracks are all anyone in town is talking about today," Maxwell said. "Apparently the woman from the paper went out to photograph them this morning, but the rain had obliterated all but some large, blurry depressions in the mud."

"I was afraid of that," Alice said.

"What did you see?"

After Hope returned with their order, Alice recounted her experience. As she spoke, she was aware of a slight stir over near the counter. Finally, the buzz grew so insistent that the sisters and Maxwell halted their conversation and turned to see what the excitement was about.

Bobby Dawson, a member of Grace Chapel's youth group, stood in the midst of a small cluster of people. The teen was gesticulating wildly. Some people were responding with expressions of incredulity, while others nodded and smiled or shook their heads and frowned.

When Hope passed their table again, Alice said, "Hope, what on earth is Bobby saying that has everyone so stirred up?"

Hope laughed. "Apparently, he found an article at the library this afternoon that made him wonder if the tracks you found are from a Bigfoot."

Alice glanced quickly at Louise. Louise had raised one eyebrow, although she remained silent.

Carefully, Alice said, "What would possess him to look that up?"

"He says he didn't," Hope reported. "He was there to research a history paper and he found the article lying near the computer."

When Alice looked at Maxwell, he was just setting down his coffee cup. "From what Alice just described, they certainly weren't from a little foot, no matter what kind of animal it was," he said.

Hope laughed. "Not a big *foot*, a *Bigfoot*. One word. Haven't you ever heard of Sasquatch? Huge man-ape creatures that no one's ever conclusively proved exist?"

"Oh, right. Bigfoot," Maxwell said. His eyes widened as he looked at Alice. "Do you think that's what the footprints could have been from?"

Alice shook her head. "I really couldn't say. It was certainly a large creature, whatever it was."

Maxwell leaned forward. "Did they find any other evidence that would lead them to believe that it might be some unknown animal?"

"I didn't hear about anything else," Alice said. "Did you, Louise?"

"No. I can't imagine what else they might have found," she said dismissively.

Maxwell looked disappointed. "I would like to go over there and inspect the site. Would either of you be interested in joining me?"

Louise shook her head. "Not I. I have a piano student coming at four-thirty for a lesson."

"I'll go with you," Alice volunteered. "But after I finish my pie, we'll have to go back to the inn to get my car."

"Hello there!"

They turned their heads to see who was interrupting their conversation.

"Here comes Florence," Louise announced. She rose. "Hello, Florence. I was just leaving. Would you like my seat?" Louise asked as she slid from the booth.

"Why, thank you, Louise dear." Florence Simpson was dressed in a navy, two-piece outfit with nautical trim and a wide, white sailor collar. From her chubby wrist dangled an expensive-looking gold bracelet with sailboat charms. Florence dismissed Louise with a wave of her hand and turned her attention to Alice and Maxwell. "Alice, dear. I have not been introduced to this young man." Then, without giving Alice a chance to draw a breath, she thrust out her right hand. "You must be Maxwell. I'm Florence Simpson. My family has been in Acorn Hill for more than one hundred years."

Maxwell rose and took Florence's hand, holding it gingerly. "That's quite interesting. My family also has a long history in Pennsylvania. My father is the sixth generation of Vandermittons to live in my family home."

Florence looked a bit deflated, although his statement had been delivered in the most pleasant tone. "Yes. Well. My friend Ethel, Alice's aunt, told me that you are staying at the inn for some time."

"Yes, I am." Maxwell smiled, waiting until Florence squeezed her bulky body into the booth beside Alice before reseating himself. "I am finishing a research project for my doctoral program, and Grace Chapel Inn is proving to be a very pleasant place to work."

"Well, yes, I can see that it would be," Florence said.

"Alice and I were just leaving," he told the older woman. "We thought we would head out to Fairy Pond for a look around. Would you care to join us?"

"Why, I'd love to." Florence's gray eyes sharpened. "My car is right outside. Ever since Ronald came home yesterday all I have heard about is those tracks. Now that silly Dawson boy is stirring up everyone with talk about mythic creatures."

"Mythic or not, I'd like to see the place where the prints were found," Maxwell said.

Alice picked up her purse, and Florence took the hint, sliding out of the booth. "I have a duty to go," she announced. "After all, it was my husband who found those prints in the first place."

Alice cleared her throat. "Well, actually it was Charles and Jason—"

"The first *adult*," Florence stressed. "Everyone knows children's impressions can't be trusted."

As they were walking out of the Coffee Shop, Nia Komonos and Carlene Moss were about to enter and stood aside to let them exit.

"Good afternoon, Nia, Carlene." Alice smiled. "*Hmm*, a researcher and a reporter. What could you two be cooking up?"

Carlene gave Alice a dimpled smile. "If you're coming out of Gossip Central, you probably already know."

Alice laughed. "Don't tell me you're giving credence to this Bigfoot theory."

"One must keep an open mind," Carlene said. She winked. "And the rumor does help to sell papers. Nia aided me in doing some research this afternoon. I'm going to publish a special edition of the paper tomorrow devoted to the prints you found and the possibility that such a creature exists."

"Landsake," Florence said. "A special edition for this? The last time you did a special edition was right after that hurricane hit the East Coast."

"A special edition?" Alice was instantly diverted. "Will you put in a notice about Wendell if I bring it by today? The sooner we can spread the word about his disappearance, the better the chance we have that someone will see or hear something."

"I'd be happy to. Now who is this young man?"

"I'm so sorry. I've forgotten my manners." Alice drew Maxwell forward. "Carlene, Nia, this is Maxwell Vandermitton. He's a graduate student staying at the inn while he works on a research paper."

"It's nice to meet you," Carlene said.

Nia smiled. "We met this morning, Alice, although I was busy and we didn't get a chance to talk." She smiled at him. "Please let me know if there is any way I can help with your research. Our library may be small but, as you've discovered, we're connected to the world via the Internet and I have subscriptions to a number of significant research sites."

"Thank you. It's a pleasure to see you ladies."

"Vandermitton is an interesting surname," Nia said. "I'm fascinated by genealogical studies. Is it Dutch?"

"Yes, my family—"

"Come on, you two. You can visit another day. My car is right over here." Florence clearly was impatient with the small talk. Alice suspected Florence feared that a discussion of Maxwell's roots would show that there were other people whose American ancestors were older than Florence's.

Bidding Carlene and Nia farewell, Alice and Maxwell followed Florence to her car.

As Florence drove past the inn and on to the pond, Alice's thoughts strayed from her companions. Once again, she wondered how Wendell had fared during the rainstorm yesterday. Sadness squeezed her heart as it did so much of the time now. She found it hard to believe that the pudgy gray tabby would never lie on her bed in a patch of sunlight again.

"Gracious! It's muddy here, isn't it?" Florence took mincing steps as they left the road and began to head around the pond.

"We don't have to go very far," Alice said. She was glad she had on her practical old tennis sneakers, which were her most comfortable walking shoes. "The tracks we saw were right ahead. But don't get your hopes up. Carlene said that the hard rain we had did quite a bit of damage."

"Holy cow!" Maxwell was looking upward. "That is a huge bird. I wonder what it is."

Alice looked in the direction he pointed, as did Florence, but missed seeing the bird. "We have hawks around here," she said. "They get pretty big."

"I once saw—well, my lands, what on earth is that?" Florence interrupted herself to point at something just over their heads in a tree.

Alice shaded her eyes with her hand, seeking what Florence had seen. "Where?"

"Right there." Maxwell sounded awed. "What is that, do you think?"

"Hair," said Florence. "Although how a clump of a hair got hung up on a branch so high above the ground…" She trailed off uncertainly. "You don't suppose it's hair from *the creature*, do you?"

Alice stifled a laugh as Florence's voice dropped to a whisper. "No," she said, "I don't."

Maxwell was looking up at the clump of brown caught in the tree branches above them. "Alice," he said, "where did you say you found those footprints?"

"Why, right over there." Alice pointed to the muddy area in the path. As she'd expected, little was left except for two indistinct depressions in the soggy soil that could have been made by just about anything heavy. Then the significance of Maxwell's question dawned on her. She turned to him. "Surely you don't think—"

He looked at her. "I don't know what to think."

"Young man," Florence said imperiously, "go up there and retrieve that hair, won't you?"

Maxwell looked at her. "Me?" He eyed the tree dubiously. "Uh . . . I suppose I can try."

As it turned out, there was a low, sturdy branch that made it easy for him to get into the tree, and several others fortuitously placed so that he could stretch out and pluck the hair from the end of a branch with relative ease.

He jumped down a moment later and presented the brownish bundle to Florence with a grimace. "Remind me to wash my hands thoroughly when we return to the inn," he said to Alice, "several times."

Alice could not prevent the smile that formed. He certainly was amusing at times, whether or not he intended to be. She stepped closer to Florence's side and the three of them appraised their find.

"It looks like human hair," Alice observed.

"It couldn't possibly be human hair, that high up in a tree." By now Florence was nearly vibrating with excitement. "It's Bigfoot hair! I just know it." She suddenly stopped and looked around. "It could be watching us right now," she said in a stage whisper. "I don't think we should be out here unarmed." And with that, she turned and began picking her way back to the road with surprising speed.

Maxwell looked at Alice. "Unarmed?"

Alice shook her head and smiled. "Florence is a force of nature," she told him.

He laughed, wiping his hands on his pants. "I suppose we may as well follow her. There isn't much left to see of those prints, as you expected."

Chapter Seven

On Saturday morning, Jane served peach-strawberry stuffed French toast. She was assured that the meal was a hit when Maxwell accepted seconds, and then thirds, and Miss Havishim asked for the recipe.

When Maxwell told Jane he was planning to walk into town again, she asked him to pick up a copy of the *Acorn Nutshell*.

While Jane was checking the reservation book to see if Mrs. Moeller, their German guest, had designated an arrival time, Alice came downstairs in her uniform.

"I may not be home until close to suppertime," Alice told Jane. "After I get off work, I thought I'd walk around the gas station and neighborhood where Wendell went missing one more time. I can't believe no one has had so much as a glimpse of him."

"Maybe we'll get some response from the notice in today's *Nutshell*," Jane said.

Footsteps sounded on the front porch and a moment later, Maxwell came into the front hallway and toward the reception desk, where Jane was standing. "Here's your paper, Jane. Good morning, Alice. Working today?"

"I am," she said. "You?"

"Yes." He waved a second copy of the paper. "I plan to get back to writing just as soon as I read the paper." He shook his head, smiling. "I can't believe there's a special issue devoted to a discussion of those tracks you found. Carlene must have stayed up very late working on it, because it even includes mention of the hair Florence found yesterday."

"Goodness." Alice looked at the paper, which Jane had spread out on the reception desk.

"I'll see you ladies later." Maxwell went on up the stairs and they heard the door of his room shut a moment later.

Alice leaned over Jane's shoulder. She drew in a shocked breath of dismay when she saw the headline: Bigfoot Visits Acorn Hill.

The entire front page was about the tracks. Jane read a section out loud:

An unnamed source tells the *Nutshell* that local folks are speculating that huge tracks observed along the bank of Fairy Pond on Thursday may belong to the North American Bigfoot, or Sasquatch. Bigfoot sightings have been reported throughout the continental United States for decades, although most sightings occur in the North and Northwest.

"Oh my gosh!" Jane said. "It goes on to mention the giant squid story as evidence that Bigfoot may exist. It sounds just like your conversation with Mark last evening."

"What a coincidence!"

"Maybe." Jane didn't sound convinced.

Alice pressed on. "It's not a big leap to say that if I thought about Bigfoot, other people also might have. Right?"

"Makes sense. But the giant squid...? You didn't mention that to anyone else, did you?"

"Of course not. It was just last night. And Carlene printed the paper early this morning, I imagine, well before any of us were up and about."

"Oh, good grief." Jane pointed to a picture. "Look at this, would you?"

Alice groaned. "Could it get any worse?"

The picture was of Florence Simpson. She was standing in front of the Coffee Shop, holding up a clump of dark hair that Alice presumed was the stuff they had found by the pond.

Jane read:

Florence Simpson, one of Acorn Hill's oldest residents, found a clump of hair from an unknown creature near the site of the tracks Friday afternoon. "Someone must do something," Simpson says, "to ensnare this monster in our midst. We are fortunate that no one has been harmed so far."

"Ensnare?" Alice repeated incredulously.

"I just read what I see." Jane began to giggle. "I think Carlene must have meant that Florence was from an old family, but it doesn't come across that way, does it? Florence is going to be hopping mad when she realizes Carlene called her old in the town paper."

Alice put a hand to her mouth as she, too, began to laugh.

"What's so funny?" Louise came into the hallway from the parlor.

Alice and Jane looked at each other and laughed harder. Jane pointed to the paper. "Florence," she wheezed as tears streamed down her cheeks.

"*Old* Florence," Alice managed.

Louise began to smile. "You two are out of control." She reached around them and picked up the paper. As she read, her eyebrows climbed higher and higher. "My heavens," she muttered. "What was Carlene thinking? Those interviews with Bobby Dawson and the two younger boys are nothing short of inflammatory. Paired with that ridiculous monster quote from Florence, this article is likely to create a real furor."

"I doubt it." Alice had calmed down enough to speak again. She drew her index fingers beneath her lower lashes, wiping away the tears of mirth. "It's a joke, don't you see?"

"Yes," Jane said. "It's meant to be tongue-in-cheek. Florence played right into Carlene's hands. But I don't think anyone— except for maybe a few kids—will believe for one minute that there's a monster on the loose in Acorn Hill."

Louise had walked around her sisters and was looking at an inside page of the newspaper. "Oh, look. Bless Carlene's heart."

Alice knew what she meant immediately. "She put the notice about Wendell in the paper?"

Louise nodded. "It's the lead article on the second page, with that wonderful picture you gave her, Jane, and it tells the whole story of his stowing away." She laughed shakily. "If anyone from

Acorn Hill happens to see him in Potterston, they'll know in a New York minute who he is and where he belongs."

"As opposed to an Acorn Hill minute," Jane returned, "which undoubtedly is twice as long as a minute from New York."

Louise smiled perfunctorily, but the lightheartedness had fled from the morning, and after a few moments, each sister went her own way.

Jane had to get the morning chores finished, but before she did, there was one more thing she wanted to do about finding Wendell. Getting out the telephone book, she laid it on the desk and began flipping through the pages until she found what she wanted.

A minute later, she dialed a number and listened while the phone rang on the other end.

"Potterston Animal Control, Wanda speaking. May I help you?"

"Good morning. This is Jane Howard from the Grace Chapel Inn in Acorn Hill. Is Jack O'Hara available?"

"Sorry. He's in the field this morning. May I take a message?"

Jane made a moue of disappointment. "Yes. Could you please ask him to call me at his convenience?" She reeled off her phone number, and the woman repeated it.

"All right, honey. Got it. I'll pass on the message to Jack. You say you're from Grace Chapel Inn? Over in Acorn Hill?"

"Yes."

"Jack's doing some patrolling over that way today so he may stop by in person if I can catch up with him."

"That would be even better. Thank you." Jane wished the woman a pleasant day and hung up.

⌒

Shortly after lunch, the reservation bell dinged. Jane was out on the back porch folding newly laundered sheets and towels. She hurriedly set down the hand towel she just had picked up and walked to the front desk.

There stood a gray-haired woman, who appeared to be in her late sixties, and a blonde twenty-something young woman.

"Hello," Jane greeted them. "I'm Jane Howard, one of the owners of Grace Chapel Inn. Welcome."

"Thank you," the woman replied in heavily accented English. She wore her gray hair in a short Dutch-boy bob, and her chocolate brown eyes were magnified by her wire-rimmed glasses.

"Oh, you must be Mrs. Moeller. It's so nice to meet you."

"And you the same, dear. This is my great-niece Amanda. She drive me from Philadelphia and take me to dinner, then go back home."

Jane thought Mrs. Moeller's grammatically garbled English was charming. She smiled at both women and then addressed Amanda. "I see. If you don't have dinner plans, Amanda, I can recommend some local restaurants."

"That would be nice," Amanda said. "I can help Aunt Clothilda get settled and then come see you."

"Oh, that's not necessary," Jane said. She reached beneath the counter and pulled out a sheet on which she had made a list of places to eat in and around Acorn Hill and Potterston. "This is what you need. There are directions from the inn to each of those restaurants on the list."

"Thank you. This is perfect." The young woman smiled.

Jane quickly completed the registration process, gave Mrs. Moeller the key to the Sunrise Room, and picked up one of the two suitcases in the hallway, while Amanda picked up the other. "I'll show you to your room now."

"*Danke* . . . thank you."

Jane smiled. "You're welcome. I'm sorry I don't speak any German, Mrs. Moeller. My sisters and I had hoped to learn a few phrases to welcome you, but we've had a very busy week and didn't find the time."

"No matter." Clothilda waved a hand. "I must practice English."

"My aunt, Ethel Buckley, is eager to visit with you. She is the one you spoke to on the telephone last week."

"Ah. Yes. I remember." The older woman followed Jane up the stairs to the second floor. "You call me Clothilda, not . . . not formal. Okay?"

"Okay. And you must call me Jane."

"Jane." It came out sounding more like "chain" but Jane figured it was close enough to get her attention. She set down the suitcase and indicated the room. "I hope you'll be comfortable here. Please let us know if there is anything you need. I'll begin serving breakfast at 7:30 AM tomorrow unless you have a need for an earlier time. Just let me know and I'll arrange to serve you at a time that suits you better."

"You are most…good. Kind." Clothilda smiled warmly. "I take a sleep right now. The travel makes me tired."

"All right." Jane gave her guest an encouraging smile, knowing that if she were visiting Germany, she'd have a lot more difficulty making herself understood than Clothilda was having in English. "Amanda, may I interest you in some tea or a snack?"

"Oh, no thank you." The young woman smiled and dug a novel out of the backpack slung over her shoulder. "May I sit on the porch? I brought a good book along so I'd have something to do while Aunt Clo rested."

"Of course. That would be fine."

"Good. Good." Clothilda nodded and smiled. "Thank you, Jane."

Jane and Amanda left the Sunrise Room. Amanda went down to the porch, while Jane went up to her room briefly and then headed back downstairs. When Jane reached the first floor, there was a man waiting at the reception desk.

"Jack! Thanks for coming by."

Jack O'Hara was the animal control officer for Potterston and the surrounding communities, including Acorn Hill.

"Hey, Jane. How are you?"

"Good, thanks. And yourself?"

"Tee-riffic." He grinned, making the tips of his handlebar mustache slide upward. "Got a message here, says you want to talk to me. Animal problem?"

Jane nodded. "On Wednesday our family cat Wendell sneaked into a guest's car and when the man stopped for gas in Potterston,

Wendell jumped out. We've been looking for him ever since. I wanted to give you his description in case you should come across him in your travels."

Jack brushed a hand reflectively across the crown of his flat-topped military style crew cut, although his brilliant red hair was in perfect order already. "Sorry to hear that. I'd be glad to keep a lookout out for him. Wanna tell me what he looks like?"

Jane nodded. "I'll do you one better." She reached beneath the counter and pulled out one of the flyers. "He's a short-haired gray tabby with white feet and a black-tipped tail. And he's fat. The picture is an excellent likeness."

"Haven't seen him," Jack said, eyeing the picture. "Can I keep this?"

"Sure. We posted a number of them around Potterston and Acorn Hill already, and Alice alerted the animal shelter in case someone was to bring him in. Is there anything else we should do?"

"Vets," Jack told her. "Take your posters around to all the local veterinarians. They usually have bulletin boards for public announcements about animals, and you should tell them at the desk, too, in case someone brings him in with an injury."

Jane shuddered. "Oh, I can't let myself think about that. But thank you for the advice. We'll do anything we can to find him." She paused, and then asked, "Do people often find lost pets?"

"Oh, sure." Jack nodded. "Not always, but I can think of quite a few situations where people have gotten their animals back. It's only been since Wednesday you say? Early days. Early days. Don't give up yet."

"All right." Jane appreciated his encouragement. "That's good to hear."

"No problem. We squared away?"

"Yes. Thanks again for stopping by, Jack. My sisters and I really appreciate anything you can do."

"Glad to be of service. Hope you find your cat."

Jane saw him out, watching as he marched down the steps and off to his truck. "Okay, Wendell," she whispered. "I'm not giving up, so you'd better not give up either."

Alice came home before supper, as she had promised. Wearily, she sank into a chair in the kitchen. "No luck," she said glumly.

"I refuse to get discouraged," Jane said as she shaped a mixture of bleu cheese, hamburger and spices into meatballs for the marinara sauce she was making for dinner. "Jack O'Hara from Animal Control took one of our flyers and promised to keep an eye out for Wendell."

"That's good," Louise said from the table where she was shredding lettuce into three bowls. "He could be a big help."

"Let's give it one more good search," Alice proposed. "Tomorrow after church we all could go over to Potterston and make one last circuit of the area where he disappeared."

"I'm game, as long as I have time to visit Mrs. Smeal for a few minutes first. I made her a batch of crème-de-menthe brownies today." Then Jane pointed to the front of the house. "Did you see your mail on the desk, Alice? There's a card there."

"A card?" Alice looked interested but she made no move to get up as she massaged her aching arches. "Who is it from?"

"There is no return address," Jane said. "Sit here and I'll bring it to you." She disappeared through the door to the hallway and returned a moment later, bearing a large ivory envelope, which she handed to Alice.

Alice examined the handwriting. "I'm not familiar with this penmanship." She tore open the flap and extracted a lovely card with a watercolor picture of a calico cat sitting on a windowsill next to a pot of geraniums. The cat was in profile as it gazed out the window decorated with lacy curtains. Opening the card, Alice said, "Oh, isn't this sweet."

Louise leaned over. "Who is it from?"

"The ANGELs." Alice reached for a tissue and read: "Dear Miss Howard, we hope you find Wendell soon. We all are saying prayers for him. Love..." She had to stop reading for a moment to dab at her eyes with the tissue. "They all signed it." She scanned the various signatures. "Every single one of them."

"That's so thoughtful," Louise said.

Alice nodded. "They are a thoughtful group. Let's hope all those extra prayers help."

Chapter Eight

After Clothilda and her niece had left for dinner, Louise went to the piano. She had purchased a new book of music suitable for wedding celebrations, and she was eager to try it out. First warming up with several of her customary exercises, she then plunged into the book.

She quickly mastered the songs, which were not terribly challenging but beautifully arranged. After playing for nearly an hour, Louise closed the book and flexed her fingers.

The sudden sound of clapping startled her, and she whipped around on the piano bench in surprise. Since all the guests had gone out for dinner, she had not thought to close the door, and so her music had drifted throughout the house.

"Quite excellent, quite excellent." Maxwell had come into the parlor sometime during her practice session and settled himself into one of the Victorian chairs. "You play quite well. Quite well, indeed."

Louise felt herself bristle. She wasn't sure why Maxwell had that effect on her but she felt as if his words were not the compliments they appeared to be, as if he were denigrating the level of skill to be found in a rural area such as Acorn Hill. "Thank you," she said politely. "You startled me."

He looked contrite. "I'm sorry. My father used to hate it when I 'sneaked up on him,' as he called it. I didn't intend to do that to you. I was just enjoying your music."

Her ruffled feathers began to lie down again at the sincerity in his tone, and Louise smiled. "I enjoy it too. Playing piano is one of the most soothing activities I can think of. I always feel more centered and relaxed when I'm done."

"The mark of a true musician," the young man said lightly.

"So are you finding the atmosphere of Acorn Hill and the inn conducive to a productive writing process?" She placed her music in the piano bench and closed the tapestry cover, then took a seat near Maxwell.

"Very much so. Everyone's been very kind, and this mysterious creature that people are buzzing about really has me intrigued."

Louise waved a hand as if to downplay the gossip. "I'm sure it will turn out to be some local creature, or perhaps a prankster."

"A prankster?" The young man leaned forward. "What makes you suspect that? Do you have any evidence?"

"No, no." Louise was a bit taken aback by his intensity. "It's just that I am quite certain no undiscovered giant creature is lurking about Acorn Hill."

"I'm not inclined to believe it, either," Maxwell confessed, "but I am keeping an open mind."

Louise felt rebuked by the statement. "I suppose I'm not, but I am very much a person who requires tangible evidence before I believe something."

"But you go to church, don't you?"

The unexpected question threw her, and she simply stared at him for a moment. "I—I—you cannot compare spiritual beliefs to the existence of an animal!" She was frustrated and more than a little annoyed that he would try to trap her with her own words.

"I'm sorry, Louise," he said immediately. "I don't mean to put you on the spot. I was not raised in a church, or with any kind of spiritual guidance."

Louise took a deep breath and said a silent prayer for patience, moved by a sudden image of a lonely little boy to whom scant attention was paid. "The whole point of spiritual faith is the ability to see the miraculous in the everyday things, and to trust that if God can create such miracles as those around us in our daily lives, then He certainly is capable of larger actions. The ultimate miracle, of course, being the risen Christ after the death of His earthly body."

Maxwell was silent for a moment. "You know," he finally said, "I consider myself highly educated compared to the average person. But I am appallingly ignorant of all but the sketchiest details of the Christian faith—or any other, for that matter. Would you and your sisters allow me to accompany you to church tomorrow?"

Louise was astonished at the request. "Of course you may. Our newest guest, Mrs. Moeller will be going with us. We would like very much for you to join our party."

Maxwell smiled. "The words 'party' and 'church' don't mesh well in my mind."

"Well, they should," Louise said. "Expressions of faith should be joyous—exuberant, even, on some occasions."

There was a short silence following Louise's words. She felt heat rise to her cheeks.

"Louise…" Maxwell's voice was hesitant. "I wonder if you have a Bible I might borrow. You have made me curious, and I think I would like to study it."

"I do, and I have something else you might enjoy. Follow me." Louise rose, heading for the library, once her father's office, where an extensive collection of faith-based volumes were still stored. "There's a book my father used to love. He gave it to my daughter Cynthia when she joined our church in Philadelphia many years ago. It is meant to be used as a study aid with the Bible and is an excellent overview of the history of Christianity. I'm sure my sisters would want me to lend it to you while you are staying with us."

"Thank you." Maxwell's voice was soft. "I will look forward to reading both books."

"And any time you have questions, Alice, Jane and I would be delighted to talk with you."

After leaving Maxwell sitting in the library with the Bible and the study guide, Louise went in search of her sisters. She was eager to tell them of the surprising turn of events.

Clothilda and her niece Amanda returned from dinner shortly before eight. Jane introduced them to Louise and Alice, and then Amanda bid her aunt farewell.

"I'll be back to get you in eighteen days," the young woman told Clothilda.

Clothilda nodded. "I will be ... okay with this good people."

Jane beamed. "Of course you will. We'll take the very best care of you. And don't forget, our aunt, Ethel Buckley, speaks German and is eager to meet you."

"Oh, good," said Amanda. "Her lack of English was my biggest hesitation in leaving Aunt Clo."

"Is not a problem. You go, come back after two weeks. Okay?"

Amanda laughed. "Okay." She kissed her aunt, said good-bye to the Howard sisters and walked off to her car to begin her drive back to Philadelphia.

Clothilda smiled at the sisters, and then covered her mouth with a yawn. "Excuse me. I am finding this traveling to be ... to make me sleepy very much."

Alice chuckled. "I work as a nurse, and I, too, am very sleepy. I'll be going to bed very soon."

"I think I go up now and maybe read and fall asleep. Thank you for your welcoming. I look forward to your breakfast and your church tomorrow."

"Wonderful," Jane said. "Good night, Clothilda."

 ❧

Jane had called Ethel on Saturday evening to let her know Clothilda had arrived. So early on Sunday morning, Jane was not surprised to see her aunt picking her way along the path from the carriage house where she made her home.

"Good morning," Jane sang out as Ethel came in the back door.

"Good morning, Jane."

"Would you like some breakfast, Aunt Ethel?"

"Why, thank you, dear. That would be lovely." She patted her hair as if a strand had slipped out of place. "I thought your Mrs. Moeller might enjoy company during breakfast this morning."

"I'm sure she would." Jane indicated the swinging door to the dining room. "She's already seated. Let me introduce you." She led the way, tossing over her shoulder, "I know you like salmon. This morning I am serving an egg dish with hollandaise sauce, along with baked apple and blackberries crepes drizzled with sweet cream, and a Black Russian breakfast cake."

"My goodness," murmured Ethel. "You outdo yourself every time I come over here, Jane."

When Jane and Ethel stepped into the dining room, Maxwell and Miss Havishim appeared to be having an animated conversation. As Jane waited to introduce Ethel, she heard mention of Freud, Bruno Bethelheim and operant conditioning.

When Miss Havishim and Maxwell sensed her presence and looked up from their discussion, Jane said, "Clothilda, Miss Havishim, this is my aunt, Ethel Buckley. Clothilda, you spoke with Aunt Ethel the day you made your reservation."

Clothilda and Miss Havishim both greeted Ethel warmly.

"Good morning, Mrs. Buckley," Maxwell said, rising courteously. "It's nice to see you again."

"And you," Ethel returned. "What kind of pie are you planning to have today?"

She and Maxwell both laughed as Ethel took a seat next to Clothilda. "Ah! Ethel," Clothilda said, her round face flushing with emotion. "You were very kind to help me when I had trouble speaking English."

"It was nothing," Ethel demurred. "I have not spoken German in many years, and it was exciting to realize how much of it I still know."

"You spoke it very well."

"Thank you. Would you like to talk in German?"

Jane slipped back to the kitchen, smiling, as the sound of the two women conversing in German flowed behind her, interspersed with two other voices murmuring about intermittent reinforcement and something about teaching sign language to monkeys.

The next forty minutes were busy ones as Jane completed her meal preparations and she and her sisters served the guests.

Alice, Louise and Jane ate their own breakfast in the kitchen and then cleared the guests' dishes. Amid all the activity, Clothilda and Ethel chatted in German. After the meal, Jane noticed that Clothilda had produced a number of papers over which she and Ethel were poring. Jane was dying to know what the two were talking about, but she was pressed for time after the dishes were done and had to hurry to her room to get ready for church.

When she came down, Alice, Louise, Maxwell, Clothilda and Ethel all were gathered in the front hallway.

"Hi-ho, hi-ho, it's off to church we go," called Jane as she got to the bottom step.

Amid a general chorus of laughter and comments, the group left the inn and walked toward Grace Chapel.

∽

The service was uplifting for Alice. Since Wendell's disappearance, she had felt as if she'd been walking under a cloud that moved in whatever direction she did. It was nice to feel that cloud dissipating, even if her concern for Wendell had not eased.

Rev. Thompson's message was about seeking divine aid to discern heavenly bidding. Last night, Louise had spoken to Alice and Jane about Maxwell's interest in learning about faith. This morning, Alice occasionally sneaked glances at him, wondering what he would take away from the experience, whether he would feel blessed by the Holy Spirit and empowered to continue to seek Christ in his life.

Clothilda clearly was a churchgoer. She looked at ease and was warm and friendly with everyone to whom they introduced her on the way to the service. To whom *Ethel* introduced her, Alice corrected herself, amused. Her aunt had taken over the supervision of their guest with the same zeal she threw into any project she approached. Alice suspected their only problem might be making sure Clothilda had time to rest during her stay at the inn.

When the service ended, Alice introduced Maxwell to several people. She was surprised at how many additional people he greeted. Apparently, he'd been spending quite a bit of time around town and had made many acquaintances.

"Sylvia," Alice said as she spied Sylvia Songer near the door. "It's nice to see you up and about."

"It's nice to be back on my feet," Sylvia told her. "That flu was no fun. Except, of course, for the meals Jane brought over."

Louise came up behind Alice and greeted Sylvia. Then she said apologetically, "Alice, if we're going to Potterston, we must leave soon. I have a rehearsal for the Easter cantata at three." Louise had agreed to play for and help direct the Easter cantata and she was a bit nervous about managing the challenging music and directing a choir at the same time.

"Of course," Alice said, taking her leave of Sylvia. "Is Jane ready to go?"

Louise indicated the road leading back to the inn. "She went ahead to make us a light lunch to take along."

"What about Maxwell?"

Louise eyed the young man, who was chatting with Kenneth Thompson, Grace Chapel's pastor. "I think he will be fine on his own. He has met an amazing number of people."

"And Clothilda is lunching with Ethel, so I suppose we are free to go."

Just then, a woman holding a young child by the hand dropped a large tote bag she had been carrying. Papers, books and crayons flew every which way. The child began to cry.

As the sisters watched, Maxwell turned and went to the woman's side, kneeling to pick up the scattered items as the harried mother thanked him profusely.

"*Hmm*," said Louise. "Looks like church was good for Maxwell."

Alice chuckled and agreed.

As one, the two sisters turned and walked back to the inn, where Jane already had lunch packed in a cooler and had brought Louise's car around to the kitchen door.

"Your car is the largest and most comfortable," Jane informed Louise, "so I volunteered you to drive."

"You're too kind," said Louise as she slipped behind the wheel.

After a visit with Penelope Smeal, the sisters left to search for Wendell. The drive to Potterston was a quiet one. Jane opened bottles of water for everyone, and then passed around sandwiches, a bag of raw vegetables and a container of the decadently delicious crème-de-menthe brownies she had saved from Mrs. Smeal's batch. Louise opted to wait until she had parked before eating, but Alice and Jane went ahead and ate so that they would be able to start their search as soon as possible.

When Louise pulled into the gas station where Wendell had last been seen, the sisters grew quiet.

Finally, Alice said, "It's only been five days but it feels like forever that he's been missing."

"I know," said Jane in a subdued tone. "But maybe today will be the day we find him."

Sadly, her hope did not bear fruit. Though the sisters fanned out and combed every inch of the neighborhood surrounding the gas station, Wendell did not appear. Worse, no one they encountered had seen a cat answering to his description.

"It's as if he vanished into thin air," Jane said sadly as they reluctantly climbed back into Louise's car and made the trip

home. Though none of them said it out loud, there was an unspo-
ken understanding that this probably was their final trip to search
the site of the escape. If Wendell hadn't heard them and
responded in the many hours they'd been searching, it was
unlikely that he was in the area.

Alice worked the night shift again on Monday evening to fill in
for a nurse who had gone into labor several weeks early during
her own shift. As she grew older, Alice found night shift work
draining. Her body did not seem to appreciate the odd hours
and unreliable sleep schedule that she followed when she
worked nights.

She was tired when she came home shortly after 8:00 AM
Tuesday, but she had to smile at the sight of Jane, Ethel and
Clothilda in the living room with papers, maps and who-knew-
what-else scattered around them. The three women were chattering like magpies, laughing and talking over each other in
both German and English. Alice was amused to think that Ethel
was the only one of the three who had any idea what both of the
others were saying.

"What's going on in here?" she asked, pausing in the doorway.

"Good morning, Alice. Come in," Ethel invited. "Clothilda is
pursuing some genealogical puzzles while she is here, and Jane
and I have volunteered to help her."

"Oh? What kinds of puzzles?" She entered the room and
perched on the arm of the sturdy burgundy chair in which Jane sat.

"Clothilda is looking for living relatives of her husband's family, the Moellers," Ethel explained.

"Moeller? One of my coworkers at the hospital is a Moeller," Alice said. She spelled the name and Jane nodded. "That's it."

"It's her married name," Alice went on, "but I could ask her if her husband knows anything about his ancestors."

"There's a Moeller family in Acorn Hill too, I think," Jane said. "Not long after I came home, I met a lady named Elspeth Moeller. We worked together on a project for a craft fair."

"Oh yes," Alice said. "I forgot about those Moellers. I wonder if they're related to the Potterston Moellers."

"I'm sure we will learn that as we go along," Ethel said, "but now Clothilda would like to trace the ancestors who made the first trip from Germany to America. She knows they booked passage on a ship coming into the Port of Philadelphia, and that many of the immigrants from that particular group settled near Potterston."

"In other words, they could have settled in Acorn Hill," Jane said. "Look at this, Alice. Clothilda's family emigrated from Germany to America in the middle of the eighteenth century. She has records from the manifest of the ship they boarded, and a translation of a letter written by her nine-or-so-times-great-grandfather before he left. And these pages are copies from a family Bible that is over two hundred years old."

"We want to visit the Potterston Historical Society," Ethel said, "and possibly find some Moeller graves in the old farm cemeteries around the area."

"I've volunteered to drive," Jane said. "I think this is absolutely fascinating." What she didn't say was that she had little choice, since Clothilda did not feel comfortable driving in the United States, and Ethel had never acquired a license, a fact the sisters found mind-boggling. Ethel had been a farm wife and, at the very least, she might have driven a tractor, but Ethel swore she'd never been behind a wheel in her life. She appeared to be quite happy with that state of affairs. Of course, now she had Louise, Alice, Jane, her longtime beau Lloyd Tynan and a plethora of friends to chauffeur her whenever she desired.

"We're going to start Wednesday," said Ethel, ever the organizer, "and we'll go to the Potterston Historical Society first. Then, perhaps, we'll search some of the local cemeteries for headstones bearing the Moeller name."

"Sounds as if you three have your excursion well under control," Alice said.

Just then, the telephone rang. Jane made a move to stand but Alice popped up from the arm of the chair. "No, you go ahead and finish your discussion. I'll answer it." She walked into the hallway and picked up the phone at the reception desk. "Grace Chapel Inn, this is Alice. May I help you?"

"*Uh*, yeah. My name's Trace Harnish. You got a pencil so you can write this down?"

"Certainly." Alice reached for a pen and pad and dutifully noted the name. "Would you like to make a reservation at the inn, Mr. Harnish?"

"No." He guffawed. "I live right over in Potterston. I seen the ad about your lost cat and I called to tell you to mail me the reward. I found him this morning and took him by the animal shelter."

"You found Wendell?" Alice hardly could believe her ears. "Oh, thank you, Mr. Harnish. This is wonderful news. What's your address?"

He reeled off the information. "You think you can get that in the mail today?"

"I'll do my best." Alice was nearly too happy to speak. "Thank you so much. I'm going over to get him right now."

"Then you can drop that reward in the mail on the way," he remarked, chuckling.

"God bless you, Mr. Harnish," she said. "Good-bye."

She put down the phone and practically sprinted back into the living room. "Jane! Come on! I just got a call from a man who found Wendell."

"What? Where? Is he all right?" Jane sprang to her feet and began to dash across the room. Then she turned back to Clothilda and Ethel. "I'm so sorry, but I have to go with Alice to get our cat."

"Go, go." Ethel made shooing motions. "We're fine."

Alice and Jane rushed out of the house and raced to Alice's car. Alice had to remind herself to drive sensibly and carefully, when she really wanted to floor the gas pedal all the way to the animal shelter, which was located on the near edge of Potterston.

Chapter Nine

Alice and Jane didn't speak much on the way to the shelter. When they arrived, Alice barely had the car in park before they were out of their seats and hurrying toward the door.

Jane pulled open the heavy door, and Alice preceded her inside.

"Good morning," Alice said, clearing her tight throat. "We're here to pick up our cat. We received a call that he was just brought in."

The woman behind the counter wore a name tag that said Luella. A puzzled look crossed her face. "You received a call from us? I didn't call you. Maybe the director did."

"Oh, I'm sorry, that's not what I meant," Alice said quickly. "A man called. He had seen our cat Wendell on a poster and he said that he brought Wendell to the shelter."

"Ah." Luella smiled. "Let me go check. He wouldn't be in the cat room yet because new animals are quarantined for a time." She rose from her seat and disappeared through a door marked "Staff Only."

Alice and Jane looked around. There was a fat orange tabby cat lying on top of a file cabinet in the office area with the longest tail Alice had ever seen languidly draped down the side. A huge tank with a turtle the size of a dinner plate swimming around in it occupied one wall in a waiting area with several chairs. Another door bore a sign that read, "Cat Rooms," with an arrow beneath it pointing to the right, and "Dog Kennels," with an arrow pointing left.

Jane read Alice's mind. As her sister took a step in the direction of the door, Jane caught the back of her pale yellow polo shirt. "Oh, no you don't. We are not taking home any new pets."

Alice turned back, smiling sheepishly. "I only wanted to look."

"*Uh-huh.* That's what they all say."

Just then the door from the staff area opened. Alice and Jane turned around to see a new face.

"Hi. I'm Erica Tremane, the executive director. Luella tells me you think your cat has been brought in."

Alice nodded eagerly, prepared to tell her tale again.

But the woman forestalled her. "What does it look like?"

"It's a gray tabby with four white paws and a black tip on its tail. I brought in a flyer with a picture on it last week."

Erica sighed. She took a piece of paper from the top of a file cabinet. "This one?"

"Yes." Jane identified it immediately. "That's Wendell."

Erica cleared her throat. "I'm afraid we don't have your cat."

"Oh, but Mr. Harnish said he brought him in a short while ago—"

Erica was shaking her head. "A man named Harnish did surrender a cat about two hours ago, and it is a gray tabby. But it's not your Wendell."

"How can you be sure?" Jane asked. "Does it have white paws?"

"Yes." The executive director beckoned. "Come with me, and I'll let you see for yourselves."

"Oh, thank you." Alice and Jane followed Erica down a short hallway past doors on the left and right. "This is the quarantine room for new cats," the woman explained, indicating a door on the left, "and for dogs." She pointed at the door opposite but continued to a second pair of doors on the right and left. "Our grooming area is over there and this is the office and lab," she said as she turned right into the room.

Alice glimpsed two cages stacked one on top of the other along the wall.

Erica led them to the cages and pointed to the topmost one. "This is the cat that was just brought in."

Alice peered into the cage, hoping against hope that it was Wendell. But one look quickly confirmed Erica's statement. In the cage was a beautiful gray tabby that looked a lot like Wendell, right down to the four white paws. But this cat had a white tip on its tail. More importantly, it was nursing a set of tiny black kittens and purring contentedly as she blinked at the newcomers.

"Oh." Jane had seen the mother cat also. Her voice broke as she said, "Not Wendell."

Alice placed an arm around Jane's shoulders, though she, too, felt like crying. "Thank you for your time," she said to Erica, "and for your patience."

"It's all right," the executive director said kindly. "Seeing is believing. I'd have wanted to be sure if he were mine." She led the way out to the public area in front of the desk again. "I'll keep your poster," she said, indicating the flyer she'd laid on the desk, "and I promise we'll call right away if your kitty comes in. Don't give up. Maybe he'll find his way home."

"From Potterston to Acorn Hill?" Jane asked. "He jumped from a car."

"Stranger things have happened," the woman said. "Animals have an uncanny ability to find their way home."

"Thank you," Alice said again. She and Jane returned to the car and slowly got in. Alice drove home with no urge to rush this time.

When she turned in to the inn's driveway, Louise was standing on the front porch, her face alight.

Jane slid down in the seat. "This is terrible. How are we going to tell her it wasn't Wendell?"

Alice sighed. "I'll do it if you'll put the car away." She braked and put the car in park. Getting out, she walked across the lawn toward Louise while Jane came around to the driver's side.

Alice could see the exact moment when her less-than-excited demeanor registered with Louise.

"Oh no." Louise sank down onto the top step, uncharacteristically disregarding the possibility of getting dirt on her good skirt. "What happened? Is he dead?"

Alice was startled. "No, no, nothing like that. It wasn't Wendell, after all."

"But Aunt Ethel told me—"

"Yes. A man called and told us he'd found Wendell and taken him to the shelter. But when we got there, the cat was a female with two kittens. She did look like Wendell, but there is no way that man really thought he'd found our male cat. I suspect he was hoping I'd put the reward money in the mail before I ever went to the shelter."

"What a miserable person," Louise said indignantly. "How could anyone do that?"

Alice just shook her head and sighed. "We were so hopeful."

The two of them sat on the steps until Jane came around the corner of the house.

"You heard," she said unnecessarily to Louise.

Louise nodded. "I'm sorry you had to go through that, both of you."

"If I ever meet that man—what was his name, anyway, Alice?" Jane asked ominously.

"I don't remember." Alice said a quick prayer that God would forgive her little white lie. But she didn't think chasing down Trace Harnish and chewing him out would accomplish much. "It doesn't matter, anyway."

"You're right." Louise rose from the step and brushed off her skirt. "We just have to accept the fact that Wendell's gone."

"I'm not accepting it yet," Jane said vehemently. "He might still come home. The woman at the shelter said she's heard of other animals finding their way home."

Alice sighed. "I'm not going to put too much faith in that, Jane. Louise is right. We need to accept it. Wendell isn't with us anymore."

Jane had tears in her eyes as she regarded her sisters. "I'm not ready to accept it yet," she said stubbornly. "He's a smart cat. We might find him yet." She started up the steps. "I need to return some telephone calls about reservations before lunch."

Alice sighed as the screen door banged a little bit in Jane's wake. "I wish I could turn back the clock, don't you?"

Louise took a breath that sounded suspiciously like a stifled sob. "Oh, you have no idea how much I would love that." Slowly, she turned to follow Jane inside. "Let's have some lunch. After that, I'm going to the piano. I do have some practicing to do, and playing always soothes me when I'm upset."

"I think I'll walk to the library after we eat," Alice said. "I have two books to return." She followed Louise into the house. "Let's try to get Jane to sit down with us for a few minutes."

The walk that afternoon did Alice good. Although she still was sad, some of the anger and frustration from the recent experience faded with the exercise.

"Hello, Alice," Nia Komonos said in a low voice as Alice entered the cool, hushed atmosphere of the library.

"Good afternoon, Nia." Alice checked her watch. "I can't believe it's ten after two. Goodness, where did the day go?"

Nia laughed, her glossy dark hair shining as she moved her head. "I know that feeling. I'm usually so busy I'm astounded when I glance at my watch. Half the time I forget to eat lunch, and I carry home the one I packed in the morning and have it for dinner."

Alice slid her books onto the counter. "I'm returning these."

"Thank you. What would you like to read next? I just got several new bestsellers that are fabulous and I—"

"What on earth is that?"

Nia stopped talking as she glanced in the direction Alice was pointing. "Oh, that? I'm putting a new display in the case."

"Yes, but—"

"I know, I know. Bigfoot is probably just a myth. But the whole idea is an excellent springboard for a display on fantastic creatures. I found a wonderful nonfiction children's book about Bigfoot. And of course, there are all kinds of stories about Nessie, the Loch Ness monster. I have the DVD of *Rudolph, the Red-Nosed Reindeer* to go along with the Yeti references since the Abominable Snowman—a Yeti, by another name—chases Rudolph in the movie, and of course there are dozens of books about creatures like dragons and griffins and unicorns." She drew in a breath and rushed on. "And this seemed the perfect opportunity to showcase C. S. Lewis' *Chronicles of Narnia.*"

Alice was still staring at the display case, which Nia had decorated with huge cardboard footprints; several enlarged illustrations of oversized, hairy creatures with long arms; and a huge banner asking, HAVE YOU SEEN BIGFOOT?

"You don't really believe there's a creature like that running around here, do you?"

Nia chuckled again, her dark eyes twinkling. "You never know. Oh, Alice, of course not," she added when she saw Alice's expression. "But it's exactly the kind of excitement that brings people—young people, in particular—into the library to research things in the stacks and on the Internet. I have to take advantage of that."

"That makes sense," Alice said slowly. "I just feel that someone's playing a great joke on us all. I mean, Ronald and I both saw that footprint and I swear it was far too large to be human. If that isn't the work of a prankster, then what could it be?"

"Alice." A masculine voice behind her called her name. "Hello. Are you walking back to the inn?" It was Maxwell, coming toward her with a computer case slung over one shoulder.

"Yes. I just returned some books," Alice told him.

"Did you find your cat? Ethel told me you went to the humane society to pick him up this morning."

Alice shook her head sadly, touched that he remembered to ask. "No. It wasn't ours." She almost smiled. "In fact, it was a mother with two kittens, although she did have coloring similar to Wendell's."

Maxwell's eyes widened. "Even I wouldn't have made that mistake," he said. "I'm so sorry."

"That's terrible," Nia said. "How could the humane society confuse things like that?" She indicated the bulletin board behind the desk, where Alice had dropped off another one of Jane's flyers. "This clearly says it is a male."

"It wasn't the humane society's fault. We received a call from a man who wanted the reward. Either it was an honest mistake or he was hoping I'd give him the money before I saw the cat. Either way, the end result is the same. It wasn't Wendell."

"Oh, how disappointing." Nia looked sympathetic. "But you keep thinking positively, Alice. Don't give up yet."

Alice nodded and said a polite good-bye, thinking that if one more person told her not to give up, she was going to bean them with the nearest object. Then she immediately felt mean-spirited. Here she was, attempting to be a Christian role model for Maxwell, and her own thoughts were far from Christian.

Lord, she thought, *mold me, shape me, help me embody Your commandments and example.*

Maxwell, walking at her side, said, "You're very quiet, Alice. I'm sure that false alarm must have been a terrible blow."

"It was," Alice said quietly. "It was." Then, making a conscious effort to shake off her morose mood, she said, "Louise told me she gave you a Bible and study aid. If you want to discuss anything, I'd be happy to do so."

Maxwell smiled at her, and she was struck by how pleasant he looked. Usually, he gave the impression of being aloof. He was perfectly friendly and polite—*really* perfectly, she thought wryly—but he often seemed to be more of an observer than one truly engaged in a conversation.

"I started with the historical background," he said. "There were selected Bible readings to accompany an encapsulated look at how the Bible came to be, and then it went on to the Old Testament. Thank goodness, all those *begats* were summarized."

Alice laughed. "Thank goodness, indeed."

"I like the way that study guide is organized, so I intend to keep working through it in the order the chapters are presented."

"It's a wonderful book," she agreed. "It was one of Father's favorites." The moment she said it, she immediately thought of Wendell. He'd been one of Father's favorites too. A lump rose to her throat and she let the topic slide.

They walked in companionable silence for a while. Then Maxwell said, "Hey," as they walked along Chapel Road. "I know just the thing to make you feel better."

"Oh?"

"June's pie," he said triumphantly.

She had to smile. "If anything can do it, June's pie probably can. Have you been in yet today? What kinds has she made?"

He nodded. "I had lunch there. She's got blackberry, blueberry, pumpkin and peach today. I had the blackberry."

"Yum, peach pie. I haven't had that in ages."

"My treat," he said instantly, stopping and pushing open the door of the Coffee Shop for her. "One piece of peach pie coming right up."

They barely had taken seats in one of the booths when Florence Simpson came rushing over, her husband Ronald right behind her. "I have a proposition to put to you. And to your sisters. You, too, Maxwell, if you're interested."

Alice braced herself. With Florence, you never knew what was coming next. "A proposition?"

Ronald nodded. "Florence has decided that our community must confront this Bigfoot menace."

"Confront?"

"Menace?"

Alice and Maxwell spoke in quick succession.

"Exactly." Florence drew herself up importantly. "Ronald is going to lead expeditions into the wild to seek the creature."

Alice wrinkled her brow, thinking the Simpsons had truly lost it. "What sort of expeditions?"

"Oh, just a few hikes," Ronald said, "around Fairy Pond and the woods, places where an animal might have left signs of its presence."

"Not just hikes," Florence insisted. "These will be significant in that the participants will be evaluating any signs they find."

"I see." Alice found it hard to believe that Ronald and Florence had taken the Bigfoot sightings so seriously. "We intend to start tomorrow," Ronald said. "Are either of you interested?"

"I work tomorrow," Alice said with relief.

"I'm afraid I must continue working on my paper," Maxwell said. "But perhaps another time. Thank you for asking me."

"Anytime," Ronald said jovially. "You're starting to seem like one of the locals."

"Thank you," Maxwell said, and Alice was surprised to see his cheeks turn pink. "That's a nice thing to say."

"I'm not just saying it," Ronald insisted. "You're becoming a fixture here at the Coffee Shop."

"That's true." The younger man smiled. "June's pies are irresistible."

"That's what we all say." Ronald grinned. "I'll let you know if we do a second expedition."

"All right."

Alice gazed after Florence and Ronald as they pounced on another customer who had just stepped through the door. "Goodness!"

"They certainly seem to have swallowed the Bigfoot theory hook, line and sinker," Maxwell said with a bemused smile.

Alice just nodded.

"I suppose I can understand how unsophisticated people might believe it, but I'm really surprised that both the librarian and the newspaper editor have bought into the Bigfoot theory," Maxwell said.

"I wouldn't say they've bought into it," Alice defended Carlene and Nia. "It's more that they saw an interesting angle to play up."

"So you don't think they believe there is such a creature?"

"I sincerely doubt it. However, you should ask each of them if you really want to know what they think."

"I must do that. Ronald and Florence certainly seem convinced, don't they?"

"Florence surely does," Alice confirmed reluctantly.

"Perhaps I will go along on one of Ronald's expeditions. Nothing like firsthand observation, you know."

Chapter Ten

As soon as breakfast was over on Wednesday morning and the kitchen was restored to its usual spotless state, Jane put on her jean jacket and met Ethel and Clothilda in the hallway.

Ethel was wearing a springy pink jacket with a flowered skirt. Clothilda was wearing a navy skirt but also had on a pink jacket.

"Good morning," said Jane. "Shall I change? I feel like a third wheel."

Clothilda's brow wrinkled. "A third wheel?"

Jane laughed. "I was teasing. It's an expression that means I feel out of place beside you two."

"Ah." Clothilda looked down at herself and then over at Ethel. "Yes. We laugh when first we see each other."

Ethel smiled. "It's up to you, Jane. If you have a pink jacket, you may wish to join our pink club. We could start a whole new fashion."

"Thanks, but I'll stick with this. Are you ready?"

"Yes. I am excited to find my family tree." Clothilda's voice carried a lilt.

Jane found her thick German accent charming. Family was pronounced "fom-ee-lee."

As she drove the familiar roads, Jane forced herself to stop thinking of Wendell. She passed the gas station from which the businessman had called that day and continued on to the center of the town, and although there was an ache in her heart, she smiled brightly when they arrived.

"Here we go," she announced as Ethel and Clothilda climbed out of her car. Clothilda carried a large black leather handbag in which she had placed copies of all the family records she had brought along.

The Potterston Historical Society was housed in a beautiful Victorian building that once had been a private home. Like Grace Chapel Inn, it had been painted in period colors. The body of the house was soft, rosy beige. The trim and shutters were done in two complementary shades of green, a soft, blue-green mossy color and a deep forest green. The imposing front door was the same forest-green shade and bore a handsome brass knocker in the classical rope design popular in Victorian times.

Inside, a delightful hostess in period costume greeted them. Her day dress was a beige-and-blue plaid taffeta with a long-waisted, close-fitting bodice. It was long-sleeved and had the high neck that Victorian modesty had demanded. The skirt was split in the front to reveal underskirts of contrasting colors and was bustled up in the back and adorned with black and blue lace trim. A tidy line of brass buttons marched down the front. Her hair was pulled up into a complicated chignon. Looking closely, Jane was almost certain it was all the woman's own hair. How long had it taken her to learn to create that hairdo? Jane couldn't imagine successfully styling her own hair that way.

"Welcome to the Potterston Historical Society," the woman said. "My name is Elizabeth. Would you like a tour?"

"Oh yes," said Clothilda. "We have the questions about finding family, but first we would enjoy to see your beautiful home."

"A short tour, perhaps, if you please," Ethel said decisively.

"Gladly." Elizabeth smiled. "It is not my home, or anyone's, anymore. It belongs to everyone in Potterston. If you'll follow me, I'll point out a few things as we go. Please feel free to ask questions at any time." Her long skirts rustled about her as she moved.

"The home is an example of Victorian architecture, built in 1871 by Edward Garling Potter, a member of one of the founding families of the town. It was owned by successive generations of the Potter family until 1979, when Miss Adelaide Potter passed away and bequeathed the home to the town with the stipulation that it house the historical society, which at that time had no permanent headquarters. After careful research, colors very similar to the original were selected..." She went on to explain the home's exterior before returning to the interior décor.

"All floors throughout the home are the original ones. In the foyer, front hallway, living room and dining room, the flooring is quarter-sawn Siberian oak, quite expensive in the Victorian era. The kitchen floor is composed of unglazed red quarry tiles laid in a staggered brickwork pattern. In Victorian times, the lovely patina on the tiles would have been created by hard-working servants frequently applying linseed oil and rubbing it in. Today," she said with a wink, "we cheat a little and use modern floor products to produce the same look with far less investment of time."

"I don't blame you a bit," Ethel said.

In the dining room, an ornate six-armed chandelier of brass had been converted to electricity from the original gas but retained its period ambience.

"Many of the furnishings came from the Potter family," Elizabeth told them. "They are the Rococo Revival, or Louis XV style, which remained very popular in the United States until shortly after the turn of the century. Rococo Revival is a graceful style reminiscent of eighteenth-century France. In general, pieces are extremely ornate and intricate. Natural figures such as flowers, vines and fruits are carved into the wood and the style includes cabriole legs. Most pieces are constructed of rosewood and black walnut..."

The bedrooms were stunning, with pieces like a tiger-oak washstand in one, and in another, a beautiful double highboy chest with the two upper doors left ajar to display several ladies' bonnets as they originally would have been stored.

The artist in Jane immediately took a flight of fantasy as she imagined what her own home would look like fully restored in a similar manner. She came back to earth, though, when Ethel cleared her throat and said, "We do have several questions for you but they pertain to genealogy rather than period homes. Not that this isn't lovely," she added hastily.

Elizabeth smiled graciously. "Let me take you to our office. All our genealogical information was catalogued electronically over the last four years by two college students with a grant from the

National Genealogical Society. We also have access to the NGS Project Registry, which is composed of thousands of genealogical projects by researchers all over the country. It's an extremely powerful tool that truly has transformed the way we conduct genealogical studies today."

Jane laughed. "So much for Victorian nostalgia. I suppose nothing can compete with modern technology."

Late Wednesday afternoon, Alice was working on her supplies for the ANGELs' senior prom in the dining room again when she heard the back door open. Moments later, Jane and Clothilda appeared.

"Hello," Alice said. "Did you have a productive day? Where's Aunt Ethel? I thought she went with you."

"She did. But she said she needs a nap after the day we had." Jane grinned. "I don't blame her."

"I, too, am very tired," Clothilda announced. "But I am happy also."

"So you were able to find some information about your family?"

"We make a start. We find in the hist-hist-"

"Historical Society," Jane supplied.

"Yes. We find in the records name of Moeller families."

"More than one family?"

"Three," Jane told her. "But the earliest ones we could find were from about 1850, which is much later than Clothilda's Moellers emigrated.

"We went to several cemeteries to look for the graves of others," Jane continued. "But like the census records at the historical society, we didn't find any really old ones."

"Perhaps the earlier ancestors are buried somewhere else," Alice said. "There are an awful lot of tiny family cemetery plots around the countryside, you know. A lot of them are still in the middle of fields. And perhaps they are not in this county but a neighboring one."

"That's possible," Jane admitted. "We may have to broaden our search."

Clothilda pulled several pieces of paper from her large handbag and held them out for Alice's perusal. "We make pencil rubbings of some of these Moellers."

Alice took one of the sheets of paper. The side of a soft pencil had been lightly rubbed repeatedly across the paper while it was lying against a smooth, hard gravestone with words carved into the surface. Alice realized she was looking at the name Klaus Moeller, with dates of birth and death years from the late 1800s. "Wow! That's interesting. How many did you find?"

Clothilda waved her sheaf of papers. "Many. Seventeen, maybe."

"It sounds as if you got a good start." Alice handed the pencil rubbings back to Clothilda. "So what next?"

"We're going to try a two-pronged approach," Jane told her. "First, we are going to begin calling all the Moellers in the area to see if any of them have done any genealogical research. It's possible they already may have what Clothilda is looking for."

"That would be most easy answer," Clothilda said, her eyes twinkling. "Less work for us."

"I'm not counting on that," Jane said. "If we don't get lucky with any of the Moellers we speak to, then we'll have to go back to the historical society and get the names of descendants of these people as far as we can go. All of them, which will be a daunting task, since a lot of folks had large families until the past half-century. Then . . . I don't know. The census office? County registrar? I'm going to have to make some calls and find out."

"And still we look for the older ones," Clothilda put in.

Just then, someone came into the front hallway of the inn.

"I'll go see who that is," Jane said.

"I, too, will go—only to lie down," Clothilda told her. "Thank you and we will talk later. Yes?"

"Yes." Jane smiled as she rose from her chair. "Have a good rest."

"Hello? Alice? Anyone home?" Alice recognized the voice of Ronald Simpson.

Jane called to him from the doorway of the dining room and said, "Hi, Ronald. We're in here."

"I'm looking for Alice," he told her.

Alice got to her feet and walked into the hallway. "Hello, Ronald."

"Hi, Alice." Now that he had found her, Ronald appeared oddly hesitant.

"The thing is . . . remember yesterday when Florence told you about the expeditions?"

"Yes . . . ?"

"Well, I led one this morning. You know, to find the Bigfoot."

Alice resisted the strong impulse to roll her eyes. "And did you? Find one, I mean."

"Not a trace," Ronald said with disgust. "I'm starting to think I imagined that footprint."

"Well, that hair Florence found isn't imaginary." Alice's instinct was to soothe.

"No, but that hair could be human." Ronald looked thoroughly miserable. "Florence is sure we're going to make the discovery of the century. But I think somebody is playing a joke on us. If a person had looked at the weather forecast and knew storms were predicted for last Thursday, he or she would know the tracks would be damaged, if not completely washed away, by a hard rain."

"Whose idea was it to go down to the pond?"

He shrugged. "I'm not sure it was anybody's. The boys were the ones who found the tracks first, remember? But anyone who knew anything about Fairy Pond would know the kids play around there all the time."

"True."

"Well," he said awkwardly, "I mostly just stopped to make sure I hadn't been seeing things." He laughed feebly.

"You weren't seeing things," Alice said gently. "Although I am inclined to think the footprints we found were not from an unknown species."

"Me too," he said glumly. "But Florence—you know how she can be—she wants to believe it and she's bound and determined to prove there's a Bigfoot out there." He sighed. "She's not going to be happy if it turns out someone is playing a joke."

He didn't have to say anything else. Alice knew well how stubborn Florence could be.

"I'm sorry," Alice said gently. "Is there anything I can do?" Her caring nature would not let her dismiss poor Ronald's distress.

But the man shook his head. "No, I don't think there is. This will just have to play out like it's going to play out. Even Florence can't create a critter out of thin air."

He turned to leave, and Alice bid him good-bye.

Jane was making a light evening meal for herself, Louise, Alice, Maxwell and Clothilda. They rarely invited inn guests to dinner, but Jane had felt sorry for both the lonely young man and the European woman so far from home, so she had asked them both to dine with the sisters.

She was washing up some of her prep dishes when she heard the front door open and close. She dried off her hands and walked toward the front of the house.

A middle-aged woman stood at the desk, fingers nervously pleating the fabric of the denim skirt she wore.

"Welcome to Grace Chapel Inn," Jane said. "How can I help you?"

"I'd like to speak to one of the Howard sisters," the woman said.

"I'm Jane Howard."

"I'm Barbara Candori. You're the folks who advertised about the lost cat?"

Jane felt her heart leap into her throat. "Yes, we are. Do you have information about Wendell?"

"I might be able to do better than that. I've had a cat hanging around my house for the past few days, so this morning I caught it."

"Have you seen one of our posters?" Jane asked eagerly. "Does the cat look like the one in the picture?"

"I haven't seen the poster," the woman said. "My friend Ella has, though. When I called her about the cat, she remembered seeing the poster in town. She lives a lot closer to Potterston than I do, so she drove in and wrote down the information. This is a gray cat with four white feet. I'm afraid I don't remember the color of its tail, and I was afraid to open the box again."

Jane tried to stay calm. "Is there a time I could come to your home and see the cat?"

"It's right out here in my car."

"Oh!" Jane followed the woman outside to a gray minivan. Barbara opened the back and pulled what looked like a sturdy fruit crate toward her. It had large slits in the sides, ensuring that plenty of air got in.

"Kitty, kitty," Jane called softly. "Come here and let me see you." She pulled the crate into the light and peered through the slits but all she could see was shadowy movement.

Carefully, she pulled back one of the flaps on the long side of the box, keeping her hand over the opening. Pulling back the other long flap, she took a deep breath as she reached in and lifted out a cat.

The moment her hands touched it, her heart sank. The fur was long and extremely silky. And when she lifted it, she didn't have to put any *oomph* behind it as she did when she lifted Wendell, who could only be described as an extremely healthy fellow. This cat was much smaller.

She lifted it out anyway. It was a gray tabby, and just like the last close call, it had four white paws. But there the resemblance ended. The hair was long and a much, much lighter gray than Wendell's. Disappointment swamped Jane. She cuddled the cat to her and closed her eyes for a moment.

"I'm sorry," she said to Barbara Candori. "I can't tell you how I appreciate your efforts, but this is not my cat." She sighed as the cat snuggled closer, obviously sensing a kind heart. "But someone must be missing this one. She's very friendly."

"She?"

"Just a guess," Jane said. "I really don't know. But it's very petite, isn't it?"

"It is. Would you like to have it? You don't have to give me a reward or anything."

Jane sadly shook her head. "No, thank you. Our cat is going to be found one of these days."

Distress crossed Barbara's face. "I can't keep it either. My husband said absolutely not. But I don't want to just take it to the shelter. You know what happens to cats at the shelter."

"My sister and I visited there and it seems like a very nice facility," Jane said. "But I understand your concern." She thought for a moment. "Let me make a telephone call. We have a friend who rescues cats all the time. Perhaps she could take this one."

"Oh, I would appreciate that so much," Barbara said.

Jane reluctantly returned the feline to its box. It had felt so good to hold a cat again. Leading the way indoors, she pulled out the telephone book from beneath the desk and quickly looked up Viola Reed's number. Dialing, she signaled to Barbara to wait while she listened to it ring.

"Hello?" Viola's greeting sounded more like a demand for information, typical of her strong personality.

"Hi, Viola, it's Jane Howard."

"Jane. Hello. How are you?"

"Fine, thanks. I'm calling because I need your help with something. I have a lady here who found a cat. She thought it might be Wendell but it isn't, and she doesn't want to take it to the shelter. It's a small, long-haired adult and seems very sweet. Is there any chance you might be able to take it?"

Viola was silent for a minute.

Jane began to think desperately of other options. She was on the verge of thanking Viola for her time when Viola said, "You know, I placed two yesterday. And I had a call from someone looking for a long-haired cat just this morning. Have your friend bring it by. Even if that placement doesn't work out, I'm sure I can find it a home."

"Oh, Viola, thank you!" Jane cried. "You are a gem. I'll send her right over."

"So you've had no luck finding Wendell yet?"

"No," Jane said. "We can't think of much else to do except pray at this point."

"I'm sorry." Viola's voice was gentle. "Cats are such special spirits. It's devastating to lose a friend like that."

"It is," Jane agreed.

Ending the conversation, Jane turned to Barbara, who was looking delighted. "Viola can take her if you don't mind driving the cat to her. She owns Nine Lives bookstore in town. She thinks she may even have a home for it."

"Oh, that's wonderful news," Barbara said fervently. "Thank you so much." Her smile faded as she realized Jane couldn't be feeling quite as happy. "I hope you find your cat. I'll pray that he is safe and gets home soon."

Jane swallowed, near tears. "That means a lot, Barbara. We need all the prayers we can get."

Chapter Eleven

D inner with their two guests was a pleasant time. Alice watched Maxwell interact with the older women. His often-stilted speech and behavior seemed to fit far more naturally among people her age than they would among young twenty-somethings like himself. She wondered what those boarding schools had been like.

She helped her sisters clear the table and wash up after the meal, and then went out onto the back porch to begin tying up newspapers. The sisters saved and recycled their newspapers and a number of other items, taking them to a local recycling center whenever they filled up their storage containers. Tomorrow she would make a run to the recycling center.

"Hello, Alice. Is there some way I may help?" Maxwell came onto the porch and stopped when he saw her.

"Oh," Alice said. "I'm just tying up these papers for recycling."

"Ah. A worthy endeavor." He stepped to her side and grabbed a stack of papers, then picked up one of the lengths of sturdy twine she already had cut. "If you'll show me what to do, I'll be happy to help."

"All right. Thank you." Alice thought it a little odd that he appeared to have no idea how to tie up the papers. "I guess they didn't teach this at your boarding schools."

The young man laughed, and once more, Alice was struck by the ease he seemed to be developing in the company of her and her sisters. "No. My education ran more to the classics, dance and deportment lessons, several languages and the all-important maths and sciences."

"Tell me about dance and deportment. I'm familiar with the rest, but my education didn't include lessons in those areas."

"Let's see . . . From the time I was about ten years old, I attended something called cotillion, where we were taught ballroom dances such as the waltz, the two-step and the rumba. We learned how to ask for a dance, how to partner the lady, and we were taught manners. We practiced basic courtesy and table manners all the time, anyway, but we learned how to take tea, how to introduce people properly and how to bow, things like that."

"Have your bowing lessons proven valuable in everyday life?" Alice asked with a smile. Good manners were important, but taking classes to learn to bow seemed to her a little extreme.

"You must understand, Alice, that I was not groomed to live an everyday life. My father socializes mainly with those with blue blood and pots of money. He expected me to do the same."

"And you aren't?"

He smiled, but Alice thought there was a sad resignation behind it. "No. I don't fit into that world any better than I fit anywhere else, and choosing to pursue higher degrees in something so far from the business world as psychology has made me even more different."

"There is nothing wrong with being different," Alice said softly.

"No. But different can get lonely." He kept his gaze on the twine he was tying.

"It can," Alice agreed. "I sometimes felt that way years ago when all my friends were marrying and having children. I wasn't unhappy in my choices, but I didn't always feel that I fit in very well."

He nodded. "Exactly. I enjoy my studies."

"What will you do once you've finished your doctorate?"

"Teaching and research. I want to work somewhere in an academic atmosphere that allows me to pursue research in a direction I find interesting."

Alice cocked her head. "And your father doesn't perceive that as a successful career choice?"

"I don't know," he admitted. "But it doesn't matter anymore. I spent years trying to show him how smart I was, to make him proud of me. He rarely seemed to notice me. So now I just worry about making choices that will make me happy."

But it couldn't be that simple, Alice thought. Inside Maxwell was a little boy to whom it still mattered desperately that he please his father.

"I haven't told anyone else this," he went on, looking over at her earnestly "but I sent resumes to several universities that have positions open on staff. There's one I particularly would like to get, but I am quite certain the competition will be fierce. I already have had an interview, but I have not received any further word, and I suspect I am not being considered for it."

"Don't give up hope yet," Alice said. "I don't know enough about your work to be any kind of judge, but I imagine you're very good at it and that you interview well."

His gaze slid away from hers. "We'll have to wait and see." He patted the bundle of papers. "Here you go."

On Thursday at lunchtime, Alice stopped in at the Coffee Shop while she was running some errands. She was curious to learn if people still were talking about the Bigfoot theory.

The moment she walked through the door, she had her answer.

"...did not find any further evidence and we believe it must be nocturnal," Florence Simpson was saying to a group around her.

The group consisted of Ronald, Fred Humbert, Maxwell and several other local people.

"Alice!" Florence sang out.

Mustering a smile, Alice turned toward the counter. She had come in to see what was going on, she reminded herself. And, boy, now was she going to find out.

"Hello, Florence," Alice said. "Hi, everyone."

"Hi, Alice," said Maxwell. "We're talking about the Bigfoot."

"Oh?"

"We took a second hike this morning," said Ronald, looking a bit embarrassed.

"We had a nice walk, but didn't find anything," added Fred Humbert. "Then again, I didn't expect to find anything."

"There *is* something out there to be found," said Florence sharply. "We must keep seeking until we find it. Just think—we could put Acorn Hill on the map."

Alice thought that putting their town on the map with the wild claim of finding Bigfoot probably would not thrill most of Acorn Hill's residents.

"Ronald and I believe the creature must be nocturnal," Florence explained to Alice what she had been saying when Alice entered. "Therefore, the key to finding it is to seek it out when it is active."

Ronald looked pained. "Florence thinks we should make an overnight expedition tomorrow near the pond in hopes of—"

"In hopes of catching it on camera," Florence interrupted. "If we could get a photograph of it, we could send the photo along with the hair and a cast of the footprint to a scientist for analysis."

"But we don't have a footprint," Alice reminded her. "Yes, Ronald and I saw a large print, but the storm—"

"I propose to have you work with an artist," Florence interjected. "You know, Alice, like the police do when they have a witness who can describe someone?"

Alice thought that was the most ridiculous idea she had heard in a very long time. "Florence, footprints don't have distinguishing features. Faces have eyes, noses, mouths, all of which can be very distinctive. All I could tell you about these prints is that they were big and broad. Period."

"Well, no matter." Florence dismissed this objection with an airy wave of her hand. "We still have the hair and the creature's picture."

"Assuming there is a creature to get a picture of," Fred said logically.

Florence glared at him. "If you're coming along on this expedition tomorrow night, you can't think so negatively. The creature might sense negative energy."

"Sorry, Florence." Fred glanced at Alice, and she read his expression perfectly. *Somebody needs to stop this silliness.*

"Alice," said Ronald, "you'll come, won't you? After all, we were the first adults to see the tracks."

"Oh, I don't think so ..." Alice wished she had work as an excuse but unless she got an emergency call to take a shift tomorrow evening, she wasn't scheduled. "I'll just hear the report when you get back."

"You have to come, Alice," said Florence. "Ronald's right. You two had the first sighting. It's important that you be there for the filming."

"Can I come?" Bobby Dawson pushed forward eagerly.

Florence frowned. She and Ronald had no children of their own and Florence was not known to be particularly maternal. "Only if your parents give permission," she said. "And one of them comes along," she added slyly.

"*Aww.* My folks hate camping," Bobby grumbled. "They'll never go for that."

"I'd like to come, if I may," Maxwell said.

"Certainly," said Florence. "The more, the merrier. Adults, that is," she added with a glance at Bobby to be sure he had gotten the message.

"I'll go if you go, Alice," said Fred. "I doubt Vera will come. Camping's not really her thing."

"Oh, pish-posh," Florence said dismissively. "Of course she must come. I wouldn't want her to miss it."

"I really don't think—"

"Why don't we plan to pursue our little expedition tomorrow night?" Florence plowed right over Fred's objection.

"All right," said Fred reluctantly. "I'll ask Vera."

"Wonderful!" Florence rose majestically from the stool where she had been holding court. "Let's go, Ronald. We must check out all our camping gear and purchase supplies."

"Supplies?"

"Well, of course. What do you think we're going to eat while we're on this hunt?"

As Ronald followed her out, Fred began to chuckle. "This should be interesting."

Alice turned and grinned at him. "You do realize Vera is going to scalp you when she learns you volunteered her to spend a night in the woods with Florence, right?"

Thursday after school, Alice's ANGELs were being driven by their parents to the nursing home. This was the afternoon that the ANGELs were hosting the nursing home residents' senior prom. As Alice began to carry her boxes of decorations out to the car, Maxwell came down the stairs.

"What are you doing?" he asked.

"Going to a senior prom," she replied with a twinkle in her eye. "These are the decorations."

"A senior prom …?" He looked totally bewildered.

Alice laughed. "You've heard me mention the group of girls I work with, the ANGELs. We're going to a nursing home to host a tea dance for the residents. Oh, it won't be a real dance," she said as she saw a question in his eyes. "Some of the residents are non-ambulatory and many of them use walkers or canes. But we plan to dress up, play music and help them move as much as they are able."

He was smiling. To Alice's surprise, he said, "I don't suppose you would let me come along, would you?"

Alice hesitated, completely unprepared for the request.

"Oh, never mind," he said. "It just sounded interesting."

"Maxwell, I would be delighted to have you come along," Alice said. "You just caught me off-guard."

"I think I caught myself off-guard," he said, sounding a little surprised.

"We can always use an extra pair of hands to decorate. Please do come."

"All right." He turned to take the last box to her car. "I'll carry this out, and then I'll run up and put on a suit."

Alice's eyebrows rose as he dashed off. He was really taking this seriously. She glanced down at her dress, a pretty floral pattern in pinks, lavenders and greens. Oh, those feather boas were going to look amazing with it, she thought, amused at herself.

When they arrived at the nursing home, they carried the boxes inside. The ANGELs began to arrive and everyone pitched in to help with decorating. Maxwell, with his height and long arms, was quite popular with anyone who needed to hang something from a higher spot. And Alice was pleased to note that he interacted very pleasantly with the girls. Ten minutes before the residents were to begin arriving, the girls rushed off to the visitors' restroom to don their "prom dresses."

They returned, bubbling and adorable, most in dresses that Alice suspected would be their Easter finery. The first of the residents shuffled in, followed by wheelchairs pushed by smiling aides.

Alice put on the first CD of music she had prepared, turning it up a little louder than she normally would have. The director of the facility had suggested doing so, reminding Alice that many of the older folks had hearing difficulties.

The girls, suddenly shy, clumped together in a group, smiling and hanging back.

"I'm ready to trip the light fantastic," one wizened little woman in a shiny red blouse declared.

To Alice's astonishment, Maxwell moved forward and bent down so that he was close to her level. "May I have this dance, madam?" He held out his hand and the tiny woman placed her delicate palm in his.

Alice blinked back sudden tears at the sight.

And Maxwell looked over his shoulder and beckoned to the knot of self-conscious teens. "Come on, girls. Grab a partner. Let's make this the best senior prom ever."

Jane checked in another guest early Thursday evening, a thirty-something woman named Ellis Andin. She was tiny and blonde, and she practically vibrated with energy.

"I'd like to stay for two nights," she told Jane in a thin, high voice that instantly brought visions of Tinker Bell to mind.

"Of course," Jane said. She launched into her usual informative chat about breakfast hours, where to take other meals, local attractions, but Ellis shook her head.

"Breakfasts will be lovely, but I will take the other meals with a friend. And I don't want you to be concerned on Friday night because I will be out all night."

"All night?" Jane wanted to be sure she had not misunderstood.

Ellis nodded. "I'll be going on an overnight camping trip that's just been planned. We're looking for Bigfoot. I'm sure you read about it in your local paper."

"Looking for Bigfoot," Jane repeated. "Oh yes, I read about it. Actually, my sister Alice is one of the two people who saw the footprints."

"Oh!" Ellis looked even more animated, if that was possible. "I must speak with her. Get her impressions. So she was the woman with Ronald?"

"Ronald Simpson," Jane confirmed. "Yes. You know Ronald?"

"No." Ellis shook her head, sending blonde curls flying every which way. "I am acquainted with his wife Florence. She e-mailed us to report her findings, and I dropped everything to investigate."

"Investigate?" Jane felt like a parrot, but this small woman was making her head spin.

"Yes. I am a member of the Sasquatch Society of America. We have investigators in every region of the country and when a sighting is reported, we mobilize to evaluate the validity of the claim."

"I see. Florence e-mailed you, so here you are."

"That's it in a nutshell." Ellis cocked her head. "I'm going to take my things up to my room. You needn't come up with me. Then, if you would be so kind, I'd like to get directions to the Simpsons' home. If you're not familiar with their residence, I can call them and ask—"

"That's all right," Jane said. "I know Florence and Ronald quite well. I'll call her and let her know you're coming, and I'll write out directions for you."

"Thank you, my dear." Ellis vanished up the stairs.

Jane shook her head. *My dear?* She picked up the phone and dialed, common sense dictating that she confirm that Ellis Andin really was who she said she was before giving out the Simpson's home information.

Florence, indeed, vouched for Ellis, so Jane promised to send the new guest over as soon as she was settled. In only a few minutes Ellis came downstairs to get the directions and head off on her mission. Alice came in the kitchen door soon after Ellis breezed out the front door.

"Hi, Alice," Jane greeted her as she pulled some things from the refrigerator. "How did the prom go?"

"Oh, Jane, it was truly wonderful. Everyone—the residents, the staff, the girls, Maxwell—had a marvelous time!"

"Maxwell?"

"Oh yes," Alice replied. "He was the hit of the afternoon. When he heard what the ANGELs were doing, he volunteered to help. He not only helped to decorate, but he kept the party going. I think half the ladies are in love with him. He was so sweet, gently guiding those elderly ladies around the floor. And he got even the shiest of the men talking."

"My my, will wonders never cease?" Jane smiled as she put the finishing touches on a casserole.

"Well, actually, today is full of wonders. You'll never believe what I heard at the Coffee Shop earlier," Alice said.

"Would it have anything to do with a Bigfoot hunting trip?"

Alice stared at Jane. "It would. How did you find out?"

Jane laughed. "Now *you're* the one who won't believe it. We have a Bigfoot specialist from the Sasquatch Society of America staying here for the next two days."

Louise stepped into the kitchen from the hallway just in time to hear the last sentence. She set down the loaf of bread she had purchased at Jane's request and said slowly, "You are joking."

Jane held up her right hand, palm out, as if taking an oath. "I swear it's the truth." Quickly, she went on to tell her sisters about Florence contacting the society and Ellis' mission.

Then Alice recounted her adventure in the Coffee Shop that afternoon.

Louise sank into a kitchen chair. "These people are under a spell. It's the only explanation."

"Maybe someone put something in the water," Jane suggested.

Alice snickered. "This really is crazy, isn't it?" Then she frowned. "Oh, and I forgot to tell you—Fred and I got roped into going on this expedition tomorrow night. Maxwell's coming too. I believe he thinks that it'll be quite a lark."

"Maybe for him it will be," Jane said.

"Vera doesn't know that she's been volunteered yet," Alice said.

"Oh my. I'd like to be a fly on the wall in the Humbert house tonight," Jane said with a chuckle.

"As I mentioned, Maxwell's quite excited about the camping trip," Alice went on. "You know, he has told me a bit about his childhood. I'll bet that Maxwell has never gone camping. Jane could be correct. This might be a grand adventure for a young man starved for any sort of normal interaction. Although interacting with Florence when she is on a mission hardly can be termed normal."

"Amen to that," Jane said.

The phone rang, and Louise answered. "Grace Chapel Inn, Louise speaking. May I help you?"

Jane saw her face change as she listened to the speaker at the other end. Her shoulders sagged, her mouth turned down and her eyes lowered.

"Yes," she said. "No, Mr. Jervis, I'm so sorry to tell you that we have not found him yet."

She listened some more, pressing her lips together. "Oh no," she said. "We don't blame you in the least. It could have happened to anyone. Wendell was—*is* the adventurous sort. We haven't given up. It's only been a bit over a week. He may be found yet… oh, you're too kind. But no, truly, we don't want you to get us another kitten. Although I appreciate the thought and I know my sisters will, also…yes, yes, of course we will give you a call…"

As she concluded the conversation, Jane said, "Oh, poor man. I feel so bad that he's worrying about Wendell. I'm glad you reassured him that it wasn't his fault, Louise."

"Well, it wasn't." From the expression on her elder sister's face, Jane was sure she was thinking that it had been her fault for getting annoyed with Wendell.

"Louise," said Alice in a tone far more severe than she normally employed, "I do not give you permission to blame yourself for Wendell's disappearance anymore."

Louise and Jane both were so startled they turned and stared at Alice.

She winked.

And all three of them smiled.

"All right," Louise said. "I am trying hard to let go of guilt. Really I am."

"I hope so," Jane said. "I told you before, I could have been the one that chased the little rascal off that table. The end result may have been the same."

"We're assuming Wendell had a reason for getting into that car," Alice pointed out. "He's a cat. He simply might have been curious and settled down for a nap. Can you imagine the surprise he got?"

Jane said, "You're right. He very well might have hopped into Mr. Jervis' car even if we'd fed him tuna that morning."

～

On Friday morning, Jane, Ethel and Clothilda went into town. Ethel had a plan.

"We'll go to all our Acorn Hill businesses and ask who knows any Moellers in the area," she said enthusiastically. "Shopkeepers and public servants get to know scads of people. We can make a list so we don't duplicate names. Then we can visit them to see if anyone knows any family history that might link them to Clothilda."

"That's a great idea," Jane said. "I also made a list of Moeller names from the telephone book. We can compare it with the list we make today to be sure we don't miss anyone. There are five families with the Moeller name in the area around Potterston and Acorn Hill."

Clothilda was not quite as spry as Ethel, so Jane dropped the two off at the library, where they intended to start their search. Then she parked the car and joined them.

Ethel already was talking a mile a minute to Nia when Jane walked in. Clothilda stood at her side, beaming and nodding.

"Oh, I have several Moellers listed who have library cards," Nia told them. "But Ethel, I cannot give out names and addresses of library patrons."

Ethel frowned. "It's not as if we're terrorists, Nia. You know us personally."

Nia shook her head firmly, her friendly smile still in place. "I wish I could help you, but I can't." Then she brightened. "I'll tell you what I can do. I can contact all the Moellers and either give them your phone number or get their permission to give you their information. Would that help?"

Jane could see Ethel's shoulders relax. "That would be a very acceptable alternative, if you don't mind the extra work."

Nia shrugged. "Not at all. I have to contact library patrons for many reasons, anyway, and it's likely that some of these Moellers already are on my list to call."

"Here." Jane dug a small notepad out of her purse and wrote down Ethel's telephone number. "This is how you can reach Ethel. I would give you the inn's number so people could talk to Clothilda, but—"

"My English on the telephone is so not good," Clothilda said earnestly. "Ethel will be much easier to speak."

"Thank you, Jane," said Ethel. "And thank you, Nia. We appreciate your help."

The three women left the library and walked around the small town, stopping at various shops, the post office and other public buildings. In each place, they left Ethel's contact information rather than requesting that any information be divulged. At the post office, the postmistress suggested that they place a notice on the public bulletin board in the lobby where the mailboxes were located. "Everybody reads that thing," she promised.

"That's a good idea," Jane said. "There could be people with other surnames who have Moellers somewhere in their family tree."

In the Good Apple Bakery, Clarissa Cottrell said, "Oh, I met someone the other week named Moeller. She just joined my art class. I'm starting watercolors," Clarissa told her. "Never tried that medium but the other club members have encouraged me, so I'm giving it a whirl. Now what was that woman's name?" she muttered to herself. Then she shrugged. "All I remember is the Moeller part. But we have a meeting coming up, so I'll make a note to ask her."

Jane held out one of the small notes on which she'd written the contact information. "Here. Please tell her that you know some folks doing genealogical research on the Moeller name and that they'd like to speak to her."

Clarissa took the paper with a grunt of acknowledgment. "Good. Now," she said, "surely you three can't leave here without a little taste of something. What strikes your fancy?"

Chapter Twelve

On Friday evening, Alice had just dragged her sleeping bag downstairs in preparation for Florence's "expedition" when she heard someone sneeze five times in rapid succession.

"God bless you!" she exclaimed as Maxwell came down behind the staircase. "Allergies?"

He shook his head. "I've never had them before. I think I may be catching something." His voice was thick and nasal-sounding.

Alice looked at him closely as he came to the bottom of the steps. His eyes appeared dull, but he didn't seem feverish.

"Vitamin C," she suggested. "Try taking it several times a day. It may boost your immune system if you are catching something. If that doesn't work, I have some over-the-counter allergy remedies you can try."

"Thank you," he said. "I had intended to accompany you on the expedition tonight, but I don't believe I am feeling up to it. I was coming downstairs to tell you."

"You should stay home," Alice said. "It's still quite cold at night. I have thermal clothing on, and I borrowed a sleeping bag from a church member who regularly camps and says this one will keep me warm down into single digits."

Maxwell shivered, and Alice couldn't tell whether it had been a chill or a reaction to the idea of sleeping outside in the cold. "*Brrr*. I'll be thinking of you while I sleep in my warm bed," he said as he climbed back up the stairs to his room.

"Thanks," Alice called after him sarcastically. But secretly she was pleased. The young man seemed to be relaxing. She hadn't heard him tease before.

Behind her, she heard Jane say, "Rats!"

"What's wrong?" she asked her sister.

"There went our last lead." Jane hung up the telephone at the registration desk. "Aunt Ethel and I have spoken with every family by the name of Moeller we could find in the area. Apparently, all of the names on our list are descended from the same couple who came over from Germany shortly before our Civil War."

"Which is about a hundred years later than Clothilda's ancestor, correct?" Alice said.

"Correct." Jane put her hands on her hips. "We're missing something. I can feel it, but I don't know what it might be."

"Why don't you pray about it?" Alice suggested. "And then sleep on it? Maybe things will look clearer in the morning."

"That's a good suggestion." Jane sighed. Then she grinned as she realized where Alice would be sleeping that night. "Maybe I'd better say a little prayer for you, as well."

Alice smiled, shaking her head. "It surely couldn't hurt."

At 8:00 PM, Alice and her fellow campers gathered in front of the inn. Along with Alice, Florence and Ronald were Fred Humbert and Vera. Ellis, the new inn guest, also was waiting, her sleeping bag in her arms.

Ellis had tried to corner Alice that morning after breakfast to ask questions about the footprints she had seen. Alice had given her the same information she'd shared with everyone else, but when the woman became more insistent with her questions, Alice had pleaded housework and escaped to the kitchen. Now she might have to fend off Ellis all night long.

Alice sighed. *Why, oh why, did I say yes to this?* It didn't matter now, she reminded herself. She was stuck with no way out. Taking a deep breath, she said, "Hello, everyone."

Her fellow campers returned various greetings.

Florence said, "I suppose you two already know each other," and when Alice and Ellis nodded pleasantly at one another, "Vera, Fred, this is Ellis Andin, from the Sasquatch Society of America."

"Hello, everyone," Ellis said in her high, flutey voice.

Vera started. "The what?"

"The Sasquatch Society of America," Florence repeated. "I invited her to visit Acorn Hill in hopes that she will be able to verify our sighting of the animal commonly known as Bigfoot."

Fred rolled his eyes, but he was standing off to one side, and Alice was the only one to see him. Vera was silent, apparently too taken aback to formulate a response.

Florence cleared her throat. "I have appointed myself official recorder for this expedition. If you have any observations, see anything unusual, please call me immediately so that I can record it." Alice noticed that Florence had a small, very costly looking video camera around her neck.

"Ronald and I set up two tents this afternoon," Fred said, "so once we get a fire going we should be nice and toasty."

The little party piled into Fred's and Ronald's vehicles for the short ride from the inn to the pond. The sky was dark by the time they arrived, and they unloaded their things and trooped back into the woods. At the far end of the pond was a clearing with a fire pit, used in the winter for bonfires to warm skaters. Earlier, Ronald and Fred had driven to the closest entry point and carried in the tents and camping supplies.

As they marched along the path, Ellis said, "So, Ronald, Alice, can you show me where the prints were and where you were when you saw them?"

Ronald, walking in front of Alice, turned and gave her a long-suffering glance. "They were over that way," he said, pointing out the spot. "As for where we were, we were standing over them, practically."

"So you could have inadvertently destroyed additional footprints?"

"I doubt it," Alice said, recalling the afternoon. "The foot-prints crossed the path at an angle from one side to another, almost at a right angle to us but not quite. It would have had to be traveling on the path for us to have destroyed prints, because it was damp that day and none of us stepped off the path."

"Ah! Very good." Ellis sounded as if she would like to pat Alice on the head. "See there? I elicited quite a bit of detailed information from you."

Alice felt annoyed, but then chided herself. *You are being silly. The poor woman hasn't done anything to you.* Still she found the expedition a terrible waste of time.

"Oh, this is nice!" Vera called out.

Alice calmed herself as she looked in the direction Vera pointed.

"I brought some marshmallows, graham crackers and chocolate bars along for s'mores tonight," Vera told the group.

Alice laughed. "Just as long as you didn't bring along any Girl Scouts!"

"No, just the six of us," Florence said, very seriously. "Too many people might spook the Bigfoot."

"Let's get our bedrolls settled," Fred proposed, "and start the fire."

"Women over here." Florence led the way to the larger of the two tents.

Stepping inside, Alice saw that there was plenty of room for four sleeping bags. Florence had procured air mattresses, which they quickly blew up, using a battery-operated pump. Vera hung a lantern from the center pole and turned it on so that there was a cozy glow in the small space.

Alice spread her sleeping bag on top of one of the mattresses and fluffed the pillow she'd rolled into the center of her sleeping bag. Vera did the same, and then she stepped to the windows and zipped closed the flaps that covered the screened squares.

Florence said, "What are you doing, Vera?"

"Shutting these windows," Vera said, and there was a note in her voice that Alice knew meant that there would be no discussion. Vera was sweet and easygoing but she had a core of steel deep inside.

Florence apparently recognized the tone, too, because she turned away and busied herself preparing her bed.

When the interior of the tent was set up, Alice stepped outside. Fred and Ronald sat on one of the logs that formed a seating square around the fire, which they had started. There was a full moon and the little clearing was so bright Alice could see easily to pick up several sticks for roasting the marshmallows Vera was opening.

"This is lovely," Vera said, inhaling deeply of the cool spring air. "A bit cold, but I think we'll be plenty warm in our sleeping bags."

"It is lovely, isn't it?" Alice accepted a marshmallow and pushed it onto one of the sticks she'd laid near the logs. "*Umm*, I love s'mores. It's been some time since I have had these."

"I've never had them before," Ellis piped up. "What are they and how do we make them?"

"To make a s'more, you break a graham cracker in half," Vera instructed as she demonstrated. "Put a couple of squares of a chocolate bar on each piece. Then toast a marshmallow, and make a sandwich of the two sections using the marshmallow as the middle filling." She set aside her stick and took a big bite of hers. "I adore these. I think there's a rule that Girl Scout troops have to make them any time they have a cookout or overnight camping trip."

Alice laughed.

"They do look delicious," Florence said. "I think I'll try one."

"Me too." Ellis copied Florence and picked up a stick. "I never was a Girl Scout."

"Hey, Vera, make me one of those, will you?" Fred said from his log on the far side of the fire.

Vera snorted. "You ask me nicely and *maybe* I will."

Everyone laughed.

"So, Ellis," Alice said, "why don't you tell us about yourself and how you came to be involved in the Sasquatch organization?"

Ellis smiled happily across the fire at Alice, and Alice felt guilty for her earlier thoughts. "I have been a science geek all my life," she said. "I was the girl in high school with the horn-rimmed glasses and a stack of books that weighed more than I did. You know, the one everyone went to for help on the chemistry test."

"Oh yes," Vera said. "I knew a girl like that. I might not have graduated if not for her."

There were a few chuckles.

"My favorite subject was biology," Ellis went on, "and I always was riveted by stories of fantastic creatures. I loved *Twenty Thousand Leagues Under the Sea*. You know, because of the giant squid."

"That story gave me the shivers," Florence confessed.

"Not me," Ellis said. "I read everything I could about giant squid, the Loch Ness monster, Bigfoot and every other unidentified creature ever mentioned. In college, I majored in biology, and one summer I had an internship at a place in South Carolina that cared for circus animals no one wanted anymore. One old man there used to tell a story about a creature he'd seen years ago, a man or an ape with long black hair that was taller than a human."

"Sasquatch!" Florence leaned forward eagerly.

"One might draw that conclusion," Ellis said, nodding at her approvingly. "Anyhow, I eventually became curious enough about his story to start researching other sightings of similar creatures. I discovered that there was hot debate about the existence of such animals."

"That's for sure," Vera said to Alice in a meaningful undertone.

Florence glared at them across the fire, and Alice elbowed Vera. "Behave," she whispered.

Ellis smiled at Vera. "Your reaction is perfectly understandable," she said. "There are many people who do not believe these creatures exist. Years after the death of one man who had claimed to have filmed a sighting, people came forward, one insisting that he had made the Bigfoot suit worn in the film and another who said he was the one wearing the suit."

"Is that the Patterson film?" Ronald asked.

"Yes." Ellis sounded surprised. "Are you familiar with it?"

"I looked up some things after we found those tracks," Ronald said, nodding.

"What's the Patterson film?" Florence demanded. Alice thought that Florence sounded as if she wasn't thrilled with Ronald's knowing something she didn't.

"It was made in 1967 near Yakima, Washington," Ellis told them, "by two men who were hoping to create a film of Bigfoot. The segment clearly shows a large female on a gravel sandbar near a creek. The men had been on horseback but the one with the camera dismounted and ran toward the creature as he filmed. At that point, the creature turned and walked back into the forest." Her eyes shone. "It is an extraordinary piece of film."

"Is the film authentic?" Florence wanted to know.

"That is still being debated," Ellis said.

"So is that sort of incident what led you to get involved with this society?" Alice asked. She really did not want to get into a debate about whether or not Bigfoot existed.

"Yes." Ellis was diverted, as Alice had hoped. "I found this little group called the Sasquatch Society of America and started volunteering. They asked me to be on the board of directors a few years later and the organization has grown steadily ever since. We have investigators in almost every state now."

"What's the most exciting thing you've ever found?" Fred wanted to know.

Ellis smiled, her pale hair gleaming in the dancing firelight. "That's easy. Five years ago I traveled to the Upper Peninsula of Michigan to investigate a report from a couple who said they had seen a Sasquatch. Not only had they seen it, they had nearly fallen over it!"

"Oh my stars." Florence looked nervous. "Did it hurt them?"

"Nothing like that," Ellis reassured her. "The woman and her husband had been hiking. She was in the lead when they came to a huge downed tree blocking the path. Her husband gave her a leg up and she scrambled onto the trunk. She was just about to leap off the other side when she glanced down and saw an enormous hairy creature in a depression half-hidden on the other side of the log."

"I would have had a heart attack," Florence pronounced. "What a scare! What did the creature do?"

"Well, the woman thought it was a bear, as we probably all would have. The creature began to rise, and she screamed, but before she could get back down off the log, the creature stood up, leaped out of the depression and ran *on two legs* until they couldn't see it anymore."

"Bears can walk on two legs," Fred stated.

"But they run on all fours, particularly when speed is needed," Ellis told him. "According to the interviews done with this couple, who both saw it, this creature had long arms that it drew up exactly like a jogger would as it ran. They also stated that once it stood up, it never went back to all fours again."

Fred whistled. "What else did they see?"

Ellis smiled. "Quite a bit. The woman, as it turned out, was an artist. She specialized in portraiture, and she was able to create a sketch based on what she had seen. The result was one of the most detailed depictions of a Sasquatch—a Bigfoot—that I have ever seen."

"Really?" Even Vera looked impressed, and Alice knew her friend considered the whole notion of a primitive North American man-ape to be entertaining science fiction and nothing more.

"Really," Ellis assured her. "She drew three different sketches. One was her initial impression of the creature lying in its nest, the second was a three-quarter profile of the face, and the third showed it running."

"Nest?" Alice asked, intrigued.

"Oh yes. I forgot to tell you that the couple had a camera. They didn't get pictures of the creature in the initial excitement, but they did photograph the spot where they had found it lying. The depression was deliberately hollowed out. You can see where the dirt that was dug up was mounded around the edges. It was filled with leaves and twigs and coarse dark hair with reddish tips. They even thought to bring back some of the hair."

"And?" Florence asked. "What was it?"

Ellis smiled. "We don't know. Or perhaps I should say we know what it is not. A DNA analysis showed that it is not a known species. Not an ape, not a bear, not a man. I believe it came from an unidentified species currently known as Bigfoot or Sasquatch. But until we actually find one, the conclusion reached by the Sasquatch Society is that it must be considered a working theory rather than a fact."

Alice was impressed. Ellis wasn't delusional as Alice had assumed. Instead, the woman spoke more like a researcher compiling empirical data and being careful not to leap to an unproven conclusion. "So exactly what does someone from your organization do to investigate?" she asked.

"Journey to the region, interview eyewitnesses and anyone else who may have pertinent information and try to preserve any evidence," Ellis said. "In your local case, the tracks have disappeared but the hair still exists."

"And what will you do with it?"

"It will be sent away for DNA analysis."

"Will you let us know when you find out what it is?" Florence asked.

"Or what it isn't," Ronald mused.

"Of course." Ellis smiled at them. "I promise you will be the first people I call."

The rest of the evening passed pleasantly. Not long after the s'mores were finished, everyone settled down for the night. It was cold, it was dark, and no one seemed to care that it was barely ten o'clock.

Alice certainly didn't. She had worked the day shift at the hospital, and her feet were letting her know it was time to rest. She lay down in her sleeping bag and zipped herself in. God wouldn't mind if she said her prayers in this position.

Dear Heavenly Father, she began, *bless each of us engaged in tonight's endeavor. Keep us safe and in Your care. Bless Wendell, wherever he is, and keep him safe too. Our hearts would be so gladdened if You led him home, Father. But if that's not in Your plan, give us the courage and grace to face it.*

She went on, asking for specific blessings for a number of people in the Grace Chapel congregation who had asked to be lifted up in prayer last Sunday morning. She prayed for the swift healing of Penelope Smeal's ankle, for the family of a woman who had passed away during her shift today, for Mark to have a successful experience in San Diego, and she prayed for herself to be more tolerant, to be kinder and more patient.

Finishing her prayers, she realized that all three of her tentmates were asleep, and she was briefly amused. Apparently no one was too worried about a Bigfoot coming into camp tonight.

She fell asleep to the sound of Florence's snoring.

Alice's eyes flew open in the dark, but she was unsure of what had awakened her. A moment later, she heard a slight but distinct movement in the thicket of shrubs and trees directly behind their campsite.

She looked in the direction of her tentmates, but without any light inside the tent it was too dark to see more than three lumps on the other mattresses.

The noise came again. Quietly, Alice slipped out of her sleeping bag, taking a bracing breath of the chilly air outside her little cocoon. Her slip-on, all-weather mocs were parked right beside her sleeping bag, and she quickly shoved her feet into them and grabbed the insulated jacket she'd brought along.

Unfastening the flap of the tent, she stepped outside and straightened up. The bright moonlight lit up the clearing and it took a moment for her eyes to adjust. She took a few tentative steps forward and stopped suddenly as she heard the rustling noise again. It was coming from the direction of the cooler and backpacks where their food had been stored away from the tents.

Alice headed across the clearing, firmly telling herself there was no such thing as Bigfoot. She hoped.

Suddenly a large raccoon popped up on the top of the cooler. Alice stifled a cry as her hand flew to her heart. He held a marshmallow in his hand, and as he surveyed her, Alice could have sworn his black eyes were laughing. A second later, he leaped off the cooler and vanished into the bushes with a last flourish of his bushy, banded tail.

Alice walked over to the cooler. She could see one of the backpacks lying open on the ground. *That little rascal!* A flash of white caught her eye and she realized it was one of the marshmallow bags that their nocturnal visitor had dragged away. She carefully picked her way through the bushes to retrieve it.

As she turned around, she was surprised to see Florence emerge from their tent. The big woman looked around and hesitated, then walked purposefully into the woods along the path that led around the pond, looking around her as she went. As she went farther and farther and the brush became denser, Alice could hear her shoving branches out of her way.

She didn't want to hail Florence across the clearing and wake everyone else, so Alice decided to go after her and was just about to cross the clearing to do so when Ronald came out of his tent, followed by Fred. The two men quickly took off along the same path that Florence had taken.

"…sounded like something big…" were the only words she was able to make out as the men vanished also.

Thoroughly entertained, Alice surmised that Ronald and Fred had heard Florence crashing through the brush. She had enough of a head start that she was completely out of sight before they emerged from their tent. Alice wondered what on earth they thought they were chasing.

Since Florence was being attended to, Alice turned back to the food and began to make sure the backpacks were secured.

Suddenly she heard Vera's voice saying, "Come on!" Alice turned to see Vera and Ellis hurry down the path.

Since there was no one still sleeping, Alice called after them, but they didn't hear her. A little dazed by the speed with which the camp had emptied, Alice stepped back into the clearing and shook her head.

Calculating Florence's progress, Alice figured she was at least halfway around the pond by now. Alice could go in the opposite direction and meet up with her to deliver the disappointing news that a raccoon had been the source of the noise that Florence had heard.

She turned to her left and began to walk around the pond. Although the path was well-marked, bushes overhung it in places, and branches downed by wind and snow during the winter made walking hazardous. She paid careful attention to her footsteps, using the bright moonlight to aid her. As she got closer to the point where the path from the road fed into the one that ran around the pond, the way became easier. More people used that end of the pond, rather than fighting their way through the brush to the far end where her friends had set up camp.

A scream split the air ahead of her. Florence! Alice began to run. She jumped over a log across the path and dodged around a tree, the noise of her running masking any other sounds, and ran smack into Florence, who was rushing her way at full speed.

Down they went in a tangle of arms and legs. Alice's breath whooshed out as the bigger woman landed squarely on top her.

"It's behind me!" Florence gasped, clutching at Alice. "I heard it."

"No, it's not," Alice said, hearing the men crashing through the brush toward them. Suddenly she realized that, like Florence, Fred and Ronald probably would not see them until they were on top of them.

As if the thought had been enough to make it happen, Ronald burst out of the brush, tripped over a root and crashed down beside them. Two seconds later, Fred fell over Ronald. He landed on his back on the ground, staring up at the sky.

Slowly, Fred turned his head. He surveyed the other three sprawled in various ungainly positions around him. "We were chasing *you*?"

"It was *you* chasing me?" Florence sat up. "I thought it was Bigfoot," she said in disgust.

Another crashing sound came and Alice realized that Vera and Ellis also would have heard the scream and were coming to the rescue as well. "Stop!" she yelled.

And just in time. The two women halted barely soon enough to avoid falling over the tangle of bodies on the ground.

Both women were panting. Ellis was looking at them all with wide eyes.

Vera took one look, immediately grasped the situation and began to laugh. "Which one of you was Bigfoot?" As she spoke, she extended a hand to Fred, braced herself and tugged him to his feet. He immediately did the same for Ronald.

"I suppose I was," Florence said sullenly. "But I thought *they* were." She pointed at the men.

Sensing a sulk coming on, Alice explained what she had seen as Fred tried to give her a helping hand. Finally, both men took Florence's arms and hauled her upright. She immediately began brushing off her clothes with an air of wounded dignity.

"A raccoon?" Ellis sounded so disappointed Alice couldn't help grinning.

"Yes," she confirmed. "That's all it was, a single raccoon, after our marshmallows."

Fred started to laugh. "Some Bigfoot hunters we are, making enough noise to wake the dead. If there was any kind of critter here, it's probably halfway to Canada by now."

"Laughing all the way," Vera added.

Ronald began to chuckle and Alice felt her own lips twitch. Ellis also saw the humor in the situation, and as the five of them laughed until they were holding their sides and wiping tears, Florence finally cracked a smile and laughed a little as well.

When the merriment abated, Alice said, "I don't know about you, but I've had quite enough Bigfoot hunting for one night. I'm going back to sleep."

"Ditto," said Vera. She began to walk along the path toward their campsite. "That rotten raccoon had better not have gotten into anything else while we're out here clowning around."

"Oh, I suspect our things are safe," Alice said. "We made so much noise I doubt there's an animal left within a five-mile radius."

Several hours later, Jane and Louise stood in the front hallway laughing as Alice recounted the night's adventures. Maxwell came downstairs in time to hear most of the story.

"At least it wasn't boring," Jane said. She almost wished she had gone along, just to see the scene Alice had described.

"Far from it." Maxwell smiled. "So were Florence and Ellis very disappointed?"

Alice shrugged. "I imagine so, although none of us dwelt on the fiasco. Ellis left this morning. She was eager to get back and file her report."

Jane was staring at Maxwell. "You sound terrible," she said. "Are you coming down with something?"

"I think I might be," he confessed. "My throat feels swollen and scratchy and I am quite congested. I didn't sleep well at all last night."

"Come into the kitchen and let me make you some special tea," Jane offered.

The young man looked surprised. "Really? Why, thank you, Jane." He followed her to the kitchen.

"Sit," she said. "This will take a few minutes."

As she efficiently began to make the tea, he asked, "What are you doing?"

"I'm mixing equal parts dried linden, elder and chamomile flowers. I use three teaspoons of this mix for every ten ounces of water." She spooned the proper measure onto a small square of finely woven linen, then secured it and set it in a mug. Then she set a spoon in the mug and poured boiling water over the linen. "There. That has to steep for ten minutes. Then you can add honey and lemon if you like. A cup in the morning and another in the evening should help until the congestion is gone."

Maxwell had a look of…almost awe on his face, Jane thought.

"That is the nicest thing anyone has ever done for me," he told her.

Jane was startled. "Good heavens, it's just a cup of herbal tea." She set down the honey and a plate with a wedge of lemon on the table near the steaming mug of fragrant tea. "There. I have to get Clothilda some information on the computer. Just wait ten minutes and flavor it to taste. I can make you more tonight."

"Thanks, Jane."

She left him there inhaling the warm, aromatic steam and went to the reception desk. Yesterday, she had had an idea that she hoped might help Clothilda. Jane was eager to give it a try. Ethel had made plans months before to take a bus trip to Longwood Gardens and she would be gone most of the day.

A few minutes later, their German guest appeared. Jane called to her from the computer. "Clothilda, over here."

The older woman waved a folder. "I have brought my records down, as you asked."

"It occurred to me," said Jane, "that we know your ancestors booked passage on a ship bound for the Port of Philadelphia. But have you ever checked to be sure that they actually were on that ship?"

Clothilda's eyebrows rose. "No, Jane, I have not tried to see this. You can help?"

"I can help. I think," said Jane. She swiveled her chair around to face the computer monitor. With a little navigating, she was able to find her way to the records from the Port of Philadelphia. They were listed by ship.

Jane perused the dates, page by page. "When does your information say they sailed and on what ship?"

Clothilda pointed to her paper. "There. I have only days, not name of ship."

Jane stabbed at the screen. "Look! I believe this is the ship. It's the only one that lists that date as the 'sailed from' that matches yours. "It looks like it arrived in Philadelphia . . . two months later. Good heavens. Could that be? I suppose in 1749 it certainly could have been." Rapidly, she scanned the list of the ship's passengers' names. "Oh, rats. I don't see it on here. There's Marckert, Matthey, Maurer, Mayer, Meer, Mehler, Meltzer, Mohr and Muller."

"No Moeller?" Clothilda's shoulders sagged.

"No Moeller." Jane wished she had better news. "What do these little marks after some of the names mean? Oh . . . the ones with no marks were copied from the original German signature. The ones with asterisks—this little snowflake thing here—were names written by a clerk. I never thought about it but I imagine some of the immigrants were illiterate."

"Ill-lit...ill...?"

"They could not read or write. They would have signed their name with a mark like an 'X' and told the clerk their name. So the clerk would have written it down." A growing excitement filled Jane. "Clothilda, is it possible your ancestors might not have been able to write their name? Maybe a clerk wrote it down wrong!"

But Clothilda shook her head. "I have the letters. Letters my family write."

"I forgot," Jane said, disappointed.

"What is this mark? This question mark?"

"I didn't see that one. Hold on." Jane scanned the information key at the bottom of the page. "The ones with question marks mean the original German name was difficult to decipher."

"So maybe my family man was bad writer?"

"I never thought of that." Jane's natural optimism returned. "A clerk could have copied it wrong if he found it hard to read." She looked up, eyes alight. "Let's compare the first names of your ancestors to the names of the people on this list to see if any are close."

"Yes." Clothilda consulted her notes. "There are three boys—brothers. First is Georg Christian, twenty-nine years. Second is Hans Jacob, twenty-two years. No good. Many, many Hans and Jacob in Germany. Third is Conrad Maximilian, eighteen years."

"So the first and third brother have somewhat distinctive names. How about their wives?"

"Georg married to Karolina. Hans married to Gertrud. Conrad not married. Georg have three children, names—Johanna, Mattheis, Ulrike. Hans have no children."

"Okay." Jane rubbed her hands together. "Now we're cooking with gas."

Clothilda looked toward the back of the house, toward the kitchen. "You must cook?"

Jane laughed. "No, it's just an expression. It means we are making progress."

"Ah. This I understand now."

"I'm going to print out the pages from the passenger manifest we found," Jane told her guest, "and then we can compare the names to names that are similar. I saw at least two that are very close: Mehler, M-e-h-l-e-r, and Muller, M-u-l-l-e-r."

"Yes." Clothilda nodded eagerly. "Let us go cook with gas."

Chapter Thirteen

Saturday afternoon, Louise asked three of her beginning piano students to come to the house for a special preparatory session before the National Piano Guild auditions. Each of the three was a first-year student and had never been through the adjudicating process. Louise wanted to be sure they understood how the auditions would work.

The first child did well, but the second child fumbled his way through his music badly enough that Louise felt the need to give him additional instruction. Unfortunately, that put her nearly ten minutes behind the time she had asked Patsy Ravin, the third child, to arrive.

Patsy was a nervous girl to begin with, and Louise was dreading the session. The second-grader's mother was determined that Patsy should become a concert pianist, and evidently she expected her to reach that goal within the first two years. Louise had rarely seen a parent pester a child so much about practicing. Poor Patsy already was so upset about the Guild auditions that Louise feared that the girl might make herself ill.

When Louise approached the living room where the little girl was waiting, she expected to hear sobbing. Instead, a raspy masculine voice was saying something in a soothing tone. She stopped in the doorway, but the occupants of the living room did not see her. She saw that the man speaking was Maxwell.

"…so when you go in there to play your pieces, don't forget that I'll be right there with you." He was speaking earnestly to Patsy.

This alarmed Louise. "Oh no," she said. "Maxwell, no one but the judge goes in with the student. I'm afraid you won't be able to do that."

"Ah, but I will." Maxwell turned and winked at her, then turned back to the seven-year-old, holding her gaze even though he still spoke to Louise. "I told Patsy here that I used to play piano when I was young and that I always got horribly nervous playing in front of other people. The trick is to tune them out, right, Patsy?"

The little girl nodded shyly.

"And do what?" he prompted.

"Pretend you're sitting right beside me," she lisped.

"That's exactly right," he told her. "I told Patsy to pretend she was just playing her songs for me and to forget about anyone else who might be listening."

Louise was so stunned that she was speechless for a moment. Finally, she found her voice. "What a very good idea." She stopped to clear her throat, surprised at the catch in her own voice. And then she had an inspiration of her own. "I'll tell you what, Patsy. Would you like Maxwell to come in with you the first time you play your pieces this afternoon? And then we can try it a second time with you pretending he's there."

When the little girl smiled and nodded vigorously, Louise felt as if they might have turned a corner. "Thank you," she mouthed at Maxwell over the child's head as they walked into the parlor.

The young man only smiled, raising his hand with the thumb and forefinger forming a circle in the *okay* sign.

∽

On Sunday morning, the sisters were accompanied to church by Maxwell, Clothilda and Ethel, just as they had been the week before.

Louise was quiet as they walked to Grace Chapel. Jane and Clothilda were talking genealogy with Ethel, right ahead of her.

"…and we realized that it had been changed to Muller, M-u-l-l-e-r, when it was copied down from the original passenger manifest," Jane said.

"Excellent sleuthing," said Ethel. "Now we can start looking for Mullers. I've heard that name before. I'm sure there are some around here."

"I cannot begin to look," Clothilda told her. "This afternoon I leave on the bus for New York City."

"Oh, I forgot." Ethel snapped her fingers. "And how long will you be gone?"

"We tour for three days, two nights. I am back on *Mittwoch*—Wednesday—in the evening. On next day we go looking again?"

"Thursday," Jane supplied. "All right. That works for me. We'll plan a trip around the area on Thursday."

∽

"Louise?" Alice's gentle voice said.

"Yes?"

Alice and Maxwell were walking beside her. Louise was quite pleased that the young man was attending church with them while he was here. It was never too late to join the flock, and Alice, bless her heart, was a particularly effective shepherdess. Louise knew Alice had spent quite a bit of her free time showing their young visitor around the community.

"Maxwell and I were just talking about the Lenten season and the reason we make an effort at sacrifice."

Louise nodded. "Jesus' death on the cross was the highest sacrifice there can be. Because we believe that Jesus was the incarnation of God here on earth, we believe that His self-sacrifice was the supreme expression of His love for humankind."

"So if you give something up for Lent, it should be something that you crave or value, something that is truly a sacrifice for you to do without," Alice explained.

"What have you given up for Lent?" Maxwell asked the two sisters.

"Secular music," Louise said with a grimace. "The only things I am playing during Lent are religious music and classical pieces. It feels a bit like cheating to include the classics," she added, "but I would not be getting adequately challenging practice if I tried to stick to only religious music for so long." She glanced at Alice. "How about you?"

"Caffeinated tea," Alice responded. "I was drinking far too much of it during my night shifts to help me stay awake."

"So how are you staying awake now?"

Alice smiled. "I'm trying to be more active. If I have a quiet moment I check on patients even if their call lights aren't on. I've found that I do well if I keep moving."

"What could I give up for Lent?" Maxwell asked. "Or is it too late?"

"It's never too late," Louise said staunchly. "What are some of the things you most enjoy?"

He groaned. "Pie at the Coffee Shop. Oh, how I love June's pies. I've been having two pieces some days. Shall I swear off pie for the rest of Lent?"

"I don't know if you need to swear off pie completely," Alice said. "June would wonder what she'd done wrong. How about having no more than one piece a day?"

The young man nodded. "I could do that. But I'm not sure it would be a very significant sacrifice."

"Just wait until the next time Hope waves that second piece of blackberry pie under your nose," Alice predicted. "You'll feel as if you're making a sacrifice."

All three of them chuckled. The group was almost at the chapel now, and as they started along the walkway toward the double front doors, one of the Trimble boys came toward them carrying a large plastic cup. Just as he reached Jane, he stumbled.

Jane gasped as the cup turned over. They all expected liquid to cascade down her pretty pale blue skirt—but the cup was empty.

"April Fool!" shouted the young boy as he rushed away.

"Morley Trimble, you get right back here and apologize." Mrs. Trimble rushed after him, looking as harassed as Louise expected she would look if she had to spend all day with the rambunctious Trimble boys. "Sorry," the woman called over her shoulder to Jane.

"It's all right." Jane laughed. "I haven't had such a good joke played on me in a long time."

"I forgot it was April first," Alice said. "Soon the late tulips will be opening. I especially love those candy-pink ones you planted against the side of the garage, Jane."

"I love those too," Jane said. "And best of all, they are perennial tulips so I don't have to plant new ones every single year. If I add some every third year, we should always have a nice display." She paused for a moment. "Last fall, Wendell was underfoot the whole time I was planting them. He was convinced there was food in the bag I was carrying."

"Still no news?" asked Ethel. "I find it hard to believe that cat just disappeared. He'll be back."

Alice took Clothilda to a large grocery store parking lot in Potterston early Monday morning to meet the bus that was taking a group to the city. On the way home, she couldn't resist driving by the gas station one more time where Wendell had jumped out of Mr. Jervis' car.

She didn't stop, although she did turn down one of the streets and drive slowly through the now-familiar neighborhood. *Oh, Wendell, whatever happened to you?* Tears stung her eyes. She had not cried this much since Father died.

That thought brought fresh tears, as she remembered how much Father had enjoyed Wendell's antics when he had been a kitten.

After driving down a few more streets without success, Alice sadly turned toward home. As she pulled into the driveway of the inn, she dried her eyes. Louise and Jane were sad enough without seeing the evidence of her own grieving.

"Good morning, Alice."

She realized she had been moping along with her head down. As she lifted her face, she saw Maxwell carrying out a white plastic bag to the large trash can near the garage.

Her eyebrows rose. *A guest doing chores?*

He began to chuckle. "You should see your face. It's all right. I volunteered. It's the least I could do after the way Jane has been making me cold remedies, and all of you have been so gracious about inviting me to dinner." He still sounded as if he were fighting a cold. In fact, Alice thought he might even sound worse than he had yesterday.

"But you're a guest. It just seems…"

"It makes me feel like I fit in. Don't take that away from me, Alice," he said quietly.

"Oh, Maxwell…" She turned and walked with him to the trash can and back to the house. "You'll find your place one of these days. You might want to try talking to God about how you feel. Sometimes answers come in the most unexpected ways."

"Grace Chapel Inn has been one of those unexpected ways for me."

"What a lovely thing to say." She turned and smiled at him. "When my sisters and I decided to turn our family home into a bed-and-breakfast, one of our hopes was that it would be a blessing to all who stayed here."

"It has been for me. I never expected to find friends on this research trip." It almost sounded as if he had regret in his voice. It seemed as if he was going to say something else, but he began to cough and the moment was lost.

"How is your research going?" Alice asked him. "You've hardly said a word about it."

"Fine, fine." He seemed quite disinclined to discuss it. "Did I tell you I am considering working on another degree as soon as I receive this one?"

Alice was taken aback. "Another degree? Maxwell, you've been in school all your life. Don't you want to be finished with it? Plus, it's expensive." As soon as she uttered the words, she remembered whom she was addressing and felt vaguely embarrassed.

He smiled, but there was a cynical slant to his lips. "My father will pay for my expenses. As long as I'm in school, he isn't obligated to see much of me or feign interest. Who knows? Maybe I'll be a student forever."

Alice did not know what to say in response to that. "I'm sorry," she said, but she knew it was completely inadequate, so she added the one thing she knew she could do to help him. "I'll pray for you, and for your father and for your relationship with him."

They entered the kitchen, and Maxwell went to his room to clean up before breakfast. Jane was at her stove, humming something under her breath as she was seasoning an omelet.

"I'm back," Alice said.

"Oh, hi." Jane said. "Clothilda got off all right?"

"She did. She was very excited about seeing the Statue of Liberty and the Empire State Building. It will be interesting to see just how much touring they can cram into three days."

"Good morning," Louise said as she entered the kitchen.

"Good morning," chorused Jane and Alice.

"Jane, did I see Maxwell carrying a trash bag when I looked out my window a few minutes ago?"

"You did, indeed." Jane grinned. "He offered. I accepted. He's starting to feel less like a guest and more like ... I don't know, a family friend. Is it all right if I invite him to eat with us again tonight? I feel bad for him, having to eat alone every evening. And he still has that dreadful cold." She took the skillet off the stove and expertly flipped the omelet, then shook the pan around in a circular motion before tilting it and sliding the omelet onto a plate, which she placed in the oven's warmer.

"It's all right with me," Alice said. "I know he often has lunch at the Coffee Shop. He's made friends there, but dinner alone can't be fun."

"I suppose it's all right with me," said Louise after a moment. "I have not gotten to know him as well as you two, but that will change if he has dinner with us again."

An odd noise on the back porch, a thump, punctuated her sentence.

All three sisters' heads swiveled as one.

"What was that?" Jane asked.

"Bigfoot," said Louise.

"Not very funny," Alice told her, "especially after I spent a night sleeping outside and rolling around in the woods."

They all laughed but quieted as they heard a second sound.

"That sounds like . . . like a scratch at the door!" Jane said in a rush. She practically flew across the kitchen and threw open the back door.

Wendell was sitting on the porch, one paw raised as if to knock. He was bedraggled, muddy and emaciated, but undeniably their cat.

Louise gasped and Alice cried out, "Oh!" as Jane fell to her knees.

"Wendell! Oh, Wendell, you precious boy. You've come home." Jane reached out and tentatively stroked the cat and his eyes closed as he pushed his head against her hand. Jane began to cry. "Look at him," she said to her sisters. "He's so thin."

Alice and Louise both came over and knelt. Alice moved very carefully as if she wasn't quite sure he was real. Louise reached out and ran a hand very lightly down his spine and he arched his back. "You silly old thing," she said, but her voice quavered.

Alice bent so she was at eye-level with the cat. "Where have you been, mister?" she asked softly. "What happened to you?"

Wendell took a few steps forward and butted his head against her.

"He's limping," announced Louise. She rose. "I'm calling the vet."

"Yes, you'd better," murmured Alice, scratching beneath his chin as she carefully looked him over. "His left ear is badly torn and the left leg appears to have some kind of open wound."

"I can't believe he's home." Jane leaped to her feet and dashed to the pantry. Wendell perked up, but appeared loath to leave Alice's stroking hands. He meowed loudly, though, when Jane returned with one of his special treat packets that she kept in the pantry. "Here you go, sweet boy."

They watched as Wendell inhaled the treat. Then he cocked his head and looked at Jane, clearly wondering where the next course was.

Jane cleared her throat. "I need to put food and water in his dishes."

"Better wait on that," advised Louise, her hand over the mouthpiece of the phone. "The vet says we can bring him right in." She held up her finger for silence and spoke into the phone, "Thank you," she said into the receiver. "We'll be there in a few minutes."

Clicking off the phone, she reached for her purse and keys, which she had laid on the table when she came into the kitchen. "I'll drive."

"I'll carry Wendell," Alice said. "I need an old towel."

Jane dashed to the pantry again. "I have a couple right here. I can't go. I have to make breakfast."

"It's all right," Alice said. "I'm sure the vet will just clean these wounds and send him home again."

"I hope so." Jane remembered her breakfast preparations and rushed back to the stove. "Come home as soon as you can."

$\backsim$

At the animal hospital, Wendell was carefully examined. The vet felt that the cat probably had sustained his wounds in a fight with another animal. She cleaned and medicated both his ear and his leg, and then put three stitches into the ear. She prescribed a course of oral antibiotics to follow for the next ten days.

"Feed him small amounts several times a day until his weight is back to normal," said the vet. "We don't want him to get sick from overeating. He clearly hasn't had much food while he was lost."

"How long will it take for him to gain back his weight?" Alice asked.

The vet shrugged. "Probably only a week or two. Cats regain lost weight surprisingly quickly." The doctor paused. "I often hear secondhand stories about animals finding their way home, but I rarely hear about them directly from a pet owner who has experienced it. You must be thrilled."

"Over the moon and beyond," said Alice.

The vet shook her head as she stroked Wendell's soft, gray-striped side. "You're a miracle boy, do you know that? Finding your way home all alone can't have been easy."

"Oh, I don't think he was alone," Alice said. "We've been praying, as has our whole church, for almost two weeks now. I believe Wendell had an angel sitting on his shoulder."

"An angel named Daniel," Louise suggested, her voice much softer than normal.

"Maybe," said Alice. "That's a lovely thought, Father helping Wendell get home again." She bent and looked into the cat's eyes. "Don't you ever scare us like this again," she crooned. "We can't take a repeat."

"Amen," the vet and Louise both said at the same time.

Then the sisters carried their cat gingerly to Louise's car and took him home where he belonged.

Chapter Fourteen

*I*f the phone rang once that day, it rang a dozen times. Alice answered the first call at five minutes before ten. They barely had been home from the veterinary clinic for an hour.

"Alice, it's Vera. I heard you found Wendell."

Alice smiled. "Actually, he found us, Vera. He made his own way home this morning."

"Is he all right?"

"Yes. He's thin and has a few minor injuries but he's going to be fine. How did you hear already?"

"Maxwell stopped at the hardware store to tell Fred a little while ago..."

"Jane, this is Wilhelm. Sylvia told me your cat came back when I ran into her at the post office. Excellent news."

"Yes, we think so."

"And you think he got here from Potterston all by himself?"

"It certainly looks that way, Wilhelm. All by himself with an awful lot of prayers from Acorn Hill guiding his way..."

"Louise, this is your aunt calling. I just heard that Wendell managed to get home. I cannot believe you did not call me right away."

"He hasn't even been back three hours yet, Aunt Ethel. We just were so excited and happy that we all completely forgot."

Ethel sniffed, but her voice was warm when she said, "You give that striped troublemaker a squeeze from me until I get over there to give him one myself. And tell him I'll skin him if he ever does this again…"

"Miss Howard. I just got home from school and my mom told me that Wendell came back to you. Is it true?"

"Sarah?"

"Oh yes. Sorry. I was so excited I forgot my manners."

Alice's eyes misted. Sarah Roberts was one of her ANGELs and just the sort of thoughtful child who would have organized something like that group card-signing last week. "It's true, Sarah. Your prayers worked."

"Cool! I'll tell the other girls…"

Wendell, oblivious to the commotion his reappearance had created, spent much of the morning happily snoozing on Alice's bed in a patch of sunlight. From time to time, as the sun moved, he got up and stretched languidly, then lay back down a few inches farther over so he stayed fully in the warm light spilling through the window.

Alice checked on him frequently. It was so good to see him there again in one of his favorite resting places. Kneeling beside the bed, she stroked him until he was purring like an outboard motor. He was lying on his side and the pads on his back paws were visible. Alice winced at their condition. The pads were scraped and torn in several places.

"You had a rough time of it out there in the big, bad world, didn't you?" she murmured.

At lunchtime, she carried him down the stairs to the kitchen, where Jane had a small meal prepared with his antibiotic pill ground up and mixed into the food.

Louise watched him eat, and then cleared her throat. "Wendell," she said, "you still can't get on the table. But I solemnly swear I will never give you a hard time again. I will just pick you up and put you on the floor if you're into something you shouldn't be."

"Gracious!" said Jane suddenly.

Both of her sisters looked at her.

"What's wrong?" asked Louise.

"Nothing." Jane made soothing motions with her hands. "Sorry. I didn't mean to scare you. But it just occurred to me that we need to call Mr. Jervis and let him know we found Wendell."

"You mean that he found us," Alice said, smiling fondly as she watched him eat.

"Well, yes." Jane rose from her chair. "I have his number in our guest registry. I better call him right now."

"Please do," Louise said. "I can only imagine how relieved the poor man will feel."

Jane left the room, returning a few minutes later with a smile on her face. "I believe I brightened his day," she said, "or possibly his entire week. He was thrilled." She walked over and inspected the bowl Wendell had finished licking clean. "Good. It looks as if he ate all of the antibiotic mixed in with the food. I was afraid he might detect the taste and refuse to eat it."

Louise lifted an eyebrow. "Since when has this cat refused to eat anything?"

"True," Jane agreed. "That's what started all the trouble in the first place."

All three sisters watched him while he sat and carefully washed himself. Then Alice carried him back upstairs.

Maxwell returned to the inn shortly after lunch and joined the sisters in the living room.

"Well, if it isn't the town crier," Jane said.

Alice laughed. "Thank you for letting people know the good news about Wendell's coming home. It saved us having to repeat it over and over."

He blushed. "I didn't think you would mind." Then he began to cough, as he'd been doing off and on for the past few days. This cough sounded deeper than before, and his thin frame shook from the force of it.

Jane was worried. "That doesn't sound good."

"It doesn't feel so good either," he said breathlessly.

"Maybe you should take it easy for a day or two," Alice suggested. "Rest a bit more."

"I didn't make you any tea this morning," Jane said. "With all the excitement over Wendell, I completely forgot."

"It's all right." He coughed again and held up a hand to indicate that they should wait until he could speak again. "I've taken cold medicine."

"For all the good that seems to be doing," muttered Jane. "Well, the tea is a homeopathic remedy and has nothing in it that could react with cold medicine. Come with me to the kitchen and let me make you some more."

He hesitated.

Alice said, "That tea really does seem to help when I have a cold."

"All right. Thank you." And he meekly followed Jane down the hallway.

In the kitchen, she quickly mixed up the tea and heated a mug in which she set the little linen packet to steep.

"Jane?"

Maxwell really didn't look well, she thought. His eyes had dark circles beneath them, and his skin was as colorless as could be. "Yes?"

"Did you ever do something you were ashamed of, and then you didn't know how to make it right? Or even to admit it?"

Jane smiled. "Of course. We all make mistakes, Maxwell."

"But can you think of anything specific?"

Jane thought for a moment. "When I was eight, I broke a vase playing tag in the house with the neighbor's kids. The vase had belonged to my mother, who passed away when I was born. I was sure Father was going to be angry because he had a rule about not running in the house, so I hid the pieces. Then, scheming little creature that I was, I went to the attic, which was filled with all sorts of old family trash and treasures—still is, come to think of it—and found another vase. It wasn't special or an heirloom, but I hoped he wouldn't notice."

"And did he?"

Jane was silent for a moment before she continued. "I hardly slept all night, worrying about how dishonest I had been. The next morning at breakfast, Father very casually mentioned that he was going to bring home some flowers that day for the vase in the hall that Mother had loved, and asked me to bring it to the kitchen so he could wash it. Well, of course he knew it wasn't there. So I, dragging my feet the whole way, brought back the substitute vase. But I couldn't stand myself anymore and I burst into tears and told Father what I had done. And guess what?"

"What?" Maxwell appeared to be hanging on her words.

"He wasn't angry. But he was disappointed and that was even worse—" Her attention was diverted as Wendell walked slowly into the room. "Hello, my buddy. How are you feeling? I bet you haven't slept so well in days."

Wendell meowed plaintively and rubbed himself against her legs.

Jane laughed. "All right. I'm sure you are hungry. But you can't tell Alice or Louise." She went to the pantry and opened the door. Wendell moved with her. Then, as Maxwell watched, Wendell rose on his hind legs and nipped a small package off the lowest shelf.

"His treats," Jane explained. "I usually give him one midmorning, but I think for a few days I'm going to give him one in the afternoon too. At least until he fattens up a bit." She bent and stroked the cat, then rose and went to the sink to wash her hands. "Now, what were we talking about?"

"Nothing important." Maxwell rose from the chair he'd taken and picked up his mug of tea. "Thank you for the tea."

The next day was Wednesday. Louise awoke with the funniest feeling of happiness and contentment, and then remembered that Wendell had come home. No wonder she felt good. Today would have been two weeks since his disappearance.

She showered and dressed, layering a toast-colored cardigan over her beige blouse. The weather had been unusually warm for the beginning of April, but first thing in the morning it could be quite nippy.

Leaving her room, she headed for the stairs. One flight down, she paused on the second floor landing. Someone was coughing and coughing.

She walked down the hall and knocked on Maxwell's door. "Maxwell?"

"Louise? I'm all right. Don't worry about me. I'm just going to rest all day as Alice suggested."

Louise hesitated. He sounded quite breathless. But he had said he was going to rest, and she supposed he'd phone the doctor himself if he began to feel really ill. "All right," she finally called. "Let us know if you need us."

"I will. Could you please tell Jane that I won't be having breakfast?"

Louise hesitated. Weren't you supposed to feed a cold and starve a fever? She wasn't sure not eating was what Maxwell really needed. Finally, she said, "Yes, certainly. I'll tell her."

"Thank you." He sounded as if he already was drifting back into slumber.

But as she continued down the steps to the first floor, she still could hear the harsh sound of coughing following her.

In the kitchen, Jane was fussing over a delicious-looking fruit plate. She looked up as Louise entered. "Good morning, Louie."

"Good morning, Janie." She smiled when her sister's head came up with a jerk.

Jane eyed her for a moment. "Does this mean we have to start calling Alice 'Ali'?"

Louise shuddered. "Heavens, I hope not." Then she remembered her errand. "Oh, Maxwell asked me to tell you he isn't coming down to breakfast. Jane, he still has that horrid cough."

Jane sighed. "I know. I heard him when I came down earlier. What do you think we should do?"

"I'm not sure there's anything we *can* do unless he asks for help. He's of age. We can't call his parents."

"Just watch me," warned Jane. "If he gets much sicker, he may not get a choice."

"If he gets much sicker, he's going to be beyond caring whom we call," Louise predicted. "The mother in me cringes to think of my child's being ill and alone among strangers."

"But he hasn't got a mother," Jane pointed out, "and he doesn't seem to think his father is too interested in where he is or what he's doing, as long as he doesn't cause any trouble."

"Well, he has us," Louise said. "Let's ask Alice to check on him later. We'll just have to keep a close eye on him until he shakes whatever bug he's got."

Clothilda was scheduled to return from her bus tour Wednesday evening. Alice had to work an evening shift and would not be home until nearly eleven and Jane was baking something for the next day's breakfast, so Louise volunteered to pick up their guest in Potterston.

As she drove to the shopping center where the bus would arrive, Louise sighed happily. Wendell was home, safe and sound. She was a few minutes early, so she drove around the neighborhood where she and her sisters had spent so many hours calling the cat. She stopped at every place she knew they had put up a poster and took it down.

Then she drove to the shopping center. The bus had not arrived yet, so she hurried into the grocery store. As she'd looked at Wendell this morning, she thought he seemed so terribly thin. Who was to know if she bought a little box of cat treats and hid them in her room? If she fed him, say, two a day, that might help to fatten him up again faster.

Feeling sneaky, she purchased the treats and squirreled them away in her handbag once she was back in the car.

In a few minutes, the bus pulled in. Stopping near the back of the lot in a wide-open area, the driver opened the doors and passengers began to exit. While the passengers searched for familiar faces or dug for car keys, the driver and the tour guide unloaded suitcases and lined them up in a neat row along the sidewalk.

"Louise. Hello." Clothilda waved at Louise with her customary zeal, dragging her red leather wheeled suitcase along behind her.

"Hello," Louise responded. "The car is right over here."

With Clothilda and her luggage safely stowed in the car, Louise began the short trip back to Acorn Hill.

"Ah," sighed Clothilda. "I am good to be back."

Louise suppressed a smile. Clothilda's interesting use of the English language never failed to amuse her. "It is good to have you back, as well." Her voice rose. "We had a surprise while you were away."

"What was it? I cannot guess."

"Our cat Wendell came home."

Clothilda looked delighted. "How wonderful! You must be so happy."

"We are." Louise went on to relate the story of Wendell's return.

"How wonderful this is." Clothilda beamed. "Jane and Alice must be very happy also."

"Oh, they are. Jane is eager for you to get home. I believe she has been enjoying your jaunts around the area."

"Jaunts? What are these jaunts?"

"Ah, travels. Short trips. Short *fun* trips."

Clothilda chuckled. "This is right. We have fun when we are on these jaunts."

"What will you do in your search for your ancestors this week?"

"We will go back to everywhere we have been and look for Mullers with a *u*. And we will begin asking everyone we meet if they know anyone by this name."

"I'm sure you'll find one sooner or later."

"Sooner is better," Clothilda told her, her sunny smile fading. "Later is bad. I must return to home in one more week. I must find Mullers before then."

She sounded oddly insistent. Louise wondered what could be so important about finding distant relatives but felt it would be impolite to ask.

When Maxwell did not come down for breakfast again on Thursday morning, Alice said, "Do you think we should check on him? I barely heard a peep out of him yesterday."

"He's still coughing a lot," Louise added. "You probably were the last one to see him, Alice. How did he seem to you?"

"Sick," said Alice frankly. "I looked in on him right after lunch, and again before I went to bed. I suggested that he see a doctor for the cough, but he said he might do it in a day or two if he doesn't soon feel better." She spread her hands helplessly. "I can't force him to take action."

Jane set down her spoon. "That coughing sounds so terrible," she agreed. "If he isn't down by the time we're done eating, I definitely think we should check on him again."

"You know," said Alice thoughtfully, "Now that I think about it, I didn't see him leave the inn at all yesterday."

Jane was beginning to look very worried. "I took him some soup at lunch time, but I'm ashamed to say I didn't keep track of him after that. I didn't see him go out to dinner, either. Did you, Louise?"

Louise shook her head. "No. After my morning visit, I did not speak to him or see him again." She picked up her napkin and delicately patted her mouth. "I'm not going to be able to eat another bite until we check on him."

"Good." Alice leaped to her feet. "I feel the same way."

All three sisters set their plates aside, even though none of them was finished completely. Alice led the way up the stairs.

They paused in the hallway outside the young man's door. Alice raised her fist and knocked gently on the door. "Maxwell?"

There was no answer.

She knocked again, quite a bit more firmly. Across the hall, Clothilda opened her door, wearing a blue robe. "*Was ist es?*"

"Sorry to have awakened you. We are afraid Maxwell may be ill," Jane told her.

Clothilda nodded. "Good to check. I hear him, ah, *husten*...cough?"

"Coughing." Jane nodded.

"I hear him coughing all the night. It does not sound good."

Really alarmed now, Alice stared at her sisters. "What shall we do?"

Louise reached out and turned the knob. The door opened.

The four women looked at each other.

"Maxwell?" Alice called in a loud, firm voice. "Maxwell, can you hear me? It's Alice. I am going to enter your room."

She waited a moment, hoping against hope that he would respond. But when she heard nothing, she hesitantly pushed the door ajar. "Oh no," she said as she caught a glimpse of the supine figure lying in the pale cream antiqued bedstead.

Alice rushed into the room, the other three women crowding in behind her. "Maxwell. Maxwell, wake up. It's Alice."

The young man moved lethargically and turned his head toward her. "Alice?" His voice was a mere croak and his face was flushed a dark, unhealthy color that intensified when his chest heaved in another deep, wracking cough. When the coughing spell ended, he was breathing in shallow gasps. "My back hurts," he said through chattering teeth. "My chest hurts. Everything hurts."

"I imagine it does." With gentle fingers, Alice tested his forehead and then lifted his wrist and began taking his pulse, holding her wrist up with its watch with the large face and easy-to-read second hand. "He's feverish, confused, shaking with chills, and I'm concerned about his breathing," she said to the others, who had followed her in and were anxiously gathered around. "And I suspect he's very dehydrated."

"Shall I call 911?" asked Jane.

Alice nodded. "I think you'd better. I doubt he can walk steadily, and none of us is going to be able to carry him if he goes down."

Jane vanished immediately.

"What shall I do?" asked Louise.

"Make sure the front door is unlocked for the paramedics. Get me a glass of water. Find his robe and some slippers or socks and shoes, and maybe a change of clothes or pajamas. See if he has a toothbrush and a razor we could bring along. And look for his wallet and check for his insurance card and complete identification."

Clothilda headed for the bathroom. "I get these things, then look for socks."

"All right. I'll get the water, unlock the door and find a bag to put his things in," Louise said.

In a few minutes, the women had a small bag with Maxwell's personal effects stored inside. Alice sat on the edge of the bed and propped up Maxwell to give him a drink, which he swallowed weakly but eagerly.

"Ah," he whispered. "Feels good."

"We're taking you to the hospital," Alice told him.

His eyes widened. "No, I—"

"Have no choice," she finished. "If you have pneumonia, you may need antibiotics. You definitely need fluids. I can't do those things here."

Jane called up the stairs. "The ambulance is here. Is he ready?"

"Bring them up," Louise called down to her.

Chapter Fifteen

$\mathcal{I}$n a matter of minutes, men and women in jackets emblazoned with the rescue squad's logo arrived. They efficiently assessed the young man's condition, covered him with a blanket, moved him onto a stretcher and maneuvered him down the stairs and out to the waiting vehicle.

Alice stood by the stretcher as they got ready to load Maxwell. He looked terribly young and defenseless lying there, and she felt a surge of maternal concern. "I'll be right behind you in my car." She reached for his hand and squeezed it.

"Thank you," he whispered.

The last things she heard were the slamming shut of the heavy doors and the sound of Maxwell coughing.

"Alice!"

Alice turned to see Louise pulling out in her Cadillac from the driveway.

"Come on." Louise waved something at her. "I have your jacket and purse. Jane's going to stay here and get Clothilda some breakfast, and then she'll join us."

Alice ran to the vehicle.

"I can't believe we didn't realize how sick Maxwell was getting," Louise said grimly.

"He hid it well," Alice said wearily. "I didn't like the sound of that cough, but he was adamant that I not call anyone for him."

"He has pneumonia, doesn't he?"

Alice, ever the responsible nurse, said, "I can't diagnose, of course, but I'm afraid he might."

Several hours later, Maxwell was installed in a private room at the Potterston hospital. As Alice had suspected, he was diagnosed with bacterial pneumonia after a chest X-ray. Laboratory tests had determined exactly which bacteria were responsible and the appropriate antibiotics to combat them were added to the intravenous fluids he was receiving. He was given acetaminophen to bring down his fever and extra oxygen through tubes in his nose.

The doctor did not want to suppress his coughing because he felt it would help to clear out the infection from his lungs, so Alice sat at his side, rubbing his back each time he suffered through a painful coughing spell.

Louise dealt with the insurance paperwork in short order, and she insisted on checking to see if a private room was covered. "Everyone knows people often get sicker in hospitals," she declared. "The fewer germs he is exposed to, the better. No offense," she said hastily to Alice.

"None taken." Alice smiled wanly. Maxwell's decline had scared her more than she wanted to admit. She was quite relieved to have him in competent medical hands. Additionally, she was feeling guilty for letting him get so sick in the first place.

Louise had called Jane after the initial diagnosis to let her know that he would be admitted. Now she said to Alice, "Would you like some coffee—no, wait, you drink tea."

The small slip told Alice that Louise also was shaken. "I would love some tea," Alice replied.

"All right. I'll be back shortly with your drink." She checked her watch. "Then I'm going to slip down to the cafeteria for a bite to eat. When I return, perhaps you can go down for a few minutes."

"Perhaps." Alice wanted to see Maxwell get a little more comfortable before she left him.

Louise brought Alice her tea and then left again. Maxwell seemed to be resting a little better at last. She had just finished the tea when a person filled the doorway of his hospital room.

"Kenneth!" Alice was delighted to see Rev. Kenneth Thompson. "Hello. How did you know we were here?"

He smiled as he advanced into the room. "Actually, I didn't know you were here. I saw Maxwell's name on the roster when I came to do my parishioner visits, and I thought I'd stop in and see what was up."

"Oh, you remembered him from church."

"Not only that, but we met for lunch in the Coffee Shop last week," Kenneth said. He moved to the bedside and laid a hand over the young man's. "Hello, Maxwell. What's going on here?"

"Pneumonia," the patient said. His voice was raspy from all the coughing. "Alice is taking care of me."

Kenneth smiled over at Alice. "She's very good at that."

Alice slipped out of the room for a moment while the two men conversed. She could hear the rise and fall of their voices, and after a few moments, Kenneth poked his head out of the room and said, "Alice, if you'd like to join us, we're going to spend a moment in prayer."

"Certainly." Alice returned and moved to the far side of the bed. She took Maxwell's free hand, and then Kenneth's as he stretched it across the young man so they made a circle.

"Dear Father in heaven, we ask that You restore Maxwell to full health and vigor. Help his body overcome this illness. We ask You to bless Maxwell as he continues his newly begun faith journey, regardless of where studies or work may take him. Thank You, Lord, for the gift of Your Son, Jesus Christ, who sacrificed Himself in Your name that we might be saved."

Alice's eyes popped open. Sacrifice! Tea! She'd completely forgotten about her Lenten vow.

"All this in Your name we pray. Amen," said Kenneth.

"Amen," echoed Alice and Maxwell.

After the minister left, Maxwell said, "Alice, I have to talk to you." His voice sounded curiously urgent.

"Yes?"

"It's about the Bigfoot tracks. I—"

"I'm back." Louise reentered the room. "Alice, you can run down to the cafeteria now. I can sit with Maxwell while you eat."

"All right. Thank you. I won't be long." She turned to Maxwell. "Don't worry. We'll have plenty of time to talk over the next few days."

Louise followed her out into the hallway. "Alice," she said in a stage whisper. She waved a piece of paper. "I found this in Maxwell's wallet."

"What is it?" Alice took the piece of paper.

"It's his father's contact information. I haven't done anything with it, but I think we should let the man know his son is in the hospital."

Alice nodded. "I know Maxwell wouldn't want us to contact his father, but I agree with you. The man should be notified." She sighed. "I'll do it right now."

Louise heaved a sigh. "Thank you. I can't stop thinking about how I would feel if that were Cynthia and I knew nothing about it."

Alice wasn't surprised to see the glimmer of a tear in Louise's eye. Her elder sister was formidable, but there was a very soft heart underneath that ever-so-capable exterior. She nodded. "His father should know. I'll try to contact him now."

"Hello, my name is Alice Howard. May I speak to Maxwell Vandermitton, please?"

"Mr. Vandermitton is on a conference call and has asked not to be interrupted." The female voice was pleasant but firm. "May I take a message and have him return your call?"

Alice frowned as she considered the woman's words. "Yes, I suppose so, but you may want to give him this message promptly. His son has been a guest at my family's bed-and-breakfast for the past two weeks. He has become very ill and this morning was hospitalized with pneumonia."

"Oh my goodness! That's just terrible. Miss … Howard, was it? Let me get your name and number and I'll see if he can talk to you." said the woman.

Alice, feeling somewhat relieved by the woman's obvious concern, relayed the information and repeated what she knew about Maxwell.

"May I put you on hold for a moment?"

"Certainly."

Alice waited through a soothing spate of elevator music. Suddenly, a connection opened again and a gruff male voice barked, "What's going on with my son?"

Alice was taken aback, first by the lack of any greeting and second by the accusatory tone of voice. She explained who she was again and told him what she had told the assistant. "He did not ask me to contact you but I felt you should know, Mr. Vandermitton."

"Right, right. Glad you called. How sick is the boy?"

"He has bacterial pneumonia, sir. His breathing is somewhat compromised, but he's on an antibiotic now that should take care of it in a few days."

"So he's not in danger of … anything?"

"Nothing lasting." *Except parental neglect.*

"All right." There was a pause, as if Mr. Vandermitton did not know what to say next. "Tell him I'm sorry to hear he's sick," he barked at Alice, "and tell him to give me a call when he gets out of the hospital."

Alice was so horrified that, for a moment, she could not summon words.

"Thank you for the call," the man added belatedly.

"Mr. Vandermitton!" Alice rarely got angry but she was working hard to rein in the unkind words that wanted to spring forth.

"I beg your pardon?"

"Mr. Vandermitton, your son needs you."

"I thought you said he's going to get better."

"He is. But that doesn't matter one little bit to his heart. You've been ignoring him for years."

"I … ignoring him? Miss Howard, I assure you my son does not want me at his bedside. He's gone to school practically year round, claimed work through holidays, to avoid me."

"That's almost exactly what he says about you."

"Look," Maxwell's father said with a weary note in his voice, "I made mistakes with Max when he was little. Losing his mother was very difficult for me. As a child, he looked a great deal like her. It was hard to see him and be reminded of what I had lost. I shoulder the blame for the distance that grew between us, but it's too late to fix it now."

"He felt more than distance," Alice said. "Being shuffled off to camps every summer gave him little opportunity to develop any kind of relationship with you."

"I traveled a great deal. I didn't want to leave him alone with a nanny all summer. I thought he'd enjoy being with other children." There was genuine shock and regret in the man's voice now. "Was that a mistake?"

"Sir," said Alice quietly. "My sisters and I have spent time over the past two weeks with your son. He is a lovely young man, but he is very lonely. Please reconsider coming to see him. I know it would mean a great deal."

"I—I will." He sounded subdued now.

Alice gave him the hospital's location, said good-bye and gently hung up the telephone. Her heart was racing. She'd never chastised anyone over the telephone before. It felt as if she'd done something very wrong. And yet, she had not known any other way to approach the man. *You did the best you could, Alice.* Whether or not her words would have any effect remained to be seen.

She took a seat in a corner of the waiting room. Before she went down for lunch, she thought perhaps it would be good for her to pray.

Thursday afternoon, Florence and Ronald walked into Maxwell's room. Florence was carrying an enormous flower arrangement studded with huge stargazer lilies and white daisies. Several balloons proclaiming, "Get well," bobbed merrily above it.

Maxwell looked positively stunned. His color had subsided to a sickly bone-white but a flush stole into his cheeks. "I don't deserve these," he said.

"Why on earth not?" Florence asked.

"You've become a part of our little community," Ronald told him. "Here." He pulled a bundle of envelopes bound in a rubber band from the inside pocket of his jacket and set it on the bedside tray. "From your friends at the Coffee Shop."

Maxwell just stared at the pile, shaking his head. "This is…you people don't know me at all."

"We think we do," Alice said gently. "You can't spend weeks in Acorn Hill without acquiring friends, Maxwell. You might as well accept it."

They all laughed, and the young man relaxed. But Alice noted that his thin fingers picked ceaselessly at the edge of the sheet all through the evening as more visitors came and went. Fred and Vera stopped by, bringing a pretty planter with African violets. Hope Collins came from her shift at the Coffee Shop, still wearing her uniform and bearing two blackberry pies from June.

"One for the nursing staff, to bribe them to take good care of you," she told him, laughing. "And one for you. Alice had better take it home this evening so it doesn't disappear."

Maxwell gave her a small smile. "You're assuming we can trust Alice with blackberry pie."

The women laughed, and Alice said, "Very good point."

Just as Hope was leaving, Jane and Clothilda came in. Louise had gone home before dinner to mind the inn so that Jane could drive over for a short visit. Clothilda insisted that she wanted to visit Maxwell too, and they stayed until seven thirty, quietly chatting with Alice and occasionally including Maxwell when he was awake. His coughing continued to shake his slim frame.

Visiting hours ended at eight PM. Alice patted the young man's hand, realizing how fond she had become of him. "I hope you are able to sleep tonight."

He nodded. "Are you coming tomorrow?" Almost immediately, he shook his head. "I understand that you're probably too busy to—"

"Stop," Alice said. "Stop telling yourself that you are not important. I'll be here tomorrow." She gave his hand a squeeze. "See you then."

∽

"Alice," Jane called when her sister came through the front door that evening. "We're in the kitchen."

Alice hung up her jacket, then trudged back to the kitchen. "Hello," she said, finding both her sisters at the table. "What a day," she said, dropping into a chair.

"It was quite eventful," Louise admitted. "That poor boy. There are few things worse than being sick when you are far away from your home and family."

Alice shook her head. "I'm not so sure Maxwell would see it that way. From what he has told us, his home wasn't a very happy place."

Jane nodded. "He's seemed very happy right here at the inn."

"Yes," Louise admitted. "He really seems to have settled in here."

"How is he doing?" Jane asked.

"About as I expected," Alice told her. "He's still coughing, but I'm hoping he'll be able to sleep tonight. And tomorrow he should begin to feel a little better. It's going to take some time, though." She yawned and covered her mouth with one hand. "Oh, I'm so sorry." She pushed back her chair and rose. "I must go to bed. I'm exhausted."

"Wait a minute." Jane held up her hand in a "stop" gesture. "I called you in here for a reason."

"I almost forgot." Louise rose, too, but she merely walked to the counter and returned to the table with a package.

"What's that?" Alice asked.

"That's what we're going to find out," Jane said. "It was delivered today but in all the excitement I set it aside and completely forgot about it until just a little while ago."

"We wanted to wait for you," Louise told Alice.

Alice leaned over and looked at the package mailing label. "This is addressed to Wendell!" she said, beginning to laugh.

"Let's take it to the parlor," Jane said, picking up the box. "Wendell's sleeping under the piano, and I really think it would be rude to open his mail without him being there."

Louise and Alice both chuckled as they followed Jane out of the kitchen.

Alice moved ahead and snapped on the light as she entered the room. Wendell lay on his tummy, his two front paws tucked in toward his chest. He swung his head around when the three women entered.

Jane set the box next to him, then knelt and began to stroke Wendell's back. "You have mail," she informed him.

He had the good grace to look interested in the package.

"Let's open it." Louise sounded surprisingly excited. "I'm dying to see what's in it. There's no return address," she pointed out to Alice.

Jane ripped away the packing tape and folded back the flaps of the box. A note card lay on a layer of bubble wrap. She picked it up, opened it and began to read:

Dear Wendell,

I offer my deepest apologies for taking you on an unwanted journey recently. Please accept these tokens of my esteem to celebrate your safe return. Tell your caregivers thank you for letting me know you arrived home safely.

I hope to see you again some day.

Yours truly,

Lyle Jervis

P.S. Next time I visit, I promise to keep my car windows rolled up.

"Isn't that sweet?" Alice found herself touched by the whimsical little letter.

"Let's see what's in here." Jane pulled out the top layer of bubble wrap. "Oh, this is pretty and so soft." She handed a royal blue pet bed to Louise. "And look at these presents!"

Jane took the three cans of gourmet cat food. "Fish, chicken and lamb. Wendell will be thrilled.

"And look at this." Jane held up a long, slim plastic stick. Attached to one tip was a length of elastic string with a feather dancing at its end.

Wendell sat up, his eyes narrowing intently. As Jane gently swished the feather in the air, he began to stalk it, pouncing just as Jane tugged it backward. One claw caught and for a second the elastic stretched. Then Jane pulled it free, and the feather bounced high in the air as Wendell made a wild leap for it, landing on the floor beside the bed.

"What a marvelous toy!" Louise exclaimed. "Our couch potato might actually get some exercise with that."

Alice laughed as she pulled one last item from the box. "Look, Wendell," she said. "A catnip mouse. Oh, you're going to enjoy this."

She was right. Wendell sniffed cautiously at the mouse she had tossed across the floor toward him. He caught it between his paws and proceeded to rub his face against it, then flopped down right on top of it and rubbed his whole body over it again and again. On his feline face was the funniest look of ecstasy Alice had ever seen.

She began to laugh. "He's acting like some of my patients do when they get pain pills. The pills make some people overly happy."

"I hope they don't roll around on the floor," Louise said, watching the cat's antics.

"You'd be surprised at some of the things they do," Alice said, laughing. "I've seen it all."

"So have I, now," Jane said. "Our cat receives a package. *Sheesh.*"

"What a nice man," Louise said.

"Yes." Jane was still watching the cat. "Tomorrow I'll help Wendell write him a thank-you note."

Maxwell had more visitors on Friday. Ethel bustled in, shaking raindrops from her umbrella before she approached the bed. She looked a bit miffed at the size of the flower arrangement that Florence had brought, but when Maxwell evinced great pleasure in the gift certificate to the Coffee Shop tucked into her gift of miniature roses in a teacup, she seemed mollified.

Around three, a candy striper came in carrying two more flower arrangements and a bouquet of balloons, all from members of Grace Chapel who had gotten to know Maxwell from his brief time at church and from the Coffee Shop. The room was beginning to look like a flower shop, and Alice smiled every time she looked around. Surely knowing so many people had thought of him would aid in his recovery.

When his dinner tray arrived, Alice helped him open containers and utensils, then sat back and watched in satisfaction as he ate. It was the first time he'd really seemed interested in food since Tuesday evening. And he appeared to be coughing less as the day wore on.

He asked her questions about the inn as he ate, wanting to know if there were new guests coming, how Louise's piano lessons had gone, what Jane was making for breakfast.

"How is Wendell?" he asked at one point. "He came home and I left a day and a half later. I hardly have gotten to see this marvelous feline."

Alice laughed. "He's doing very well, I believe. His injuries seem to be healing cleanly.

"Oh, I almost forgot," she added, "you mentioned Bigfoot yesterday and we were interrupted. The furor appears to be dying down a good bit this week. There haven't been any further developments, and only Florence still seems to believe it was something other than a teenager's prank."

Maxwell was silent for a moment. "You never really believed it, did you?"

Alice chuckled. "Well, I admit to having a few nervous moments when we found that huge footprint at the pond. I was sure something was going to leap out of the bushes at us. But I suppose I am too much of a skeptic. There is so little tangible evidence of Bigfoot, I simply can't imagine that there really is a huge creature running around out there."

Maxwell nodded. "A very sensible view. One with which I agree."

A nurse appeared in the doorway then, beaming at Maxwell. "Here he is," she said to someone out of sight in the hallway.

The nurse stepped back and a man came in. He wore an expensive-looking black suit, a starched white shirt and a red silk tie, and he carried an overcoat across one arm. He had steel-gray eyes and a long, thin face and . . . he looked like Maxwell, Alice realized.

The young man had fallen silent. He was staring at the new visitor as if he was seeing a ghost. "Father?"

"Hello, son." He stepped closer to the bed and held out a slim, flat package. "I brought you a book. It's a first edition of the first published paper of Sigmund Freud, in the original dust jacket."

"Really?" Maxwell sounded surprised. "Thank you. I'm interested in psychology. It's my area of study."

"I know."

"You do?"

His father nodded. "How are you feeling?"

"Better. I'm on antibiotics."

The two stared at each other for a suspended moment. Alice cleared her throat and rose. "I believe I'll go down to the cafeteria for some tea," she said to Maxwell.

"Oh, wait," the young man entreated. "Alice, this is my father, Maxwell Alexander Vandermitton, Junior. Father, this is Alice Howard. Alice and her sisters run the inn at which I have been staying."

"Miss Howard," murmured the older man. He took the hand she offered and shook it gravely. "We have spoken," he told his son. "She's...quite a remarkable lady."

Maxwell beamed as if his father had praised his judgment. "Isn't she?" Then his face changed. "You've spoken?"

"Yes," Alice said. "I called him. I thought he should know you'd been hospitalized."

"There was no need." Very formally, he said to his father, "I'm sorry if you worried needlessly. I'll be fine in a day or two."

"Rubbish!" said his father. "I already spoke to the doctor. You were very sick and if you don't take care, you could relapse. Maxwell, I'd like you to come home with me when you're released."

"Home?" The younger man said the word as if he'd never heard it before. "What do you mean, home?"

"To my home. Our home. I have canceled my travel engagements for the next six months. I would like you to consider coming to stay for at least that long. Longer, if you like. It's your home too."

Maxwell appeared dumbstruck. Cautiously, he said, "I wouldn't want to be in your way. You shouldn't have canceled your plans because of me."

With equal care, his father replied, "There is nothing more important to me than you. The travel can wait. Please, son, just think about it. You and I need time to talk, to get to know each other." The man took a deep breath. "I've made mistakes, pushed you away when I should have pulled you closer. I can't change the past, but I'd like a chance to create a happier future."

The room fell silent. Alice wanted to leave, but she was afraid these two might never breach the walls that separated them if she didn't do something. "Maxwell?" she prompted.

Her young friend turned his head and looked at her. "I don't want him here because you made him feel guilty. And I don't want your pity."

"It's not pity I feel," Alice told him. "I'm very fond of you." She smiled down at him and then continued, "You've been to church with us. You've begun to learn that a large part of being a true Christian is forgiving. Can't you consider forgiving your father?"

"I didn't think it would be so hard." He sounded like a sulky child.

Alice smiled, silently praying that her young friend's heart was as big as she believed it to be. "Maxwell, your father is here, asking you to give yourselves a chance to start over. Do you or do you not wish to accept?"

She could have heard a pin drop in the silence that followed. A hollow feeling began to gather in her stomach.

"Yes," Maxwell said. He looked at his father and offered a hand. "I accept. I would like to come home to live for a while, Father."

The elder Vandermitton closed his eyes for a moment. Then he moved across the room, ignored his son's outstretched hand and gathered him into an embrace.

Alice slipped out of the room with tears in her eyes. With a little luck and a lot of prayer, perhaps the two men would be able to let go of the past and become a family again.

Chapter Sixteen

With Maxwell in good hands, Jane, Clothilda and Ethel decided to begin their hunt for people with the Muller name following lunch on Friday. After another fruitless pass through the cemeteries they already had visited, they drove to several small churches in the surrounding countryside.

The first two churches were tiny, rural parishes, both of which fell under the ministry of one part-time pastor. The clergyman and his wife, who acted as secretary and treasurer for both churches, happily shared their records with the women, but none of the old rolls showed either the Muller or Moeller name.

"You know," said the pastor, a small man who had served the parishes for more than fifty years, "that name rings a bell. Used to be a feller over near Merriville that showed up occasionally at the farmers' market. I'm thinking his name might have been Muller. The oldest cemetery in the county is over there too."

"Thank you," said Jane as the three women climbed back into her car. "Ladies, I guess our next stop is Merriville."

"There's a little church on Main Street, as I recall," said Ethel, "That would be a good place to start."

It was a short drive to Merriville. Ethel's accurate memory directed them straight to the church, and they were pleased to see a car in the parking lot.

Opening the door to the dim interior, Jane called, "Hello. Anyone here?"

"Why, hello." A woman of about Ethel's age walked toward them with a youthful step. Her hair had been allowed to turn a striking silver and was cut in a very chic, extremely short style that was charmingly disordered. Up at the altar was a bucket full of glorious spring blossoms that she apparently had been arranging for an upcoming service. "I'm Violet Rabb. May I help you?"

"We hope so," Ethel replied. After making introductions, she explained Clothilda's quest to Violet and asked, "Would it be possible for us to see the church's records from the eighteenth and nineteenth centuries?"

The woman's face fell. "Oh dear. I am sorry to tell you, but our first church burned to the ground in 1837, and everything before that date was destroyed. You are most welcome to examine what we have, though."

Jane could see that the other two were as disappointed as she, but she nodded when Ethel politely said, "Thank you."

"Muller," said Violet thoughtfully. "I am trying to recall where I have seen that name before. I'm fairly certain it appears in our post-fire records, but that's not the thing that's teasing my memory. Ah, well." She threw up her hands and then beckoned. "Come with me. I'll think of it eventually."

They followed her to a surprisingly modern little office with a computer system, fax and huge color copier. Violet dropped into the chair in front of the keyboard and quickly called up a list on the monitor.

"We have all our old records since the fire computerized now. Tell me how to spell the name and we'll see if there are any listed."

Clothilda gave her the information, and a moment later squealed in delight as three lines popped up on the screen.

"Three Mullers," said Jane. "This is the most luck we've had yet. Thank you so much."

"I've remembered where I saw this name. The oldest cemetery in the county is about ten miles down the road. Some of the graves date back to before the Revolutionary War. I'm sure there are Mullers in there." Violet hit a button and printed out two copies of the information on the screen. "Computers are amazing, aren't they?"

"Yes, but so confusing," said Ethel. "However did you become so comfortable using one?"

"I took a class for adults that they offered at the high school," Violet said. "I can give you the information if you're interested."

Ethel shook her head. "No, I think I am content to let Jane do any computer things I need done. I don't want to start all over learning a new skill at my age."

Violet's eyes twinkled. "We're only as old as we feel."

Jane could see a light in Ethel's eyes that meant a "difference of opinion." Hastily, she said, "Thank you so much for your help. We'll check out that cemetery." She gave the papers to Ethel and before her startled aunt could recover, Jane hustled them out into the sunny parking lot again.

Ethel eyed her niece narrowly. "Don't think that escaped me, Jane Howard. I know I was 'handled' in there."

Jane smiled innocently. "Sorry. I didn't think we had time for an extended discussion."

"*Humph.*" Ethel turned and got into the car without further argument.

Jane smiled as she slid into the driver's seat. It was not often that one got the better of Aunt Ethel. She might write down the date so she wouldn't forget it.

Alice came home from the hospital around three on Friday afternoon. Maxwell's father intended to stay with Maxwell through dinner until visiting hours were over, at which time he planned to come to the inn for the night. She had felt comfortable leaving the two men together, and she certainly had things to do at home that she had neglected during her time at the hospital with Maxwell.

She could hear Louise in a lesson with one of her older students who got out of school before the little ones. As she walked into the kitchen to get a drink of water and to check through the mail she had brought in with her, Wendell greeted her with a plaintive meow.

"It's not dinner time," Alice told him as he rubbed along her ankles, nearly making her trip. But as she looked down at him, her heart was pained to see how thin he was. What a hard time he must have had. "Oh, all right. I'll give you a little something to tide you over until Jane comes home and feeds you your dinner."

Tomorrow, she promised herself, she'd make up some of the little packets of treats that Jane gave Wendell. If she kept them in her room, she could let him snack occasionally until he regained his weight.

It was after three and Jane was ready to begin the trip home. But Clothilda and Ethel badly wanted to check out the little cemetery that Violet Rabb had mentioned.

So Jane turned left instead of right and drove several miles down the road. Two more turns as Violet had directed brought them to a small, winding road along a pretty creek. Cows grazed in a nearby pasture. Several ducks were serenely gliding across the water.

The cemetery was next to a small church that had closed its doors. Jane pulled off onto the grassy verge and parked, and the three of them began to wander among the gravestones.

"Wow!" said Jane. "Here's one man who died in 1802."

"Look at this." Ethel pointed to a large stone with a number of smaller ones at its foot. "This man had two wives—not at the same time, of course—and at least eleven children who died in infancy and childhood."

Jane stood over the sobering reminders of an earlier time when illnesses like Maxwell's routinely killed people. "How very sad. I can't imagine."

"Very bad," said Clothilda. "Very, very bad."

"I wonder how many survived to adulthood," Ethel said. "One of my grandfathers had more than twenty children, although I believe fewer than half of them lived past their first few years."

They hadn't been there ten minutes when Clothilda called, "I have found one! Many ones!"

Jane and Ethel hurried to her side. There, in the soft spring grass, were headstones bearing the names of several Muller family members who had passed away many decades before.

"Gracious sakes alive!" Ethel pulled the folder of information from under her arm and opened it. "Look. There's Georg. And Jacob. And their wives."

"There are more over here," Jane said from around a broad old tree, kneeling. "Looks like their children. Infants and ones who died young are here." She stood and glanced around. "The second son is over here, but I don't see any others. I wonder why the youngest brother isn't buried here."

"The youngest was only eighteen when they emigrated from Germany," Ethel reminded her. "He could have fought in the Revolutionary War and died who knows where, or married and moved far away." She pulled out large sheets of blank white paper and pencils and distributed them to Jane and one to Clothilda. "Let's get busy, girls. Start rubbing."

As they worked, Clothilda said, "Jane, Ethel, thank you so very much for helping me with this. I still wish to find living Muller-name people, but this, this is very good start."

"You're welcome." Jane thought Clothilda seemed a bit more emotional than the discovery warranted. "Are you all right?"

Clothilda smiled. "I am very all right. For many years I have wanted to make trip, but it was much money." She began to chatter in German, apparently lacking the vocabulary to express herself in English, and Ethel started to translate for Jane.

"She thought maybe she was wrong to spend so much money, but now she is hopeful. She really wants to find living descendants, to talk with them about . . . about a rare genetic disorder in the family. Her granddaughter has this disorder. It is a form of dwarfism and causes a wrist defect, she says. It's nothing fatal, but she wonders if anyone in America has had it and if American medicine has discovered any treatment they aren't aware of."

"A wrist defect?" Jane said.

Clothilda nodded. "Floppy." She held up her arms and bounced them loosely, letting her hands flop up and down in an exaggerated fashion. Then she began to speak in German again.

"The skeletal structure of the wrists is bad, things are not connected," Ethel went on. "The child lives a relatively normal life but she has little grip strength. It affects her ability to do a number of routine tasks, such as opening jars and containers, carrying or holding anything heavy such as a laundry basket, opening heavy doors, driving long distances. She also has difficulty completing tasks that require manual dexterity, such as painting walls, playing piano or working at the computer."

"I see," Jane said. "And you hope someone in this family has it and has been able to find a cure."

Clothilda beamed. "Yes. Probably not to happen, but I think this ... passed from generation to generation."

"Ah."

"Well," said Ethel, "we are running out of time today, but the next time, we shall start in Merriville. We're only a few miles from there, and they have a lovely old brick library there that may have records or other information that would be helpful."

Ethel had invited Clothilda to dinner at the carriage house Friday evening. With Maxwell still hospitalized, the sisters sat around the kitchen table to enjoy the steaming lasagna Jane had made yesterday and baked this evening. As they finished their prayer and began to eat, Alice recounted her surprise when Maxwell's father had appeared, and explained the awkward beginning of the subsequent reconciliation. "He will be arriving here later after visiting hours end, so we'll need to make up a room for him."

Jane gave a squeak. "You could have let me know earlier. I have to lay out clean towels and be sure the room is dusted. I suppose we'll put him in the Symphony Room—"

"Breathe, Jane," said Louise. "You know as well as I do that the Symphony Room is immaculate, and it only takes a minute to put out towels."

Jane sat back. "You're right. Sorry, Alice, I didn't mean to snap at you. I'm tired, I suppose. It was a long day, driving around and chasing through cemeteries again." She brightened. "But we had success at last."

"Do tell," said Alice. "You mean you found Clothilda's ancestors?"

"We did," Jane said triumphantly. "Some of the earliest exact names from her list are buried in a Merriville church cemetery. One of her ancestors was born in 1753 in Germany and lived to the ripe old age of eighty-two, which was quite ancient back then. He was buried in 1835."

Louise raised an eyebrow. "That is quite remarkable."

Jane proceeded to share the whole story, including Clothilda's real reason for the hunt. "So she is wondering if the condition is genetic, as she suspects, and if anyone has been born with it recently. She is hoping there is a medical intervention that would help the grandchild gain better use of her joints."

"Oh, I hope someone can help her," Alice said sympathetically. "What is it called again?"

"Leri-Weill Syndrome."

Alice shook her head. "I've never heard of it, but if it's a rare orthopedic condition, that's not surprising." She rose and went to the window as they heard a car pull into the driveway and continue back to the parking lot. "That must be Maxwell's father. I'll go out and greet him."

"Oh, rats!" said Jane. "I was hoping for a little more time."

"I can clean up these dishes," Louise said, "if you would like to dash up to check the room."

"Dash," said Jane. "I like that. Yes, I believe if you don't mind, I'll just dash up, lay out fresh towels and chase down any stray dust bunnies I see hopping around."

 ~

"I'm allowed to go home!" Maxwell crowed when Alice came through the doorway of his room Saturday morning. His father, who had gone to the hospital immediately after breakfast, greeted her with a smile.

"That's wonderful," said Alice. "Did they give you any restrictions?"

"The doctor doesn't want me to fly for a week or so, and I have to take it pretty easy, but nothing major." He smiled. "I can still go to the Coffee Shop for my one piece of pie every day."

Alice laughed. "Only one more week. Tomorrow we celebrate Palm Sunday and next Sunday is Easter. You're almost there." Then something occurred to her. "You're not going home with your father?"

He shook his head. "I am but not until after Easter. I'd like to go back to the inn, if you'll have me." He smiled. "I've been quite a troublesome fellow, it seems."

Then his face sobered. "Alice ... there is something I need to tell you. I've been trying for days but either my courage fails or I get interrupted." His gaze darted to his father, who stood at the foot of the bed.

"Would you like me to leave you two alone to talk privately?" asked the elder Vandermitton.

"No, no." Maxwell shook his head. "You might as well hear it too." He looked so gloomy that Alice could not imagine what he could be about to say. "You both might change your mind about having me come home after you hear this."

His father slowly sat down. Alice took another chair and pulled it close to the bed. "What's wrong?"

Maxwell took a deep breath and blew it out. "It's about Bigfoot." He looked into her eyes. "There isn't one."

Alice said, "What do you mean, 'there isn't one?' How do you know?"

The young man hung his head. "The tracks and the hair . . . I left those. I also put that article in the library where someone could find it easily." His shoulders slumped.

Alice took a moment to absorb the information. Surprisingly, she *wasn't* all that surprised. For days now, some sixth sense had been lightly stirring every time the Bigfoot topic came up in Maxwell's presence. Finally, she knew why.

"The mud on your shoes that day came from the path around the pond."

Maxwell nodded, looking miserable.

His father, seated a bit apart from them in a corner, looked concerned and confused.

"You knew it wasn't real when you walked out there with Florence? And when we went on that ridiculous overnight expedition of Ronald's?" Memories continued to flood back.

He just nodded.

"Why? Why would you do that?" She was struggling with a strong sense of betrayal. "You were laughing at us the whole time?"

"No!" He looked shocked, then contrite. He squared his shoulders. "Well, perhaps I was amused, at first. You see, it's part of my research. I am comparing and contrasting small town residents to people who live in large cities. How are they alike? How are they different? When presented with the same information, how do they deal with it?"

"You've pulled this stunt before?" his father asked.

Maxwell nodded. "Well, something similar in Philadelphia. Before that, I studied control groups in two other similar small town and city areas."

"And how did people react in Philadelphia?"

Maxwell shook his head. "Most of them didn't, after the first rush of sensationalism. There were a few who wanted to believe, just as there have been here, but the hubbub passed quickly. Actually, I've been a little surprised at how similar the two communities have been. The primary difference is the speed at which news travels. In Acorn Hill, it moves like lightning and…and you don't care about that," he said miserably.

Alice didn't know what to say or how to feel. She could not believe Maxwell had been using Acorn Hill, all the people who had befriended him, as…as test subjects. "Did you overhear me talking about the giant squid? Were you the anonymous source who talked to Carlene?"

When he only nodded, she said, "Why tell me now?"

"I had to." He leaned forward, pointing at the cards, flowers and balloons that made the sterile hospital room look so much more warm and inviting. "In the city, people usually don't befriend you unless you reach out first. They don't even meet one another's eyes on the street. Here, everyone says hello, everyone invites you to join in whatever community thing is going on. Here, I have friends." His gaze dropped. "Or at least, I did have friends. Once they find out what I did, I imagine most of them will wash their hands of me."

Alice didn't correct him. She still was trying to understand how he could do such a thing.

There was a silence in the room. Maxwell's father still looked puzzled.

Finally, Alice said, "You could have just gotten well, finished your visit and left, and no one ever would have been the wiser."

The young man hesitated. "You took me to church with you. I began to think about dishonesty. And yes, while no one else would have known, *I* would know. If I'm really going to begin to consider what God expects of me, how could I just leave?" He swallowed. "I committed a sin. And I think the only way to absolve myself *is* to confess and ask forgiveness."

Alice stared at him. "You're going to tell everyone in Acorn Hill that the Bigfoot signs were a hoax?"

He set his jaw. Nodded. "Yes. I don't expect forgiveness from them. But at least I'll know I tried to make things right."

Chapter Seventeen

On Saturday morning, Jane, Ethel and Clothilda decided to visit the library in the little town of Merriville.

"We need to look for Georg and Jacob's grandchildren," Jane said. "If we can get that far, we should be into the mideighteen hundreds, and there might be town census records from sometime close to that."

They had learned that the library closed at 2:00 PM, so the women arrived there shortly after it opened at 9:00 AM. A young, dark-haired librarian welcomed them and directed them to the Civil War Room, where they searched for and found two Muller men, both of whom had fought for the Union. Unfortunately, it appeared that both men had perished, one at the Battle of Antietam in Sharpsburg, Maryland, and the second later in the war at Cold Harbor near Richmond, Virginia.

"Well, rats," said Jane. "For this to be helpful, they would have to have lived and procreated."

"They may have left wives and children," Ethel pointed out.

"Unlikely," Jane said. "The older boy, who died in 1862, was only eighteen. His brother, who was a year younger, lived two more years and died at the age of nineteen. I know people married young back then, but there is no information about wives left behind, nor is there any record of a marriage for either boy. They probably joined the army as soon as they were of age."

Clothilda shut the book she had been searching through. "What do we think to do now?"

Jane shook her head. "Let's go ask the librarian if the town has census records and, if so, where they are located."

They returned everything to its proper place and trooped back downstairs to the librarian's desk. The woman was on the telephone and she held up one finger to indicate that they should wait.

Jane looked around while they waited for her conversation to conclude. The library was housed in what apparently had been a grand old mansion on the main street of town. The circulation desk was just to the right inside one of the huge rooms and a large spiral staircase curved upward from the spacious foyer. They had used the staircase to get to the Civil War Room, where the young woman had directed them first.

Finally, the librarian hung up the telephone. "Thank you for your patience," she said, turning to face them. Her name tag read Mrs. Hall. "Did you have any success locating family members from the Civil War era?

Ethel made a face. "We did," she told the woman, "but they died young. The eldest brother was killed at the Battle of Antietam."

"What we are seeking," Jane said as she gestured toward Clothilda, "is a living descendant of this lady's ancestors who first came to this area from Germany more than two hundred years ago. Are there census records, or anything else you can think of, that would assist us?"

The young woman looked quizzical. "If you want live folks, how about the phone book?"

There was a silence, and then Jane said, "What a good suggestion. We are from Acorn Hill and while we did check our local telephone book when we first began our search, I forgot that Merriville would have a different book of listings."

Mrs. Hall smiled. She reached beneath the desk and pulled out a telephone book, which she laid on the desk. "What is the name?" she asked. "I can check for you right now."

"Muller," said Ethel. "M-u-l-l-e-r."

The young woman's eyes widened. She began to laugh as she closed the telephone book. "Your search has ended. My maiden name was Muller."

Clothilda babbled out a rapid stream of German that Ethel struggled to translate quickly.

"She wants to know if there are any other Mullers around that aren't related to you. She would like to visit your parents, if they're willing to meet with her. We found some Mullers buried in a little cemetery near here. Are they your ancestors?"

"Whoa." Mrs. Hall held up a hand. "There are a number of Mullers here, but they all are related to me somehow. I'm sure my mother would be delighted to talk with you. Genealogy is one of her passions. And . . . what was the other thing I wanted to mention—oh yes, the Civil War vets are in our family tree. If you're sure they are in yours, it's quite likely that we are related."

She beamed at Clothilda. "This is so exciting! Why don't I give my mother a call right now and see if she has time to talk with you? She's retired and I never know what she might be up to," she warned. "But you may get lucky and catch her at home."

She placed a call to her mother. Unfortunately, the woman was not available just then but she invited them to visit later in the afternoon, an invitation they accepted with alacrity.

Late on Saturday morning, Maxwell was discharged from the hospital, and his father brought him back to the inn. Alice had directed Mr. Vandermitton to stop near the back porch steps, and as soon as he rolled to a halt, she and Louise went out to greet Maxwell. Alice had not told anyone about Maxwell's deception. If he wanted people to know, the responsibility for telling them had to be his.

When the car door opened, Maxwell's gaze immediately flew to Alice.

"Did you tell your sisters?" he asked in an undertone as she helped him from the car.

Alice shook her head. "That's something you must decide to do."

"Welcome home." Louise stepped forward and gathered him into a warm hug that surprised Alice. Louise normally was not one for such displays of affection.

"Are you sure he should be out of the hospital so soon?" she asked Alice.

Alice smiled. "I know he still sounds terrible, but he actually had a fairly mild case of pneumonia. The antibiotics have killed the bacteria by now, so it's really just a matter of taking it easy until he recovers." Her face sobered. "But I'm sure you can see why this kind of illness is so lethal to our elderly patients."

Louise and Alice brought in the flowers and assorted other get-well wishes that Maxwell had accumulated during his hospitalization. His father got his son's small bag. Then he and Alice helped Maxwell upstairs and into bed, where Alice checked his temperature.

His eyes drooped as she leaned over him. "Trip tired me out," he said drowsily.

"Just rest now," Alice advised. "There will be plenty of time to do the things you want to do."

"Think I'll be able to go to church tomorrow?"

Privately, Alice doubted it. But she was not about to discourage him. "We'll see," she said noncommittally. "It may depend on how you rest tonight."

And then the visitors began to arrive. Florence and Ronald were the first to come, followed by Rev. Kenneth Thompson, Nia Komonos and Fred and Vera Humbert. Maxwell's father looked on in surprise at this outpouring of welcome.

"Your son has made quite a few friends in Acorn Hill," Alice told him at one point.

"So I see." His father looked pleased. "His mother always made friends easily. I was never as good at socializing."

Alice only smiled, recalling Maxwell's stilted manner when they first had met. Goodness, how he had changed.

Patsy and Henry Ley were the next to arrive after lunch. Patsy carried a small basket with two sealed canning jars of soup inside. The lids were decorated with a pretty red-and-white gingham cloth square tied with red ribbons.

Patsy took one out to show Maxwell. "Homemade chicken soup," she said. "My mother's recipe. I'm sure it can't compare with Jane's cooking, but my mother always made this when one of us was ill. She swore it helped us get better faster. I don't know about that, but it sure is tasty."

The three genealogy musketeers had a leisurely lunch in a Merriville tearoom, strolled through town and then headed off for their afternoon visit with the librarian's mother. Lacy Hall opened the door with a welcoming smile after Jane rang the doorbell.

"Please come in," she said. "My mother is so eager to meet you."

They followed Lacy through a charming country-style cottage with overstuffed chairs covered in floral patterns, handwoven baskets and pieces of glazed blue pottery scattered about. She led them out a side door onto a stone patio surrounded by azaleas that were not yet in bloom. Beautiful tulips in pinks and lavenders were scattered among the bushes. In the center of the lovely little area stood a wrought-iron table and chairs beneath a sun umbrella.

A dark-haired woman in a broad straw gardening hat stood on tiptoe beside a bird feeder, adding some sort of small seed mix to it.

"Mom," said Lacy, "here are the ladies I told you about."

The woman turned and stripped off gardening gloves, then advanced with a hand outstretched. "Hello, I'm Lucinda Muller." She shook each of their hands as Lacy introduced them. "Please, have a seat. Would you like some lemonade? It's a gorgeous day. I thought we could sit out here and chat."

"I'll get it," Lacy volunteered. "You go ahead and sit down with your guests."

"What a peaceful retreat," Jane said as all four women took their seats. "You've done some lovely landscaping."

"Thank you," Lucinda replied. "I am a Penn State Master Gardener. I have some extraordinary rare and choice plants that I've acquired from other Master Gardeners over the years. I love playing in the dirt," she confided with a grin.

"I enjoy it too," Jane told her. "What exactly is a Master Gardener?"

"Penn State established the program more than thirty years ago to help educate the public about horticulture and good environmental stewardship. Master Gardeners receive training in return for volunteering time to teach good horticultural practices."

"That sounds fascinating."

"It is to me, but as I said, I love gardening. My specialty is shade garden plantings."

"Hostas and astilbe are two of my favorites of the shade plants," Jane said, "and of course, coral bells. They seem to be coming out with new, improved varieties every year now."

"Yes, there are some wonderful improvements on some of our old standards," Lucinda said. "If you're interested in the Master Gardener program, I'll be glad to give you some information and a link to the Web site."

Lacy came out of the house through a set of French doors. She set a tray carefully on the table and placed a glass of lemonade in front of each woman, leaving on the tray a large pitcher filled with more lemonade, as well as a plate of butter cookies.

"Enough about gardening," said Lucinda. "I know you came here to discuss tracing our family connection." She looked across the table at Clothilda. "So my husband was your cousin about twenty times removed?"

Clothilda looked a little confused. "*Was ist es?*" she asked Ethel, who promptly replied in German.

"I am so sorry," exclaimed Lucinda. "I did not realize you don't speak English."

"I do some," Clothilda told her, "but I am not familiar with this 'removed.'"

"I meant that you and my husband's family appear to be related through a common ancestor many generations ago."

"Yes." Clothilda opened the folder they had brought along. "I came here to find more Moellers, M-o-e-l-l-e-r, but instead we learn that the name changes to Muller with a *u* when they got off the ship."

Lucinda sat up straighter. "Wait a minute. You're telling me you have traced your family back to the port they sailed from, and that when they disembarked here, the name was changed?"

Clothilda glanced at Ethel, who nodded. "Yes. That's exactly it."

"This is fabulous!" exclaimed Lucinda. "Before he passed away, my husband and I had traced the Mullers back to the family that came out of the Port of Philadelphia, but we never could go back any further. If you and I share information, we'll have a connection across the Atlantic." She leaned forward. "How many generations back have you gone in Germany."

"Nine," said Clothilda. "Too far in back, there are no more written records."

"Nine," repeated Lucinda reverently. "That's amazing. We have ten here, if we include my children's children. May I see your work? No, wait." She popped up out of her seat. "Let me go get my notebook first. Then you can look at my research too."

Off she zipped into the house.

Jane smiled. "Goodness, but she has a lot of energy."

"You don't know the half of it," Lacy replied. "She makes my sister and me tired just watching her sometimes."

"I want the name of her vitamins," Ethel said, and they all laughed.

"I called my sister a few minutes ago," said Lacy. "She's on her way over so you'll get to meet her too," she said to Clothilda.

"Lacy," said Jane, "Clothilda is seeking a genetic link to a condition that has been passed down through her family."

Clothilda rattled off something in German and Ethel spoke for her. "She says that her granddaughter, her husband's grandmother and one other great-great-something all had the same kind of condition. She wonders if you know of anyone in your family who might have it."

"What kind of condition is it?" asked Lucinda, who had returned bearing a hefty notebook that she placed on the table with a thud.

"It's called Leri-Weill Syndrome," Ethel told the mother and daughter. "It's characterized by short stature and a wrist deformity."

Lacy and Lucinda exchanged glances and Lucinda nodded. "We're familiar with it."

"You are?" Jane was nearly as excited as Clothilda and Ethel. "Someone in your family had it?"

"*Has* it," corrected Lucinda. She beckoned to someone just coming through the French doors. "Haley, come and meet our guests." She turned to the three visitors. "This is my younger daughter Haley and her friend Akiko. Akiko's family just moved here last year from Tokyo."

Jane turned with a smile to greet the newcomers, and her eyes widened in surprise.

Haley, Lacy's younger sister, was pretty and dark-haired like her mother and sister, but she was only about four-and-a-half-feet tall.

Chapter Eighteen

At dinner Saturday evening, Jane, Ethel and Clothilda told Alice and Louise about the discovery. Maxwell, though he had begged, was not allowed to come downstairs for dinner, so Jane made up a tray for his father and him to dine together in his room.

"What a burden," said Alice sympathetically as they spoke of the girl they had met.

"Not really," said Jane. "The young woman is extremely petite, but her stature does not appear to hamper her. She can do most ordinary things. Lucinda said she keeps several small folding stools around the house to make it easier for Haley to get items out of higher cupboards and reach into the washing machine."

"And you would never know she has weak wrists. She compensates well for that too." Ethel closed her eyes as she chewed a piece of bacon-wrapped chicken breast stuffed with banana-nut bread. "Jane, this is just delicious."

"Thank you," Jane smiled. "Maybe it would be more accurate to say that others compensate for her. I saw her quietly hand a bottle of water to her sister to open for her, and the young friend who was with her while we visited picked up a heavy backpack for her without even being asked. I thought it was very nice that they didn't even seem to think about it."

"So what did they tell you about the family history?" Louise asked. "Were there others who had it?"

"There were," Ethel confirmed. "Lucinda said her husband had a great-aunt who was tiny and had weak wrists all her life, and apparently the great-aunt remembered someone even further back on the family tree who was the same."

"When Haley was a teenager," Jane went on, "she began to have pain in her wrists. Radiographs showed an unusual skeletal structure, so she was referred to a specialist for testing. That's when they discovered that she had this specific syndrome linked to a form of dwarfism. And that's when Lucinda recalled the great-aunt."

Clothilda said, "I wanted to know if there was any treatment for this wrists."

"Apparently, in some cases in the past, surgery has helped with the appearance of the deformity," Jane said. "Haley has never had anything done because her case is fairly mild. But for people with significant wrist deformity, there is a surgical procedure that can stabilize the wrists. The problem is that the patient loses some flexibility because they have to fuse certain bones together."

"So if she has surgery, she loses range of motion," Louise restated.

"I have a question," Alice said to Clothilda. "Did you look for a doctor in Europe? Surely there is someone who could do it there."

The German woman shook her head. "Surgery Jane talks of is done by very few. But no one knows anything to do to stable— stabilize wrists without taking away motion." She demonstrated her meaning by twisting her wrists back and forth, up and down and every which way.

"And that's what you are hoping to find for your granddaughter?" Louise asked Clothilda.

"Yes. Lucinda gave me the name of doctor who has talked about new surgery. Lotte, my granddaughter, has more troubles than Haley. More bad wrist. But to choose bad wrists or no motion," she shook her head. "I wish to see if American doctor can help more."

"Clothilda is going to give her daughter the name of the orthopedic surgeon Lucinda recommended," said Ethel. "They can send her history and X-rays to him. If he thinks it might help, then Clothilda might try to find a way to bring Lotte over here for the surgery."

"Expensive," said Clothilda grimly. "I help with what I can, but still expensive for daughter."

"I imagine so," said Alice. "I will keep your Lotte in my prayers, Clothilda, in hopes that you and your family will be able to discern what might be the right thing to do."

"Thank you." Clothilda looked around the table at her four friends. "Coming to Grace Chapel Inn was very good for me."

Maxwell pestered Alice half to death until she gave in and agreed that he could attend church on Palm Sunday with them. By that time, his course of antibiotics had eliminated the chance of passing on the infection.

His father reluctantly took his leave immediately after Sunday breakfast. "I left a number of loose ends when I rushed out of my office," he told Alice. He extended his hand to her. "Thank you for everything, Alice. Without your help, Maxwell and I might never have been able to overcome the distance between us."

Alice shook his hand as she smiled. "I suspect it would have worked itself out someday," she said modestly. "But I'm glad I could be an instrument of change for you both. Have a safe trip, Mr. Vandermitton. Please visit us again someday."

While Maxwell and his father said their farewells, Alice discreetly gave them some space. Then she walked to the front porch with Maxwell, and they both waved good-bye until the rental SUV drove out of sight.

He sighed. "Alice, I don't know how to thank you. I suppose it sounds silly to thank you for ignoring my wishes, but if you hadn't, my father and I would never have had this chance to talk."

"So you're feeling better about your relationship with him?"

The young man nodded. "Much. Neither of us is perfect, and we both made unfortunate choices that kept us from really seeing the other. But that's in the past now, and I think we've made a very good start on a closer bond."

"That's wonderful, Maxwell," she said sincerely. Then the nurse side of her personality kicked in. "How are you feeling? Coming downstairs for breakfast may have been enough for you—"

"No, Alice, I want to go to church. It's only a short walk," he protested. "I feel all right. Honestly. And I can sleep for the rest of the day if you think I need to."

"I propose a compromise," she suggested. "You can go to church *if* you allow one of us to drive you and drop you off at the door. It sounds foolish, I know, but that short walk is enough to get you coughing again if you're not careful."

"All right," he said. "Anything you say, as long as I can go the Palm Sunday service."

Jane drove Maxwell to the church just before the service was to start. The others had arrived at Grace Chapel a few minutes earlier and were there to walk with Maxwell into the church. Jane observed that there were ripples of smiles and waves directed at Maxwell as their fellow congregants noticed him.

When Louise began to play "The Palms" prelude, pleasure and peace stole through Jane as she prepared for worship. The Palm Sunday service always had been one of Jane's favorites. When she was small, the children of the chapel were dressed in simple white choir robes and lined up in order by height. Each child received a small bundle of palms, which they were instructed to hold with both hands. As the stately music began, the children started to wave their palms and step forward. The biggest children started off because it was too risky to try to get the smallest, newest palm-wavers to walk up the aisles first. Every other child went left and right down the outside aisles of the church until they met in the center. Stopping to lay their palms on a growing pile before the altar, they came back to the center aisle, two by two, to the rear of the chapel.

Step-together, step-together, step-together, slowly in time with the music. Dip your palms twice to the right and twice to the left.

Seeing the children of Grace Chapel continuing the same tradition in which she had participated so long ago brought tears to Jane's eyes.

When the palm processional ended, the congregation rose to sing "All Glory, Laud, and Honor." Jane enjoyed hearing the voices around her, though she usually didn't sing at all or just mouthed the words. As some unkind music teacher had once told her, she "couldn't carry a tune in a bucket" and she was loathe to inflict her voice on anyone.

The service flowed on smoothly, Rev. Thompson delivering a stirring sermon before administering Holy Communion. The choir sang a beautiful four-part voice arrangement of an old standard, "Were You There When They Crucified My Lord?"

Glancing over, Jane noticed Maxwell paying rapt attention throughout the service. She tried to imagine what it would be like to be experiencing one's very first Palm Sunday service as an adult. She had been away from the church before moving home to Acorn Hill, but the childhood memories associated with the church and congregation were such a part of her that she could not imagine who or what she would be without them. Someone with a void in her spirit, she supposed. Perhaps that is the way

Maxwell felt, before coming to Christ as an adult. What a wondrous feeling to have that void filling with the Holy Spirit.

The service concluded with a final, heartfelt hymn, "Hosanna, Loud Hosanna," another of Jane's favorites. As the postlude began and she turned to speak to those around her, she was amused to note that Maxwell had been inundated with well-wishers wanting to hear the details of his illness and to ascertain that he really was feeling better.

"Thank you all," he was saying. "I can't tell you how much your cards, flowers and other expressions of caring meant to me while I was hospitalized. Acorn Hill truly has welcomed me with open arms."

The young man looked as if he was on the verge of tears. Jane glanced at Alice, who usually knew just what to say in situations like this, but she was looking at the floor, apparently distracted and unaware that Maxwell was struggling.

Jane stepped forward. "I hate to bring this love fest to an end," she said, evoking chuckles, "but Maxwell needs to get home and rest again. The last thing we want is to put him back in the hospital."

There was a murmur of agreement, and in moments the crowd had dispersed.

"Thank you," he said gratefully to Jane.

She took him by the arm and urged him to sit down again in the pew, noticing that he seemed breathless and that his color wasn't good. "I'll go get the car." To Alice, she added, "Meet me out front in a couple of minutes."

Maxwell slept most of the afternoon. He'd been exhausted by the time they got home from church. Even eating some of Patsy Ley's tasty chicken soup had seemed to sap his energy. Fortunately, the ugly cough he'd had just a few days ago had all but disappeared, and he slept soundly.

Just before dinner, Alice was in her room feeding Wendell one of his packs of treats when she heard her name being called up the stairs.

"Alice?"

"I'm up here. Just a minute." She recognized Maxwell's voice. Apparently he was standing at the foot of the flight of steps to the third floor.

She tossed the incriminating wrapper from Wendell's treat in her trash can and descended the steps. "Hello," she said. "It's almost five o'clock. You had a nice, long nap."

"I feel much better." He shook his head. "I must seem ridiculous, needing so much rest and napping like a two-year-old."

"You were sick enough to require hospitalization," Alice reminded him. "It's not at all uncommon for patients to need significant amounts of rest after an illness like pneumonia."

"Alice…"

"Yes?"

Quietly, he said, "I need to tell Jane and Louise tonight. Will you be there, for moral support?"

"Of course," she said immediately. "Before dinner?"

"Yes. Then, tomorrow, I must tell a number of other people. I know having a whole string of individual discussions will be tiring for me, but that's what I should do."

"What if you make a list of all the people you believe you need to tell, and perhaps I can help you sort the names into two or three groups."

"That sounds a lot more manageable," he said with relief. "Thank you." He turned and headed for his room. "I'm going to start on that list."

An hour before dinner, Alice walked into the parlor. Louise had been playing piano, and she looked up as Alice entered. "Hello."

"That was beautiful," Alice told her. "I so enjoy hearing you play."

"Thank you." Louise stood, lifted the lid of the piano bench and neatly laid several pieces of sheet music inside.

"Uh … could you come into the living room, please? Maxwell would like to talk to you."

Louise raised one eyebrow. "To me?"

"Well, to you and Jane."

"Not you?"

"I'll be there."

"Alice, are you being deliberately cryptic? What is this all about?"

"Maxwell will tell you." Alice vanished from the doorway.

Louise finished putting away all her music, then walked into the living room.

Alice was seated in the corner in the rocker that had belonged to their mother. She had a gold-covered pillow on her lap with her arms loosely hugging it. Jane sat on the burgundy sofa. Her gaze met Louise's and, reading the question there, she shrugged. *I don't know what this is about either.*

Maxwell was standing in front of the fireplace. As Louise seated herself beside Jane on the couch, he said, "Thank you for joining me. I realize you both have things to do, so I'll make this brief." He walked over and sat down in the overstuffed chair so that he could face them.

Holding Louise's gaze for a moment, he said, "There's something unpleasant I have to tell you about myself." He hesitated. "I have a confession to make. I did something . . . well, I suppose you'd call it sneaky, at best." He hesitated again.

"Please just tell us," said Louise. "Dancing around it isn't going to make it go away."

"All right." He took a deep breath. "I was responsible for the Bigfoot evidence."

Both women were silent for a moment as they digested the statement.

"All right," said Jane finally. "Do you mean you made those tracks?"

He nodded. "And planted the hair, which I got from my barbershop before I arrived here."

Louise was beginning to feel stirrings of anger as the meaning of his words sank in. "I presume you have an excellent explanation for this," she said in an icy tone.

Maxwell nodded cautiously. He clearly had caught the anger underlining her words. "I'm not sure it's an excellent one," he said, "but it's the only one I have." He twisted his fingers together nervously. "I was doing a project for one of my classes. A compare-and-contrast-communities sort of thing to gauge reactions to fantastic stories. I studied a control group in Philadelphia and in another small town called Nottingham, then introduced a hoax in a different neighborhood in Philadelphia. For the second small town, I chose Acorn Hill."

"Did the Philadelphia hoax involve Bigfoot?" Louise's voice was tight.

"No." He shook his head, looking at the floor. "It involved a giant alligator in the sewers."

"Well, lucky us," said Jane.

Maxwell hung his head. "I never intended to hurt or embarrass anyone. To be truthful, I didn't even consider the feelings of the people involved. Until I came here, I had never been a part of a community like this."

Maxwell cleared his throat. "I know I don't deserve your friendship. I apologize sincerely for upsetting you and anyone else who was affected by my behavior."

Jane rose. "I accept your apology," she said, very seriously, "and I appreciate your honesty. Your friendship is something I am going to have to think about for a while." And she turned and left the room.

Louise understood Jane's feelings. Jane had worried over him, made him special remedies and fed him well. She felt betrayed. Louise felt the same way herself, but she was going to do her best to let go of it. The young man had made a mistake, as everyone did in youth. Such mistakes simply were part of maturing. And it was clear that he had grown and changed for the better since his arrival in Acorn Hill.

"I," she said, "am going to forgive you, Maxwell. As a mother, I understand that young people make mistakes as they learn about the world around them. You made an error, and I believe you have learned from it."

"Thank you, Louise." He bowed his head.

"You're welcome." As she began to leave the room, she stopped and laid a hand on his shoulder. "It took courage to confess to us," she said. "And we were probably the easiest ones you're going to have to deal with. Don't expect everyone to let you off so lightly."

Clothilda had gone to dinner with Ethel and several of Ethel's friends. Apparently Jane had not invited Maxwell to dine with them that evening. Or perhaps she'd *un*invited him or he'd just assumed he was not welcome. In any case Louise saw that the table was set for three.

After saying grace, the sisters picked at their food in silence. Louise savored a bite of the succulent pecan-crusted mountain trout Jane had prepared. "This is excellent," she said. "I wonder if you could serve this as a breakfast entrée."

A wisp of a smile flitted across Jane's face. "I just might try it sometime." Then she sighed. "I just can't believe he did that to us."

There was no need to clarify who "he" was.

"I know," Alice said. "It was an insensitive—"

"Callous, thoughtless and . . . and just plain *mean* thing to do," Jane finished.

"This really struck a nerve with you," Louise observed.

"And it didn't with you?" Jane leaned forward. "I feel so, so, I don't know . . . taken advantage of. Don't you get it? He chose us because in his eyes Acorn Hill is a backward little burg filled with backward little people. That's pretty insulting."

"I agree completely," Alice said.

"You do?" Jane looked shocked.

"I do. Initially, I believe that's very much what he thought. But we surprised him. We weren't backward. He's met accomplished musicians and artists. He's eaten four-star food at a top-rated inn. He's talked with people who have traveled the world. *And* we all were warm and friendly and accepting. If he'd been doing a paper on hospitality, we'd have gotten the blue ribbon."

"You're right, Alice," Louise said. "We did surprise him. And what's more, we have changed him." She lifted her chin and raised her eyes toward the ceiling, indicating the floor above. "That young man is a very different person from the one who arrived here. I have to confess I didn't care much for that one. Not much at all. This one, however, I am growing to enjoy quite a bit."

"That's true." Jane appeared to be giving their words some thought. "He is quite different from the young man who checked in weeks ago. Recently, I haven't seen those little flashes of superiority that I don't even think he knew he was displaying."

"No, and he's far more aware of and concerned about others than he was," Alice added.

"He carried three boxes of things for Goodwill out to the car for me the other day." Jane's gaze was distant, examining the memory. "He told me they were too heavy for me. I don't think he would have done that before he came here."

"No," said Louise dryly, "he'd have hired someone."

Alice chuckled. "And the other day, when it stormed and I was racing around closing windows, he was a big help. He had the whole first floor finished before I even got half the guest rooms done."

"Again," said Louise, "not something he would have done a few weeks ago. He really is beginning to think of others, isn't he?"

Jane looked down at her half-eaten plate of fish. "He certainly didn't get much guidance from his father when he was a child. You wrought a miracle there, Alice, bringing those two together." She took a bite, then said, "I suppose I'm going to have to forgive him."

Louise chuckled. "You wouldn't be our Jane if you didn't, dear."

$\backsim$

After dinner, Alice brought a piece of paper into the kitchen, where Jane was putting dishes in the dishwasher and Louise was wiping the counters.

"Here," said Alice. "Maxwell made this list of people he felt he needed to tell personally before he contacts Carlene. Rather than risk exhausting himself with dozens of meetings, I suggested he separate them into two or three groups and ask them to come here. I thought he could manage to make his speech a couple more times. I would like each of you to look over these groups. I helped him divide them. If there's anyone you think might be less...difficult in another group, please tell me."

Jane and Louise looked at each other. Louise thought *Florence* and she suspected Jane was thinking the same thing. Alice must have been, too, because she said, "I know that Florence is going to take this badly. She really embraced the notion of this creature frequenting Acorn Hill."

Jane snorted. "Alice, you're so tactful it slays me. Why don't you just say Florence was cuckoo on the subject and be done with it?"

Louise tried not to laugh but a small chuckle escaped. "Definitely less tactful," she informed Jane.

Chapter Nineteen

On Monday evening, right after supper, the doorbell rang. Opening the door, Alice found Vera and Fred on the doorstep. "Come on in," she said. "Maxwell is in the living room."

There were more people coming up the walk so she continued to hold open the door. Zach and Nancy Colwin, Jason Ransom, Charles Matthews and all four of their parents completed the first group. When they filed out a short while later, there were a lot of sober faces. But as he was leaving, Zach Colwin winked at Alice and said, "If that's the worst thing the fellow ever does in his life, won't he be lucky?"

The second group arrived not long afterward. It was composed of June Carter, Hope Collins, Florence and Ronald Simpson, Clarissa Cottrell and Rev. Thompson. Alice had decided not to remain in the room during each confession session, and she was particularly concerned about how Florence was going to take the news. She had hoped including Grace Chapel's pastor in that group might defuse any huge explosions.

After a surprisingly short time, the door opened and the group came out. June and Hope looked ... disenchanted, but Alice suspected they would forgive Maxwell once they had an opportunity to reflect on the situation. Ronald came next, shaking his head and raising his gaze heavenward, as if asking for patience. She could hear Florence's voice, clearly agitated, and Kenneth's deeper, calmer tones still in discussion. Maxwell said something once but a sharp tone from Florence apparently silenced him. Alice bit her lip. It didn't sound good.

After what seemed like forever, Florence came stalking out of the room. Tonight Florence had worn a light cape over her clothing and it snapped around her rapidly moving figure like a raised sail on a windy day.

"Well," she said as she reached Alice. "I never. The nerve of that young man. He should be tarred and feathered."

"Oh, Florence," Alice entreated, "don't you remember doing anything foolish or ill-advised when you were young? All of us make mistakes. The important thing is that we learn from them. And I believe Maxwell has. He truly regrets this whole debacle."

"He should," said Florence grimly. Without another word, she stomped out the door.

Alice felt as if she'd been wrung out and hung up to dry. She couldn't imagine how exhausted Maxwell must feel. Jane had brought drinks and cookies in for each group as they arrived, and Alice walked into the room and filled an extra glass with ice water. She walked across to where Kenneth was speaking with Maxwell.

Both men turned toward her as she approached. Kenneth's expression was sober but his eyes were warm. "We were just having a brief prayer," he told her. "I thought Maxwell could use a little support from the Almighty."

"I suspect you're right." Alice searched the young man's face, looking for signs of illness. His color had drained to a pasty white, but she imagined he could get through one more of these horrid meetings. "How are you feeling?" she asked him, just to confirm her impressions.

"All right." He nodded. "This is going a little better than I expected."

Alice raised her eyebrows. "Really? After seeing the way Florence left, I find that hard to believe."

Kenneth smiled. "Florence's pride took a hit. She has a difficult time when she appears foolish, as you know, and she certainly felt foolish tonight. She'll come around." He extended a hand and firmly clasped Maxwell's. "What you are doing takes courage," he told the younger man. "Never doubt that the Lord is with you right now. He'll carry you if the going gets too tough."

Alice saw the pastor out, and just a few minutes later, the final group arrived as Jane was setting out fresh drinks and cookies. It was composed of Ethel, Nia Komonos, Carlene Moss, Henry and Patsy Ley and Clothilda. They all wore barely disguised looks of curiosity.

"We were here early and we saw Florence storm out," Patsy whispered. "What on earth is going on?"

Alice shook her head. "It's not my story to tell. Come into the living room and Maxwell can explain."

It was a relief to see the last group leave.

While Alice ushered them out, Jane gathered up glasses and several empty plates. The only ones who lingered inside were Ethel, talking to Alice in the hallway, and Carlene, who was hot on the trail of the story.

Maxwell looked tired enough to collapse, and Jane finally took pity on him. "Maxwell," she said, "I know you and Carlene want to finish your conversation, but can't it wait until tomorrow? You've had an exhausting day. You can call Carlene tomorrow."

Carlene smiled, her dimples winking. "I'm sorry, Maxwell. I completely forgot you'd been ill. Call me tomorrow."

"I'll do better than that," he said. "I'll come to your office, and I'll bring along a statement you can print in Wednesday's paper if you like."

"That would be fabulous." Carlene scribbled a reminder to herself on her small notepad, and then stuffed both pencil and pad into her bag. "You did a good thing, coming clean," she told him. "I know there are a few folks who are going to be miffed for a little while, but they'll get over it. It took guts to tell everybody what you've been up to."

Maxwell began to cough.

Alice appeared in the doorway, looking as stern as she possibly could. "Bed," she said succinctly to him. "And don't forget your antibiotic or that cough medicine. I've already filled the humidifier and turned it on for you."

The young man looked grateful. "Thank you, Alice. I'll be asleep two minutes after my head hits the pillow."

Carlene stood to leave. "Goodnight, all. I'll just let myself out."

Jane and Alice both trailed her out to the hallway. Louise had come out of the parlor and was talking with Ethel, and they all said good-bye to Carlene.

Just as the door closed behind her, Wendell came sashaying down the steps.

"Good gracious sakes alive!" Ethel was staring at the cat.

"What's wrong?" Louise asked.

"Apparently nothing," their aunt said. "I swear that cat is almost as fat as he was before he took off. How did you pork him up so fast?"

Jane looked a little mystified as she studied the cat. "You're right. He *is* fat. I've been giving him one extra pack of treats per day, but that shouldn't have done it in just a week."

Louise cleared her throat. "I, ah, also have been giving him treats that I kept in my room. I thought it might help him regain his strength faster."

"He regained something, that's for sure," Ethel said.

Alice started to laugh. "You're not going to believe this, but I've been giving him treats from a stash in my room too. I made up some extra packets, Jane, from the kitchen."

"I thought I was getting absentminded," Jane said, beginning to chuckle. "I went in there the other day and there was a lot less food than I thought there should be."

Louise and Ethel joined the laughter as the four women watched Wendell waddle the rest of the way down the steps. As he rounded the newel post and walked back up the hallway toward the kitchen, his belly swayed from side to side. They all laughed harder.

"Don't think you're getting a bedtime snack," Jane called after him.

⌒

On Tuesday morning, Jane made oatmeal-apple pancakes paired with a salad of oranges, grapefruit and kiwi.

A young couple on their honeymoon had arrived the previous afternoon. They were on their way to Fort Rucker, an army post in Alabama, where the young man was to be stationed.

"Ms. Howard?" The young bride, Emmaline Morning, raised her hand as if she was still in school, making Jane chuckle inwardly.

"Yes? May I get either of you another helping of anything? Perhaps some more tea?"

"Oh no," the young woman said, smiling. "I'm beginning to feel like an overstuffed ball. Teddy can just roll me down the driveway to the car."

"But then who's going to roll *me*?" her husband asked plaintively. "Those pancakes were very good."

"I'm glad you enjoyed them," Jane said. "I was looking for a recipe for oatmeal cookies last week when I came across the pancake recipe, so you're the first people who have tasted it."

"Two thumbs up," Mr. Morning told her. "You definitely should add those to the menu."

"Would it be possible," his wife said hesitantly, "for me to get that recipe from you? I've just begun collecting recipes and I would love to make those for Teddy."

"Certainly," Jane said. "I will copy it down for you as soon as we clean up the kitchen. I'll just slip it under your door later if you are not here."

"We probably won't be," the young husband said. "We're meeting a tour guide in Potterston who is taking us to Lancaster County to learn more about the Amish."

"That should be interesting," Jane said. "One caution—most Amish consider photographs of themselves to be prideful, if that's a word, and don't allow you to take pictures of them."

"Thank you for letting us know," said Teddy Morning. He rose and came around the table to pull out his wife's chair in a courtly gesture that Jane found endearing. "We'll be heading out soon."

"Enjoy your day," Jane called after them.

Alice breezed through the swinging door just after the couple left. She wore a comfortable pair of jeans with a red-and-white striped blouse. "Louise is taking out the trash. I asked her to cut a few fresh daffodils for the reception desk," she said as she began to clear the table.

"Oh, good," Jane responded. "The ones we have there now are beginning to wilt."

Maxwell was seated at the far end of the table so it was a relatively easy matter for Jane to make small talk with Clothilda and avoid speaking to him. Her anger at his deception had faded somewhat, but she still was not sure that she wanted to be friendly with him again.

As she turned and backed through the swinging door, she saw that the young man had followed her, carrying a precariously wobbling stack of dishes he had gathered.

"Oh, careful," she warned. "Let me get those." She quickly put down her load and took his.

He handed them over with relief and a small smile. "I thought I would help you clear the table. I never realized waitresses needed to be so adept."

"It's a skill," Jane agreed.

There was a small awkward silence.

Then Maxwell said, "Well, I suppose I'll go up to my room now and work on my paper."

"Do you plan to include our reactions to the news that you'd been tricking us for days?" Jane asked, looking him squarely in the eye.

He did not squirm, as she expected him to. "Yes," he said very seriously. "I don't have any control data with which to compare that aspect, but I think it is an important part of the whole experience. I have learned a great deal from it, at any rate." He sighed. "And I really am so sorry, Jane. I wish I could go back and fix the clock so that I'd never even considered the idea."

"I wish you could too," Jane said. Then, honesty compelled her to add, "But since you can't, I think what you did last evening is the next best thing."

Alice came into the kitchen at that moment with a load of dishes she had cleared from the dining room. She glanced curiously from one to the other, and then said to Maxwell, "Oh, good, you're still here. Do you remember when I showed you our mother's Depression glass and we talked about flea markets?"

He nodded. "We never got around to seeing one."

"Would you still like to? There's one in Riverton today. It'll be there all week, in fact. It's an indoor flea market slash antique sale."

"That would be interesting. Thank you, Alice, I would love to. When would you like to leave?"

"How about ten?"

"Ten it is." He turned and headed for the door to the hallway. "I'll meet you in the foyer then."

"Don't forget your jacket," Alice called after him. "It's supposed to be warm today but that could change."

Jane was methodically rinsing dishes, and Alice began loading the dishwasher. "Don't let him tire himself out."

Alice chuckled. "Yes, nurse."

Jane blushed. "Well, you know what I mean. I know you'll keep an eagle eye on his health."

"So have you forgiven him?"

"I think so," she said. "Every once in a while, a little kernel of anger pops up, but I do believe he's sincerely contrite."

"I do too," Alice said. "It would have been much easier for him not to tell us, ever. After all, who would have known?"

"I think perhaps I might have liked not knowing," Jane said wryly.

Louise came into the kitchen then, carrying a basket of fresh daffodil blooms and the vase from the hallway with a bouquet of rather sad-looking flowers. "I felt as if my name were Jane, puttering about in the garden."

Her sisters laughed.

"Two Janes in one family would be problematic," Alice said.

Louise smiled. "The tulips are doing nicely."

"I love tulips," Jane and Alice said in unison. They looked at each other and laughed.

"That's a very pretty scarf, Jane," said Louise.

"Thank you." Jane was wearing a yellow shirt and pants, and around her neck she had tied a beautiful paisley scarf in shades of yellow, green and brown. It had called her name the day she'd seen it in a store in California, and she'd gone back for it three days later after thinking about it constantly.

Alice said, "I'm going to run to the store before Maxwell and I leave for the flea market. Do you need anything?"

Each of her sisters shook her head.

"No," said Jane, "but before you leave, I have a proposal to make to both of you."

"A proposal? This sounds serious." Alice took a seat at the table while Louise walked to the sink with the flowers.

"I got to thinking about Clothilda," Jane said, "and her financial concerns for her family if they do bring her grandchild over to this area for evaluation or treatment. What would you think of offering them a week's lodging here?"

Alice sat up straight. "Oh, Jane, what a good idea."

"It's a thoughtful one," Louise pronounced, "if we can afford to do it."

Jane grimaced. "I know. That worried me too, but I believe we could manage. Not indefinitely, of course, but I thought a week would be helpful to them."

"I should think so," Louise responded.

"What a lovely gesture," said Alice. "I vote yes."

"As do I." Louise stopped arranging flowers in the vase. "Who wants to tell her?"

"Why don't we all tell her?" Jane suggested. "Her niece is returning tomorrow to pick her up. I could make up a gift certificate on the computer and we could present it to her before she goes."

"Excellent idea," Louise said.

"Thank you, Jane," said Alice. "Just let us know what time she is leaving so we can arrange to be here."

Wednesday morning, Alice walked into the Coffee Shop around ten o'clock and picked up a copy of the *Acorn Nutshell*. Before she could pay for it, Hope came whizzing by with a tray loaded with food. The waitress paused long enough to say, "Check out the front page."

Alice slipped onto a stool at the counter and unfolded the newspaper. ACORN HILL HOAX read the headline. She groaned inwardly. She had hoped Carlene would understand the sensitive nature of Maxwell's confession and downplay it.

"Hey, Alice, want a cup of tea?" Hope returned and stopped near her.

"Sure. I may need it after I read this article."

Hope smiled. "It's not that bad. His statement will go a long way toward softening any hard feelings people may have."

His statement? Really curious now, Alice began to read. Carlene went through the sequence of events that led to the Bigfoot theory. The newspaper editor simply reported the facts. Near the end of the article, Alice found out what Hope had meant.

Carlene reported that Maxwell had prepared a statement, which she printed in its entirety. Alice read every word.

… In my zeal to create a research experiment to discover whether urban dwellers react differently from those in rural areas to rumors of extraordinary events, I went too far in creating the Bigfoot hoax. I made the tracks and planted the hair that was found. I deeply regret my deception. The people of Acorn Hill have shown me hospitality, kindness and friendship such as I have never experienced before. For the first time in my life, I have enjoyed the bonds of community. I recognize that my actions were a breach of trust, and I humbly ask your forgiveness.

Alice looked up from the article as someone tapped her on the shoulder. Florence stood directly behind her.

"Well?" the older woman demanded.

Alice raised an eyebrow in her best imitation of Louise, who could intimidate anyone with that expression when she so chose. "Well what?" she repeated.

"What do you think?" Florence asked. "Of the article?" Alice glanced back down at the newspaper. "I think he's young, he's poorly acquainted with true friendship, and he's extremely sincere. I think he will never do something like this again."

Florence mulled over Alice's words, and Alice prepared for a blast of ire. Finally, Florence said, "I guess you're right."

"I am?" Alice was stunned. "Does that mean you're not angry with him anymore?"

"I wouldn't say that," Florence sniffed, "but I suppose I am willing to forgive and forget."

Privately, Alice doubted the last part. Florence never forgot any perceived slight. But at least she was willing to take a step in the right direction. "That's very generous of you, Florence."

"It is," agreed Florence with a self-righteous nod. "After all the trouble he put us through."

Ronald, standing at his wife's side, chuckled. "Oh, come on. Admit it. This is the most excitement we've had around Acorn Hill since the Y2K scare."

"*Humph*. Another thing we could have done without," grumbled Florence. But Alice noticed when Ronald put his arm around her and squeezed, she leaned into his shoulder and briefly rested her head against him. It appeared all would be well in the Simpsons' world, Bigfoot or no Bigfoot.

When Alice got back to the inn, Maxwell was waiting for her in the hallway.

"Did you get the paper?" he asked in a rush. "How bad is it?"

Alice smiled as she handed over the newspaper. "Not bad at all. Even Florence agreed that you deserve forgiveness."

Maxwell's head jerked up from the paper. "Are you serious? I heard she wanted to tar and feather me."

"I didn't say she wasn't still annoyed," Alice cautioned. "But she's softening."

"Hey." Jane poked her head out of the living room. "Alice, could you come in here? We want to tell Clothilda about our offer."

"Coming."

Maxwell started up the stairs. "I guess I'll read this and see if it really is safe for me to walk into town. Thanks, Alice, for everything."

Ethel was in the living room with Jane, Louise and Clothilda when Alice arrived.

The sisters had tried every gentle hint in their repertoire to encourage Ethel to take her leave, but it was as if she sensed something was up, and she wasn't about to miss it.

Alice barely had taken a seat when Louise said to Clothilda, "Alice, Jane and I have something we would like to talk to you about."

Clothilda's eyebrows rose, and a moment later, her forehead wrinkled. "Did I do the something wrong?"

"No, no." Jane leaned forward and patted the woman's hand. "You have done everything just right."

"We—" She glanced at Ethel. "—sisters have been talking and we have an offer to make to you. If and when the time comes to bring your granddaughter here for evaluation or treatment, we would like to provide you with a week's free lodging here at the inn."

Jane rose, took an envelope from the mantel and walked to Clothilda's side. "Here," she said, extending the envelope. "This is a gift certificate. It is good for one room for a week, and you can redeem it anytime."

"Although," said Louise hastily, "it is helpful to have as much advance notice as possible so that we can reserve a room for you before the inn fills up."

Clothilda slowly took the envelope from Jane, looking at it in disbelief as her eyes filled with tears. "You ladies," she said, "have been so kind. God smiled on me when I greeted you."

"Met you," corrected Ethel gently. "When I met you."

Clothilda laughed. "Thank you, Ethel. Without you, I would have had the more difficult time speaking English." She rose and embraced each sister in turn, thanking them individually.

Ethel cleared her throat. "Clothilda?"

When the German guest turned to her, Ethel smiled and said, "I can't let my nieces show me up with their generosity." She beamed at all three of them, then looked back at Clothilda. "When you bring Lotte over, I would be honored if you would allow me to purchase her airplane ticket."

"Aunt Ethel!" Jane gasped. "That's a wonderful thing to do."

"Yes," said Alice. "Extremely generous."

Clothilda rose from her seat and grabbed Ethel in a firm embrace, her shoulders shaking. With her mouth muffled in the navy wool at the shoulder of Ethel's spring sweater, she said, "You, dear friend, also are too kind. I will treasure you all forever."

"As we will treasure you," Ethel said in return.

The sisters smiled at each other, their own eyes misting.

"Goodness," said Jane. "Aren't we just a bunch of crybabies?"

"Apparently so," Alice replied, dabbing at her eyes.

"Why don't we take this party into the kitchen," Jane suggested. "I just made a new batch of those crème-de-menthe brownies we all loved so much."

"Excellent idea," said Louise.

As one, they all walked toward the kitchen with Louise in the lead.

Suddenly Louise stopped and everyone else nearly plowed into her.

"What's wrong?" Ethel asked as she stopped a pace away from Jane's back.

Louise silently pointed.

There, sitting right in the middle of the table, was Wendell. There was no food in sight, but he looked perfectly at home. And quite pleased with himself.

"All right, you smarty pants," said Louise. "You think you're the king of the castle now, don't you?"

"He *knows* he is," corrected Alice, and she went to retrieve the fat feline from the table as the others began to laugh.

About the Author

*A*nne Marie Rodgers has published nearly three dozen novels since 1992. She has been a finalist for the prestigious RITA award and has won several Golden Leaf awards, among others. In addition, she has been a teacher of handicapped and preschool children.

Anne Marie has been involved in animal-rescue efforts for many years, and her family is used to sharing their home with furred, finned and feathered creatures in need. After Hurricane Katrina, she volunteered at the Humane Society of Louisiana, caring for animals left behind during evacuation efforts. She and her loved ones also have raised puppies for Guiding Eyes for the Blind.

Anne Marie and her family live in State College, Pennsylvania. Her favorite activities include ice skating, needlework, amateur theater and dance, canine training, and scrapbooking. She considers irises, beaches and babies of any species some of God's finest creations.

A Note from the Editors

We hope you enjoy Tales from Grace Chapel Inn, created by the Books and Inspirational Media Division of Guideposts, a nonprofit organization. In all of our books, magazines and outreach efforts, we aim to deliver inspiration and encouragement, help you grow in your faith, and celebrate God's love in every aspect of your daily life.

Thank you for making a difference with your purchase of this book, which helps fund our many outreach programs to the military, prisons, hospitals, nursing homes and schools. To learn more, visit GuidepostsFoundation.org.

We also maintain many useful and uplifting online resources. Visit Guideposts.org to read true stories of hope and inspiration, access OurPrayer network, sign up for free newsletters, download free e-books, join our Facebook community, and follow our stimulating blogs.

To learn about other Guideposts publications, including our best-selling devotional *Daily Guideposts,* go to ShopGuideposts.org, call (800) 932-2145 or write to Guideposts, PO Box 5815, Harlan, Iowa 51593.

Tales from Grace Chapel Inn

Once you visit the charming village of Acorn Hill, you'll never want to leave. Here, the three Howard sisters reunite after their father's death and turn the family home into a bed-and-breakfast. They rekindle old memories, rediscover the bonds of sisterhood, revel in the blessings of friendship and meet many fascinating guests along the way.